THE AURA

A novel by

Carrie Bedford

For James, Madeleine and Charlotte
with love and thanks

CHAPTER ONE

Waking up didn't end the nightmare. It just kept going. At first light, I bolted from sleep with a headache unlike anything I'd ever felt before. It pinned my head to the pillow and poked daggers into my eyes when I opened them. Easing myself out of bed, I hobbled to the bathroom and splashed water on my face. I'd have to work out how to shower when I had more time. My legs were bandaged from mid-calf to mid-thigh; pain stabbed at my knees when I moved them.

Back in my room, I pulled some loose-fitting black pants from a hanger. They would hide the bandages better than a skirt and tights. I found a silk shirt to dress them up, pulled my hair up into a ponytail, and smoothed concealer under my eyes to hide the dark circles that had gathered overnight. While I drank a cup of tea, I weighed the many advantages of going back to bed, but I knew I couldn't take any more time off work. I'd already missed the first two days of the week. I imagined my desk sinking under the mass of paper that must have accumulated by now.

Dumping my cup in the sink, I made my way down three flights of stairs by clinging to the banisters, and limped through rain-slicked streets to the nearest Tube station. Every painful step reminded me of what had happened in Tuscany over the weekend. I joined the other commuters in a crowded carriage that smelled of damp wool. When a man pushed his way past me and swung his briefcase into my leg, I realized this would have been a good day to treat myself to a taxi.

Needlepoints of rain stung my face when I came out the Tube

station. I walked as quickly as I could to reach the shelter of the office. Bradley Cohen, the architectural firm where I worked, resided in what must be one of the ugliest buildings in the city. Undoubtedly considered the height of contemporary style when it was built in the 1960s, the four-story office block now cowered in the shadow of newer construction, as though ashamed of its metal window frames and weather-darkened aluminum siding. Still, the interior was elegant and comfortable, the lobby and offices filled with sleek blonde furniture from Sweden, while creamy plaster walls served as a backdrop for large and colorful paintings by several London artists.

Unable to face the stairs, I opted for the elevator, which was empty this early in the morning, but, just as the doors started to close, a beefy hand appeared between them and they slid open to reveal my boss, Alan Bradley. His perma-tan glowed orange in the florescent light, clashing with a pink Polo shirt that stretched tightly over his paunch and was tucked and belted into beige chinos. He wore his usual frown.

"You look frightful, Kate. Been out partying?"

He didn't wait for me to answer. "You young things have all the fun with your concerts and bar-hopping. I, on the other hand, have a house and garden to slave over, as if I don't have enough to do at the office."

I doubted that Alan did his own housework or gardening. He was co-owner of Bradley Cohen, and his Tudor-style mansion in Surrey was more than large enough to accommodate a nanny, a housekeeper, and probably a gardener too.

"Poor you," I said, summoning up a smile. Staying on Alan's good side would make the rest of the week less stressful. "I'm going to get some coffee. Do you want one?"

"You were out yesterday, weren't you? And Monday too, come to think of it." He followed me into the kitchen, where I poured two cups of coffee and gave him one. I edged my way past him to rummage in the fridge for milk or cream, hoping he would tire of asking about my absence.

"No milk," I said, handing him a packet of nondairy creamer.

"This bloody stuff tastes like petrol," he said. "Now can you explain to me why you missed two days of work?"

"She had an accident," came a voice from the door. It was Josh. "Hit and run," he said. "Who'd think something like that could happen in idyllic Tuscany?"

A quick jolt of guilt made my cheeks feel warm. There was, I realized, a big difference between telling the truth and being honest. I had, in fact, been in Tuscany and there had been a car. That part was true. But I couldn't tell anyone what had really happened; no one would believe me. Josh came into the kitchen, took the small sachet of powder from my hands and finished opening it for me.

"Well, I hope you find the driver," said Alan, tipping more creamer into his mug. "So that you can sue him for lost wages."

I leaned against the counter and tried to slow my breathing. Everything hurt, my hair needed washing, and I couldn't remember if I'd put on any mascara. I was sure I looked hideous. Of course Josh wouldn't say anything; he was far too considerate for that.

He grinned, undaunted by Alan's sardonic humor. When he smiled, his eyes, which were the color of sea glass, crinkled at the corners. I envied his ability to make light of our boss's acerbic manner; Alan often made me feel off balance, as though I'd done something wrong or was about to commit some terrible blunder. Which, of course, I had, by taking days off at a time when the team was working frantically for our prestigious new client.

"You two should be at your desks preparing for the Montgomery meeting," Alan said, when he'd adjusted his coffee to the color he wanted. "I'll see you in the conference room at three. Don't be late."

"Have a nice day, Alan," I muttered once he was out of earshot.

"Are you sure you should be here?" Josh asked. "Shouldn't you be resting?" He had a faint Scottish accent that I loved, with its rolling 'r's and flowing vowels. "Thanks for texting me, by the way. I'd been worrying about where you were. Did you fly in last night?"

I felt myself blushing, and bent my head over my cup of coffee.

"Yes, and I'm okay," I said. "Just a bit sore. How was your weekend?"

"Fantastic. I went to the Chelsea game and then to that new comedy club on Marshall Street. We could go there together some time."

I nodded. "Some time, yeah."

"Well, we should get started on our presentation then, okay?"

"Of course."

I followed him to his office, kicking myself for my half-hearted response to his offer. It didn't take long for me to realize how much I had to catch up on, but I found it hard to concentrate. Even the feel of my pencil on paper, normally so soothing, wasn't enough to alleviate the throbbing in my head.

We ate sandwiches at our desks, and worked without a break until three o' clock rolled around. At least, once the meeting started, I could sit in a comfortable conference room chair and listen to Josh give the presentation we had prepared. He would outline the design concepts for the building, and propose a timeline. He was a good speaker, and all our clients adored him.

I took a seat at the conference table and watched the visitors file in, Peter Montgomery leading the way. Several minions in dark suits trailed after him. He was a well-known real estate developer, and had awarded our firm a major contract for a new commercial building in the City. He was an attractive man in his forties, but he looked as though he'd spent more time doing his hair that morning than I had. When his liberally applied aftershave made me sneeze, Alan glared at me. I sank back into my chair, determined to be unnoticed for the rest of the afternoon.

Montgomery glanced at his Rolex. "My Financial Director will be joining us today, but she's running a little late, so let's get started."

Alan signaled to Josh to turn on the projector and pull down the blinds. A few minutes later, the door opened and a woman entered. At once, I recognized her.

"Rebecca!" Everyone in the room looked at me. So much for my invisibility plan. Rebecca and I had gone to university together, sharing a dorm room for our first year. We'd been quite close for a while, but we had drifted apart by the time we graduated. She smiled and raised a hand in greeting before taking a seat.

In the semi-darkness, I tried to concentrate, but my thoughts kept veering off in the direction of Tuscany and what had happened there. The memory had kept me awake all night. My lack of sleep, the twilight room and the soft tone of Josh's voice were soporific. My eyelids drooped and I resorted to an old trick of using pain to keep myself awake, pushing the fingernails of one hand hard against the palm of the other.

Finally, Josh switched off the projector and pulled the blinds up, submerging the room in thin, grey light. I blinked myself fully awake. Montgomery was nodding his head, obviously happy with the designs that had been presented.

Rebecca asked a question about permits. I swiveled in my chair to look at her while Alan answered. When I breathed in sharply,

Alan paused for a second, darting a quick look in my direction. I seemed to be acting like a magnet for his disapproval today. Picking up a pencil, I pretended to write notes on the paper in front of me, waiting for him to start talking again.

Head still lowered over my notepad, I raised my eyes to look at Rebecca and the air dancing over her head. It was very faint, barely visible, but it was definitely there, an unusual crown on her mane of red hair. It looked like heat rising in waves from hot asphalt.

When Josh nudged me with his elbow, I sat up straight, feeling everyone's eyes on me. Peter Montgomery looked at his Rolex while Alan glowered.

"When you're ready, Kate," he muttered. "Mr. Montgomery asked you a question."

Josh rescued me by repeating the question for me. I flipped through my notes and answered, even though I felt that all connections between my brain and my mouth had been severed. I described the lobby design, pointing out relevant points on the diagram spread out on the table. But my mind was on Rebecca and the odd visual hallucination I seemed to be having.

It seemed to take an age for the meeting to come to a close but, finally, everyone stood up and packed up their briefcases. Josh and Alan moved towards Rebecca to introduce themselves. Her striking hair, alabaster skin dusted with freckles, and wide green eyes had quite an impact on them, but she seemed oblivious. As soon as everyone had left, Rebecca threw her arms around me.

"Kate, it's so nice to see you again! I had no idea that you were working in London now. We'll have a great time working together on the project but let's meet for lunch and catch up? Are you free tomorrow? Even better, why don't you come for dinner? Tomorrow night, my place."

I wasn't sure I could face an evening out, but I'd always liked Rebecca and looked forward to getting to know her again. And perhaps if I spent some time with her, I could work out what that weird rippling air meant.

She gave me her address, we exchanged cell phone numbers, and I watched her walk away with Peter Montgomery and the rest of the team. A glance at my watch showed that it was almost a decent time for me to leave too. We often worked late, and I certainly owed the company a couple of late nights to catch up on all the work I'd missed, but I was aching and tired. I needed an early night.

Back in my office, I collected my coat and bag, realizing I'd left my umbrella at home. The rain was beating against the windows like a feral animal, blurring the outline of the building opposite. The indistinct image vaguely resembled the strange undulations I had seen around Rebecca. I put my hand against the glass, grateful for the feel of its cold, solid mass. I had no idea what was happening to me, but I was scared.

CHAPTER TWO

The following evening, I took a cab to Rebecca's address in Belgravia. In the encroaching darkness, under a fine drizzle, the tall Georgian houses lined the square like soldiers on a parade ground. In the center, protected by wrought iron railings, trimmed lawns and flower beds sheltered under the branches of old oak trees. Private gardens like this one were reserved for the use of the local residents, a rare perk that many Londoners dreamed of.

The cab pulled up outside a four-story house with elegant white columns and topiaries in pots flanking a black and white tiled entryway. I rang the bell and Rebecca buzzed me in through the glossy black front door, telling me to come to the third floor. Inside, I paused to admire the spacious lobby, where an exotic flower arrangement stood on an antique table. Oriental carpets covered the tiled floor. The flowers alone would barely fit in the cramped hallway of my building.

I walked slowly up the curved stairway, running my fingers along dark wood banister rails that gleamed under the soft light of the wall sconces. On the second floor landing, two men were standing at a door with briefcases and umbrellas at their feet. Young, tall and very good-looking, they were dressed in black jeans and matching cashmere jackets, one tan and one ivory.

"Hello," the tan one greeted me. "I'm Nick. Are you a friend of Rebecca's?"

"Yes, just going up to have dinner," I said.

"This is Gary and he thinks I've lost my key, but I know it's here somewhere." He patted his pockets, then pulled out a key, holding it up in triumph.

"Ha, I knew I had it. Have fun with Rebecca. Bon appetit and all that."

I climbed the stairs to the third floor, where Rebecca waited at her door. She greeted me with a hug, pulling me towards her and straining my knees under their bandages. I almost lost my balance and, when she frowned, I realized she thought I was leaning away from her.

"I'm sorry," she said. "Too huggy, my dad says."

"No, it's okay," I said, embarrassed. I didn't want to say anything about my injuries. "It was my fault. I'm such a klutz."

I gave her the bottle of wine I'd brought. She led the way into the living room. The walls were painted a pale duck egg blue, reaching up to a high ceiling with plaster moldings. Two white sofas faced each other across a glass coffee table laden with glossy magazines and a vase of white roses.

"Wow!" I said.

Rebecca blushed. "Thanks. It's nice isn't it? I love it here. Come and see the kitchen."

I focused on the Poggenpohl cabinets and tried to ignore the air that hovered over her head. It seemed to be moving faster than when I'd seen her the previous afternoon.

"You can put your bag and jacket on the bed in my room if you like," said Rebecca, pointing along the hall. "I'm going to finish cooking."

A grey cat sat in the doorway, watching me until I got closer. It ran and hid under the bed.

The bedroom looked like something in a five star hotel, with Wedgwood blue walls, luxurious silky linens and matching drapes at the windows. A photo in a silver frame caught my attention. It was a snap of Rebecca standing next to a tall man with wide shoulders, very blue eyes and curly dark hair. His arm was draped around Rebecca and they both smiled at the camera.

I limped to the bathroom and, while washing my hands, noticed that the door of the cabinet over the sink was partially open. I couldn't resist a peek. On one shelf was a messy array of cosmetics and hair products. The shelf above held several tubes of shaving cream and an embossed flacon of Amouage aftershave. There'd been a big promotion for it at Harrod's recently and I knew it was expensive. I lifted it out, unscrewed the lid, and sniffed. It had a distinctive musky and slightly smoky scent. Rebecca must have a boyfriend with good taste.

"Kate? Are you ready?" Rebecca called down the hallway. I put the bottle back in the cabinet and left the door the way it had been. I'd never thought of myself as the prying kind, but I couldn't help being curious about Rebecca's situation. Her flat was luxurious and in one of the most expensive areas of London. Admittedly, she had a good job with a successful company, but it was hard to imagine she was making the kind of money that this apartment would cost.

Back in the kitchen, I sipped a glass of Cabernet while Rebecca tossed a salad. Not a sensible idea to drink on top of the painkillers I was taking, but the wine felt warm in my throat.

"Did you meet Caspian?" she asked.

"That would be the grey cat? Yes, sort of, but he ran under the bed."

"He's shy. But I love him to bits. I talk to him all the time. Here, sit down and I'll bring the plates over."

We sat at a table near the kitchen window. Night had fallen. The fenced garden was now nothing more than a black hole absorbing light from the windows on the other side of the square. While we ate steaks with pepper sauce and green beans, we talked about our jobs and what we'd been doing since college. After a while, and another few sips of wine, I was able to ignore the moving air that rippled over her head.

Rebecca told me she loved working at Montgomery Group, where she'd recently been promoted to the position of Financial Director. Her eyes shone as she praised the company's accomplishments and track record. "The people are so nice to work with. I can't wait to get into the office in the mornings. How about you? Do you like Bradley Cohen?"

I didn't even contemplate telling the truth. "Fantastic," I said. "The bosses are wonderful, nurturing and encouraging, and the team works together really well. I'm very lucky."

"And you're doing something so creative," she said, carrying the empty plates to the sink. "I think I would have liked to be an architect, but I have no graphics skills at all. Still, I love money!" She laughed. "Well, I mean I love working with money. Although I rather like having it too."

While she measured coffee grounds into a complicated-looking espresso maker, she seemed preoccupied, perhaps contemplating what she'd just said. To break the silence, I asked her if she had a boyfriend. When she didn't answer immediately, I wondered if I'd missed something. In college, she'd been surrounded by guys. Her social life and mine hadn't been vaguely comparable. She'd had her pick of dates and parties while I hung around the Student Union drinking cheap wine with my friends and their nerdy boyfriends.

"Yes, I do," she said finally. "But he travels a lot. How about you? Do you have anyone special?"

I shrugged. "No one right now. What's his name? Your boyfriend? And what does he do to travel so much?"

Rebecca hesitated before answering. "His name's Edward, and he works in technology. Let's take our coffee into the living room."

"Does he live here with you?"

"No, not yet," she said. "He plans to move in one day but..." Her eyes wandered towards the window and she didn't finish the sentence.

We settled on opposite sides of the coffee table. I kept my eyes on my cup, nervous about spilling on the pristine white upholstery. It also helped not to look at the air over Rebecca's head. We talked about old friends from University. Rebecca said one of them had gone on to be an actor.

"He's in a play at the Apollo and I'd love to see it," she said, picking up a copy of Time Out and flicking to a page of theater listings. "It opens in two weeks. Would you come with me?" Without waiting for an answer, she continued. "Why don't we talk later in the week? I'll know more about my boyfriend's schedule and then we can decide when to go?"

"Okay," I said, wondering why she wasn't planning on going with Edward. Maybe he wasn't the cultural type. Suddenly, I felt exhausted and my head began to pound. Perhaps the combination of wine and coffee hadn't been a good idea. Putting my cup and saucer down on the glass coffee table, I leaned back against the down-filled cushions.

"You look pale. Are you feeling all right?" Rebecca asked with real concern in her voice. My skin felt cold and goose-bumpy. I wanted to tell her about the air that moved around her, but what could I say? She'd think I was crazy and, even if she believed me, which was unlikely, I couldn't tell her what it meant because I didn't know.

"I had a painful encounter with a car over the weekend," I said, deciding to share part of the story. "I was visiting my Dad in Tuscany. It's not bad, but my knees hurt and I hit my head too."

"Oh goodness," she said. Putting her cup down, she came around the table to sit next to me. She took my hands in hers and rubbed them. "You're freezing. You should have said something before. I wouldn't have dragged you all the way over here if I'd known you weren't feeling well. Did you go to the hospital?"

"No, really, it's not serious. My dad's friend is a doctor and he checked me out and put dressings on my legs. I'll be fine in a day or two."

Recalling the events of Saturday afternoon made my heart bang around my chest like a bird trying to escape from a cage.

"I've never been to Florence," said Rebecca.

I wanted to change the subject from my injuries. "We should go together some time," I said. I meant it. There was something comforting about being with Rebecca, an old friend from a simpler time, when classes and social events were all we had to think about. I'd enjoyed every day at college, reveled in the work and late-night studying. Sometimes, I thought of going back for another degree, but I knew I was fortunate to have the job at Bradley Cohen.

"My dad would love to meet you," I said. "Think how much fun we'll have. We could meet a couple of Italian gigolos and drive around in their Ferraris. Or, knowing my luck, their Fiats."

She laughed. "Yes, please. I never go anywhere interesting nowadays. Let's plan it soon, can we?"

"You tell me when you have a weekend free, and we'll go," I said. "If we fly out of City airport we can be at Dad's house in less than three hours, with plenty of time for a late Friday night dinner."

Rebecca clapped her hands together. "Perfect. I can't wait."

"Now I really should go home," I said. "Work tomorrow, bright and early."

Half an hour later, I stood on the doorstep of the Victorian house in Islington where I lived. Fumbling with my keys, which were cold and slippery in the rain, I finally managed to open the front door. The maroon carpet in the hall was worn in places and the walls were covered in a brown and orange geometric wallpaper that would have been popular in the 'seventies. I clambered up the stairs, holding on to the banisters for support, hearing the beat of music from the first floor and the faint sound of a television on the second.

I reached the top floor, let myself in and flipped on the light switch. Several table lamps came on, revealing a cozy living room nestled under the eaves of the old house. The walls were painted in my favorite color, a green-gray that reminded me of olive leaves. The room was furnished with a cream Ikea sofa and a colorful Persian rug that had been a present from my parents. At one end, a granite counter separated the living room from a small kitchen lined with painted cabinets and rather old but functional appliances. I loved my apartment, and looked around with affection, thinking that I wouldn't be as comfortable in the stark whiteness of Rebecca's living room.

I went straight to bed, but sleep was elusive. My mind was too crowded with thoughts of the strange moving air. After a while, I got up, put the kettle on and set my laptop on the coffee table. Several cups of tea and a couple of hours later, I'd worked my way through a multitude of websites, searching for information about air that moved around people. Nothing seemed to correlate with what I had seen over Rebecca. The wavy lines people see over hot asphalt or hot sand in the desert, it turned out, are caused by refraction, the bending of light waves, which occurs when light passes between substances with different refractive properties, such as cold air and hot air. Interesting, I thought, but it didn't seem relevant.

More searches yielded pages of descriptions of high and low pressure zones and how air moves between them; information that might come in handy if I ever took up flying or sailing. The only phenomenon vaguely related to what I was seeing was described on a site for mediums and psychics. It talked about auras, which could come in a rainbow of colors, apparently, and could surround a person from head to toe. But there was no reference to the manifestation of clear air rippling around someone's head.

I closed the laptop, listening to the rain on the windows. It was only September and England's much anticipated Indian summer had failed to materialize. While the rest of Europe bathed in the golden glow of autumnal sunshine and unseasonable warmth, poor London was drowning under the onslaught of torrential rain and swirling mist. It had been hot in Tuscany over the weekend, almost like summer.

The moving air had to be connected with what had happened on that hill in Tuscany. A hallucination caused by the fall? Had I suffered brain damage? Or did I have a tumor? That would explain a few things. Fear crawled across my skin, and churned my stomach. I stood up and limped to the bathroom, where I stared into the mirror, straining to see a glimpse of moving air. I ran my hand through the space over my head but felt nothing. Saw nothing. It was time to get some help. I'd call the doctor first thing in the morning.

CHAPTER THREE

On my way to work, I got a doctor's appointment for noon. The receptionist chirped on about how lucky I was that there had been a cancellation and sounded ecstatic that she could get me in so quickly. I wondered if she expected a gift or a medal. On the Tube, I noticed air swirling over a middle-aged man with red blotchy skin and a morose expression. When he saw me staring at him, he frowned at me and turned away; it was never a good idea to make eye contact with anyone on the Underground. I pulled up the hood of my raincoat and stared at my iPhone screen for the rest of the journey, anxious to avoid any more visual encounters with my fellow commuters.

After a few hours at work, I was so immersed in my design that I was no longer aware of my aches and pains. The persistent sense of dread that I'd felt since the weekend faded away. The neat lines on the page began to form an image of what would become a fully functional building; I could imagine the open spaces and the wide stretches of glass with expansive views over London. As always, the feeling of pencil on paper calmed me.

Josh walked in with a cup of coffee for me and looked over my shoulder at the sketches.

"Those look really good, Kate. You draw so much better than anyone else here." When he leaned forward to trace a line with his finger, I inhaled his scent of soap and freshly-laundered shirt.

"Perhaps you could make that wall eighteen inches longer and it would intersect here for a more interesting angle," he said, pointing at one of the lines I'd just drawn.

"Good idea," I agreed. "You've got a better eye for detail than I have."

He grinned. "We make a good team then, don't we?"

Alan walked past the door and beckoned to Josh.

"Wish me luck," Josh whispered. "See you later."

I twirled my pencil in my hand, feeling the smoothness of it against my skin. Any residual dysphoria had melted away under the warmth of Josh's words and I went back to work with renewed energy.

An hour later my cell phone rang and I glanced around to check that Alan wasn't in sight before answering it. We weren't supposed to take personal calls at work. The caller ID showed that my brother was on the line.

"Hi Leo." I kept my voice down. I walked to the window, from where I looked down at the street, thronged with workers on their lunch hour. A pallid sun hung behind a veil of thin cloud, barely casting shadows, but at least alleviating the gloom of the previous few days.

"Katie, how are you doing? Dad called to tell me what happened. Do you need me to come up?"

"I'm fine. Everything is healing quickly. Paolo came over and looked after me. It was nothing. Just a silly accident."

"Uh huh."

"What does that mean?"

"It means that you're not telling me everything," he said. "Dad sounded really worried about you and said something about... well, he seemed to think you were suffering from a concussion."

I shifted my weight, aware again of the ache around my knees. "Can I call you when I get home?"

Leo paused. "Why don't you come over this weekend? The boys would love to see you, and you can bring me up to date on how Dad's doing."

I thought for a minute. Rebecca and I were planning to see a movie on Sunday evening, but I had nothing else to do. The drive to Oxford would be a good distraction.

"Yes," I said. "I'll come for dinner tomorrow and stay the night."

"Good, great." Leo sounded relieved. He was worried; my Dad was worried. I had to get better quickly so everyone would stop worrying about me.

At lunchtime, I took a taxi to the doctor's office. I was tense with anticipation, half hoping that the doctor would easily identify the cause of my visual disturbances, half dreading that the diagnosis would be unspeakably terrifying. The visit was inconclusive, however. The doctor, a portly, middle-aged woman with grey hair and bad teeth, examined my eyes and ears, pressed on various parts of my skull and wrote out an order for a CT scan. Then she offered me a prescription for antidepressants, which I refused.

As soon as I was out of the doctor's office, I called the radiology department of the local hospital to make an appointment for the scan. To my relief, they were able to fit me in on Monday afternoon. At least I wouldn't have to wait too long, in suspense.

I got back to my desk, had my coat off and was working when Alan came in with Josh and another team member, Ben, in tow.

"Team huddle," Alan said. "Just want to be sure you're all working your asses off on the Montgomery project. This one is crucial. Get it right and we'll be deluged with new contracts. Jack will be coming in for the next meeting and we all want to look good for Uncle Jack, don't we?"

I liked Jack Cohen. He was the other founding partner and had acted as my mentor since I joined the firm. Older than Alan, he didn't work full time, but I gathered that he networked, lunched with influencers and came in a couple of times a week to see how things were going. Alan referred to him as the 'big gun'. "We only wheel him out for special occasions," he'd say. "And for the Christmas party."

When Alan walked towards the door, I sighed with relief. At least he hadn't referred to my time off again. But, just when I thought I was safe, he swung around to look at me.

"Kate. You're outstanding at what you do, but I'm sensing a lack of commitment. Too much time off, and a recent tendency to distraction. Step it up, young lady, and give these two guys the full benefit of your talent. I'll be keeping an eye on you."

Ben smirked, his small dark eyes glistening with amusement. Josh told him to cut it out and, as soon as Alan had gone, leaned forward across the desk towards Ben and me.

"We need to cooperate if we're going to get everything completed on time," he said. "We'll split the project into parts and we'll each handle the details we're strongest at. Kate, you'll have functional design and Ben will work with..."

I tuned out, thinking it was ironic that Alan was picking on me just when I was starting to feel like my old self and finding enthusiasm for the project. But he was right. I'd been distracted ever since my mother died. The shock of her death had knocked me sideways. And now this thing with the moving air. It was going to be hard to get through the coming weeks of long hours and constant review, but I would get back on track. I owed it to Josh, if no one else. I wouldn't let him down.

CHAPTER FOUR

By mid morning on Saturday, I had cleaned up my apartment, done my laundry and packed a bag for my stay at Leo's. I seemed to have regained my usual energy and still had a few hours to spare before picking up a Zipcar for the drive to Oxford. A run would do me good. Just a short one to see how my knees would hold up. The night before, I'd removed the bandages and examined the damage. My legs were dotted with small red scars where each piece of gravel had left its mark. One or two spots were still raw but the rest had healed well. I jogged slowly to the park a couple of blocks away. The air was heavy and humid, and ominous black clouds loomed in the distance. My knees ached, but not as much as I'd feared.

After doing a slow circuit around the park, I sat at the end of a green wooden bench to retie my shoelaces. One broke off when I tugged on it too hard. I took the shoe off to re-lace it with what was left of the white cord. A young woman pushing a stroller and talking on a cell phone stopped in front of me. Positioning the stroller at the other end of the bench, she sank on to the wooden seat and lit a cigarette. Annoyed, I stared at her. I didn't understand why anyone would use cigarettes around children. The dangers of second-hand smoke were well-known, but the woman, oblivious, carried on her conversation, taking deep drags and coughing occasionally.

I worked faster on my shoe, anxious to get away from the smoke. A little girl climbed out of the stroller. She was about three, with blonde curls peeping out from a pink beret. Her pink raincoat matched her wellingtons and she clutched a small brown teddy bear. I didn't think of myself as much of a maternal type but I smiled at the sweetness of all that pink. The mother didn't seem very maternal either when she snapped at the child, who was climbing up on to her lap.

"For goodness' sake, Sophie, get down. You're too heavy to sit on me."

In spite of the harsh words, Sophie remained where she was. I winced to see the smoke being blown into the child's face. I slipped my shoe back on and stood up, just as Sophie dropped her teddy bear. She scrambled down to pick it up. Immediately, I saw that the air over her head was trembling. I sat back on the bench, trying not to stare. There was no doubt that the rippling air was there, shimmering over the pink beret and blonde hair. I glanced at the mother, but she wasn't even looking at the child, focused instead on using her phone. I opened my mouth to say something but closed it again. I couldn't tell her about the aura. The woman would think I was a lunatic.

Sophie began singing to her little bear, swinging the toy from side to side in time to the song. She took a few steps away from the bench, across the asphalted trail and on to the grass on the other side. She turned to look at her mother, who seemed to either not notice or not care, and then she ran a few yards further.

Alarmed, I spoke to the young woman. "Your little girl," I said, pointing, but she waved my words away with an outstretched hand.

"What? Sorry, somebody interrupted me," she said, settling further back into the bench.

I turned my attention back to the child, who was skipping towards the trees on the other side of the grass. She was moving fast for being so small. Deciding there was no point in waiting for the mother to make a move, I set off after Sophie. The girl had already reached the trees, where she disappeared for a moment between the dark trunks.

To my left, I caught sight of a man in a jacket with a hood up over his head. He was also walking towards the trees. My mind filled with thoughts of pedophiles, I broke into a jog. Reaching the tree line, I saw Sophie still scampering ahead of me; any second now, she would cross his path. What would he do? Snatch her and run? I darted forward, aware of stabbing pains in my knees, and saw the little girl pass just a few yards in front of him. He didn't even look at her, but kept walking, white earphone cables dangling from under his hood.

Thunder rolled above us and a flash of lightning brightened the purple sky. Fat drops of water began to fall. Within seconds, rain cascaded through the trees, soaking my running shirt. Swollen black clouds hung so low that they seemed to be ensnared in the leafless branches. I wiped the rain from my eyes with a corner of my running shirt and then realized that the girl had disappeared from sight. Panicked, I ran in the direction where I had last seen her, my feet slipping on the wet grass. A glimpse of pink off to my right. I breathed again. Leaving the trees behind, I saw her on the other side of an expanse of lawn. In the lurid light of the storm, the grass looked black, like the surface of an angry sea.

It took a minute for me to register the danger. Sophie was standing on the concrete rim of a boating pond, looking down into the water. On sunny days, kids brought remote-controlled boats and raced them around the pool, but today it was deserted. Green water churned under the torrential rain.

"Sophie!" I shouted. "Get off the wall."

My words were drowned out by the gusty wind and crash of rain. In slow motion, the stuffed bear slipped from Sophie's fingers into the murky water. She leaned forward, hand outstretched. She seemed to slip, tried to catch her balance and disappeared from sight over the rim of the pond. I dashed towards her. Stepping up on to the low wall, I saw a pink outline under the surface. I reached down, but the water was deeper than I'd thought. I couldn't get hold of her. I plunged in, feeling the cold water hit my skin with a shock like an electric current. When my feet touched bottom, the algae-filled water was over my head, and my eyes burned.

Lunging towards Sophie, I tried to grab at her arm. She had drifted a few yards away, her pink raincoat rendered grey in the muddy, opaque water. I took several strokes towards her and reached down to gather her into my arms. Twice I tried to grab her and failed, my hands slipping on the plastic macintosh. Then, desperate, I caught hold of her hair to pull her towards me. Her body was limp, her eyes were closed, and blood was leaking from her head, trailing through the water like tendrils of black smoke.

I held her face above the water and dog-paddled back to the rim. There, I shifted my grip on her, while scrabbling at the wall with my free hand. The side of the stone basin was slick with frothy green scum and I couldn't get a firm hold. Scraping my arms and legs against the concrete, I finally managed to grab the slippery wall and push Sophie over the top of it. Then I clambered out, my breaths short and ragged, my chest burning. I scrambled to my feet, stripped off my shirt and wadded it against the wound on Sophie's head. She must have hit the rim when she fell in. I felt for a pulse but there was nothing. Frantic, I started gentle chest compressions, trying to remember what I had learned in girl scouts about CPR.

I shouted for help while I did the chest compressions, wondering how it was possible that I was in the middle of one of the busiest cities on Earth and yet so alone. At last, a man's voice sounded close by.

"I'm calling for an ambulance," he said, striding towards me with a cell phone at his ear. It was the young man with the hooded jacket.

I nodded and kept working. After what felt like an infinite span of time, the wail of an ambulance siren cut through the steady drumbeat of the rain. Sophie's eyelids fluttered and my heart lifted. Thank God.

"Is she your daughter?" the stranger asked, holding the shirt that was now red with blood tight against her wound. I shook my head.

Before he could ask any more questions, a scream echoed over the pond. I glanced up to see Sophie's mother running towards us, ungainly in her shiny padded coat and tight jeans.

"Sophie, oh my God. What did you do?" she shouted at me.

Then the grassy area was suddenly crowded with paramedics, calm, strong men in yellow jackets, with blankets and oxygen tanks. An ambulance parked a hundred yards away at the edge of the lawn, its blue light whirling.

I stood up and moved away to give the paramedics room to work. Sophie's mother screamed and yelled while I sank to my knees on the wet lawn, vomiting up foul green water. I couldn't stop shaking. The child had been well and happy just ten minutes ago. Now she was fighting for her life.

Images from the past flashed past my eyes. Visions of a tiny white casket, mourners in black, the smell of white carnations and blue hyacinths. So long ago, yet it felt like no time at all. This couldn't be happening again.

One of the paramedics came over, wrapped a blanket around me, took my pulse and listened to my chest. His face was close to mine and he smelled of peppermint and something herbal, eucalyptus maybe.

"Good," he said. "Pulse a little high but steady. No water in the lungs. But you should come in for a check-up at the hospital."

"No, I'm okay. Just look after the little girl."

"She's in good hands," he said. "And you did a terrific job."

Just as he walked away, a uniformed police officer appeared, helped me to my feet and led me to the steps of the ambulance, where he asked a lot of questions about what had happened. I did my best to answer them, aware the whole time of the screams of Sophie's mother.

Finally, the officer thanked me and helped me into the back of a police car. He told the driver to take me home. My legs were like pillars of lead. It took forever to climb the stairs to my apartment. I tore my soaked running pants and sports bra off, threw them with the blanket on the bathroom floor, and pulled on my robe.

In the kitchen, I put the kettle on and stared, mesmerized, at the steam rising from the spout. It looked like the moving air over Sophie. It had been there, clear and distinct over her little pink beret. What did it mean? After I'd showered and dressed, I drank a cup of tea, leaning against the counter, watching my hand shake as I lifted the china mug to my lips. I wasn't sure I should drive to Oxford, but I also knew I had to go. Leo was already concerned about me. If I didn't turn up, he'd be at my door in a few hours.

CHAPTER FIVE

"Hi everyone!" I called as I let myself into my brother's house, a red brick, semi-detached on the outskirts of Oxford. I'd made good time on the drive up from London, in light of Saturday afternoon traffic.

"Hi Aunt Kate."

Aidan and Gabe were leaning over the coffee table with remotes in hand, concentrating closely on whatever computer game they were playing. Their blonde heads were almost touching, and their long legs were splayed out in identical blue jeans and Converse sneakers so it was hard to tell which limbs belonged to which boy. I continued on to the kitchen where I could hear the clink of dishes.

"Kate!" Leo straightened up from loading the dishwasher. He leaned forward to give me a peck on the cheek. He was six inches taller than me, his lean body clad in a black t-shirt and skinny jeans. His dark brown hair was thick and glossy, and he had the same blue eyes and long dark lashes as me. Everyone said we looked like twins.

"What do you have there?" he asked, eyeing the bags I was carrying.

"Dinner," I said, pushing a pile of plates to one side and unloading everything on to the counter. "I thought we could go Italian. I brought prosciutto, Parmesan, those little stuffed peppers you like, and olives. Bread of course, and a bottle of Brunello..." I stopped when I saw Leo's expression.

"What?"

"I promised the boys we would have fish and chips tonight," he said.

"They can have fish and chips any night."

"No, they can't because I won't let them," said Leo firmly. "It's a treat because it's Saturday and first day of their half-term break."

"Well, let the boys have fish and chips. We'll eat this. All the more for us."

Leo nodded. "All right. You open the wine while I run to the chippie to pick up our order. I'll be just ten minutes."

I put plates and cutlery out on the kitchen island, retrieved two dirty wineglasses from the dishwasher, washed and dried them. There were no napkins to be found, so I folded pieces of kitchen towel into triangles and laid them by the two plates. I opened the wine, poured a little of the deep red liquid into each glass, then took a sip. It tasted of sun and warm earth. I rotated my shoulders, trying to roll the tension of the morning away. I wanted to check in to make sure Sophie was recovering, but didn't know which hospital she'd been taken to. I didn't even know her second name.

In the living room, the boys were shrieking in excitement and I wondered how Leo managed to stay so calm. He was a great Dad, single since his wife ran off with the realtor who had sold them this house two years ago. He was a math professor at Oxford University. Somehow, he managed to juggle his teaching with ferrying the boys to and from school, sports clubs and music lessons. I knew that cleaning and laundry came pretty far down the to-do list; the house had a faint odor of cooking fat and sweaty socks.

"What are you doing, Katie?" Leo came in with two white carrier bags. The smell of fish and malt vinegar filled up the kitchen.

I jumped. "Just straightening things a little."

"You were arranging the mugs so the handles all point in the same direction," he said accusingly, looking at the shelf holding the offending crockery.

"Well, it makes it easier to get them down that way."

"Here, help me dish this up. The boys can eat out of the paper. It'll save washing up later."

I realized that Leo had ordered enough for all four of us and felt a pang of guilt. It had never struck me to ask whether he would have preferred to eat fish and chips. We gave the boys their food, although I winced at the thought of what havoc the greasy meal would wreak on the sofa. Then Leo and I settled on the stools at the kitchen island.

"Cheers." Leo clinked his glass against mine. He looked serious. "Are you all right?" he asked. "You seem a bit jumpy."

I told him about the near-drowning in the park that morning. "The little girl will be all right," I said, "but it was scary."

"Goodness, Katie. That's rough. Good for you for saving her."

He paused, took a sip of wine. "I've been worried about you ever since Dad called. How are you feeling? Dad said your legs were pretty banged up. It can't have helped to be jumping in and out of ponds like you did this morning."

"I'm fine. Everything is healing quickly and no harm was done today, apart from to my nerves."

I tore a piece of bread in half, the white fibers stretching and breaking under the assault.

"What did Dad tell you about the accident?" I asked.

Leo looked at me over the rim of his glass. "Just that you had a bump on the head and seemed a little confused about what had happened. He sounded rattled, to be honest. It must have scared him to see you hurt like that, especially after Mum... Well, you know."

I took a gulp of wine. I'd had all week to think about what had happened and still didn't understand it. Was I going to tell Leo the truth or the anodyne version I'd stuck to with everyone else? I'd always confided in him, looked up to him when we were kids, shared with him my dream of becoming an architect. But he wouldn't want to hear this.

And then there was that strange moving air that I could see.

"Dad says the police are trying to trace the car, but that you didn't get a plate number, so he doubts they'll find anything." Leo paused. "Katie? What are you thinking about? You've got that million miles away look on your face."

Of course they wouldn't find anything, I thought.

Leo began eating with enthusiasm, apparently forgiving me for depriving him of his fish and chips.

"So until that happened, how do you think Dad was doing? Is he okay?"

I'd gone for the weekend to keep Dad company for his birthday, and ended up staying until Tuesday because of my accident. I knew Dad enjoyed seeing me. Or he had until the day after the accident. Things hadn't gone so well after that.

"Dad's okay. He's gardening and writing, and hanging out with Paolo." I paused and took a sip of wine. "And Francesca's spending a lot of time there. I think she has a crush on him."

Leo put his glass down. "You're not serious."

"Yes, really. Either Dad is totally oblivious or he's keen on her as well. She's been there cooking for him and now she's eating with him too. She calls him 'Feeleep'."

"It could be worse, I suppose," said Leo. "I like Francesca. She's been very nice to us all since we were kids."

He was right. My parents had first bought the villa as a vacation home and, whenever we visited, our neighbor Francesca would open the house up, air it out, and stock the fridge with food and milk. She always left treats, lollipops for the kids and biscotti for Mum and Dad. In the last few years, she'd lost both her son and her husband and now lived alone in a rambling villa close to my father's.

"I like her too, but it's too soon. Dad's lonely, I know, but he shouldn't hurry into another relationship."

"He's sensible enough not to move too fast. But some people, men anyway, need a partner. They're just not cut out for living alone."

"Not like you," I said. "But don't you miss Marie sometimes? Or think about finding someone new?"

He picked up his wineglass again. "I never miss Marie. And there is someone, actually. Her name's Olivia. I'd like you to meet her next time you're here. She's a psychology professor at the university. I think you'll like her."

Surprised, thrilled that Leo was finally showing some interest in dating, I nodded enthusiastically and was about to launch an inquisition when the phone rang.

"Aidan, get that, will you?" Leo called. There was no movement in the living room. When the ringing continued, Leo pushed his stool back, the feet scraping on the tile. I heard him pick up the phone in the hallway, followed by a murmur of voices. He came back to the kitchen looking shaken, reached for his glass and took a swallow of wine.

"That was Dad," he said.

"Is something wrong?" I felt my heart rate rocket.

"Francesca's dead."

I gripped the edge of the counter with one hand to steady myself. "What?"

"She had a stroke, probably yesterday evening, and her body was discovered a few hours ago. Dad's upset. She'd invited him over for dinner last night but he'd planned on playing chess with Paolo. Now he thinks that maybe she would have survived the stroke if he'd been there. They say the first hour is critical."

"Shit." I felt queasy. Francesca dead, so suddenly.

"The funeral will be next week some time," continued Leo. "I told Dad I'd fly over with the boys. It's half-term, so they'll be out of school."

There was something flickering at the edges of my brain, a memory of something that had happened with Francesca.

"Kate? Are you all right? You're not saying anything?"

"Sorry," I said. "Just a bit shocked, that's all. I mean, I saw her a few days ago and she was fine."

Francesca had come on Sunday morning with a beautiful cake to celebrate Dad's birthday. When she realized I'd been injured, she stayed to help look after me. She'd cooked lunch, which I'd hardly touched, fussed over me and helped me wash my hair, even though the whole time, I'd been mad with her for being there, flirting with Dad, taking my mother's place.

I took a big swallow of the fruity red wine. I didn't recall much of the day after the accident. Dad's friend, Paolo, the village doctor had come in to check on me, bandaged my legs and given me a couple of powerful painkillers. They'd left me woozy and light-headed. But now, suddenly, I remembered. I'd seen air swirling around Francesca's head, fast and sinuous, just like the air over Sophie and Rebecca.

I thought back to the park that morning. Was the air still moving over Sophie when the paramedics got there? I couldn't remember. I'd been so focused on the chest compressions that I hadn't thought to check.

"You're looking a bit green, Katie. Are you all right?"

"Not really."

Tears welled in my eyes and spilled down my cheeks. Leo put his glass down very carefully, as though it were made of the finest crystal.

"What's going on?"

"I have to tell you something, but you need to promise me to keep an open mind."

"Okay," he said slowly.

"My accident. It wasn't a hit and run. Something happened up there. And now..." I couldn't finish the sentence.

"Come on. Let's go sit in my study," he said. "It's more comfortable."

"All right," I said. "Bring the wine."

CHAPTER SIX

I slid into the corner of the geriatric brown couch in Leo's study. I felt hot and a little nauseous, but I knew I had to tell Leo everything. That was just the way it was between us. He pulled his desk chair over to sit opposite me. I took a deep breath, and pulled my knees up to my chest, hugging my legs more tightly than was really comfortable. I was glad the room was dark, lit only by the lamp on Leo's desk and a soft orange glow from a streetlight.

"On the day of the accident," I said. "Dad and I drove up the strada bianca to get to the top of the hill. We wanted to look at the view, you know, as we often do. Florence is always so beautiful from up there. It was a lovely day, warm and sunny, and the air smelled of thyme and lavender. We parked the car and walked to that gap between the olive trees. You know where I mean?"

He nodded.

"Then we heard a car engine coming from the other side of the hill."

"From the old farmhouse?"

"Yes. It was odd. I mean, the place is abandoned and the road doesn't go anywhere."

I shivered, remembering, recapturing every detail. The view, which usually delighted me, had made me feel wistful and melancholy. Anxious too, although I couldn't think why. My unease had grown, together with a vague feeling that I was being watched. The leaves of the tree behind me had sighed softly in a sudden breeze, and I'd glanced back over my shoulder. There was no one there. Only waves of heat that rose from the gravel road, making the air above it shimmer.

Leo waved his hand in front of my face. "Come on, Kate. Don't leave me hanging. What happened?"

"Okay, sorry. I went to the edge of the road, curious to see who would be driving up there. I know sometimes teenagers go to the old farmhouse but not usually in the middle of the afternoon. The engine was straining and then a silver car crested the hill. I couldn't see the driver because the windows were heavily tinted. Like a mafia car or something. Then the car stopped a few yards away from me and the back door opened. Dad came up behind me and put his hand on my arm. I think we were both nervous.

"A woman got out. Her hair was loose around her shoulders and she was wearing a blue and white flowered dress. Leo, it was Mum."

Leo didn't move. He was completely still, looking at me intently. I imagined him scrutinizing his students that way, looking for signs of understanding or for a burst of brilliant insight.

"I ran forward and Mum held out her arms to hold me."

I remembered the scent of face powder and perfume. The feel of her soft hair against my cheek. "She told me that they had let her come back to say goodbye, and that she knew how devastating her death had been for us all. She was sorry she'd left with no warning."

My heart pounded against my ribs. I was finding it hard to breathe.

"Kate?"

"Mum told me she loved me, and you and Dad too. And that Toby needed her. She said that he wanted me to be happy. Then she let go of me and got back into the car. I begged her to stop, to stay with us, but she blew me a kiss and pulled the door closed. The engine restarted and the car began to pull away.

"I was desperate, Leo. I grabbed hold of the door handle and tried to open the back door but it was locked. I began to jog alongside the car, banging on the window with my other hand. The wheels were spitting up jagged stones that stung my legs. Even when the car picked up speed, I ran alongside, my feet sliding along the gravel. I heard Dad shouting my name and then I fell, landing hard on my knees. My head hit the ground and I lost consciousness. When I woke up, I was in bed, with Dad and Paolo sitting there, watching me."

The silence that followed was heavy and black, reeking of

disbelief and shock, like an old musty blanket; there was nothing warm and comforting about it. The metal lamp on the desk creaked as the light bulb heated it. I heard Leo breathing, heard the monotonous drip of rain on the roof outside the window.

He shifted, uncrossed his legs and came to sit next to me on the couch. "You know that didn't happen, right?"

"But it did, Leo. I know Dad says it didn't. He says a car hit me and kept going but that's not what happened. I saw Mum. I spoke to her. I swear it. When I told Dad, he was upset and angry. We hardly spoke for two days."

When Leo put his arm around my shoulders, I leaned into him. It was easier not to look at his face, which was taut with anguish.

"Kate, think about it."

"There's something else."

I felt his arm muscles tense where my cheek rested against them.

"Since the accident, I've seen something, like air moving around people's heads and shoulders. It's clear air and it ripples."

"Like air rising from hot gravel?"

"Exactly."

He pushed me away gently so that he could look at me.

"It's a mirage, Katie. You saw the air rising over the road that day, and now you imagine you can see it in other places. Probably something to do with banging your head."

I didn't blame him for trying to rationalize things. What I was telling him was too implausible, too unbelievable. Yet I plunged on, telling him how I'd seen the moving air over the little girl at the park. And that I'd seen the air over Francesca too.

"And now Francesca is dead. I feel so guilty about that, Leo. I was angry with her and now ..."

"Stop right there, Kate," Leo said. He got up and walked to his desk, where he made some space by shoving a pile of papers off to one side. He perched on the edge, the way he sat when he was in class. I'd been to one of his lectures, advanced calculus that was way over my head, but I'd enjoyed watching him teach. Now I braced for a lecture on a different subject.

"You know, Kate, your life has been governed by guilt and regret. First about Toby's death and then about Mum's. Guilt is like..." He paused as though searching for the right phrase. "It's like a pernicious weed. It grows and grows until there's no room for positive thought or feeling. You have to cut it out before it destroys you."

Wrapping my arms around myself, I shrank back into the corner of the couch. I didn't want to hear what he was saying.

"And now you're saying you feel guilty over what happened to Francesca. Well, that's crazy. Being angry with someone doesn't kill them."

He shifted, leaned forward towards me.

"Kate, I grieve for Toby too. And you have no idea how much I miss Mum. You can feel sorry for what happened, but not guilty. Neither of those deaths was your fault. Grief serves a purpose, but guilt doesn't. You have to let it go. You have so much potential and you're burying it under a granite mountain of self-condemnation and regret."

"A bit strong on the metaphors, Leo," I said, hoping to ease the tension.

He smiled, stood and retrieved our glasses from the floor where he'd left them. He sat down next to me. "I'm sure I'm right, Katie. That blow to the head has caused this. Have you seen a doctor?"

"I have a CT scan scheduled for Monday."

"Good. Then we'll know more." He squeezed my hand. "It'll be all right."

We sipped our wine. This time the silence was consoling. I knew he wouldn't say any more tonight; he didn't believe in superfluous conversation. I wished, of course, that he had believed me, but that was just wishful thinking. There was no way my brother could accept what I'd told him. He was a scientist and a purist. From my earliest memories of him, he'd analyzed everything. How high a swing could go depending on the length of the chains. Why custard went lumpy if the heat was too high. If he couldn't measure it or weigh it or explain it with a formula, then it didn't exist.

I finished my wine and wished there was more. I knew Leo was right about one thing. For as long as I could remember, I'd been weighed down by guilt; as though it was an anchor, something that kept me stable. If I let it go, I'd be cast adrift, floating with no direction. I couldn't imagine my life without the heft and mass of my failings to keep my feet on the ground.

"I should clean up the kitchen," I said, stretching my legs out and testing how my knees felt before putting all my weight on them.

Leo stood up, looking relieved that my confession was over. He took his laptop from his desk. "I'll go online and book some flights.

At least the boys will be excited to see Grandpa. Can you come?"

"I can't risk taking any more time off," I said. I half-wished I could go, to spend time with Leo and the boys and Dad, but was relieved too that my workload gave me an excuse to miss Francesca's service. I wasn't sure I could face a second funeral so soon after my mother's. Or that I could handle Leo and Dad together, both trying to convince me that the accident hadn't happened the way I described it or that the moving air was a figment of my wild imagination.

CHAPTER SEVEN

While Leo booked flights, I helped Aidan and Gabe to pack their cases. Then I headed for bed, bone-tired. Just as I turned out the light, Rebecca texted me to say she couldn't make the movie the following evening. She suggested lunch instead and we agreed to meet at my favorite Chinese restaurant.

In the morning, I dropped Leo and the boys off at Heathrow for their flight to Italy. We hadn't spoken any more about my accident or the moving air. The boys were excited and noisy in the back seat; I was glad they were focused on seeing their grandfather, and not so much on the real reason for the trip.

Back in the city, after dropping off the Zipcar, I reached the restaurant at the same time as Rebecca. The air was eddying around her head, faster and more visible than ever.

The owner, a tiny trim woman in a red mandarin jacket, hurried to the table when she saw me.

"Where is your boyfriend?" she asked. "He's not with you?" It sounded like an accusation.

I shook my head. "He isn't my boyfriend."

The woman laughed, showing small, perfect white teeth.

"Of course he your boyfriend," she said, clapping her hands together. "I see the way he look at you. And you at him." Still laughing as though I had told her a funny joke, she turned away to greet some new customers.

"What was that all about?" asked Rebecca.

"A friend," I said. "We come here quite often, but he's not my boyfriend."

"The good-looking guy with the dark hair? What's his name, Josh?"

I nodded.

"Why not?" she asked. "Why aren't you dating him? He's gorgeous."

She sighed, and yet again I found myself wondering about her own love life.

"Well, he hasn't asked me out," I said. Then I realized he had, sort of, the other day. I hadn't exactly jumped all over the invitation and now perhaps he wouldn't ask again.

I picked up the menu. "Let's eat."

After ordering, we drank jasmine tea while we waited for the food. Although I asked a few questions about her boyfriend, Edward, Rebecca didn't seem to want to talk about him, so instead I asked her about her family.

"My Mum and Dad are in Bournemouth," she said. "They retired there a few years ago. They like the beach and the sea air."

We paused while the waiter put down plates of potstickers, rice and kung pao shrimp.

"You don't have any siblings?" I couldn't remember ever meeting Rebecca's family. At graduation, when I might have met them, we were in different sections of the hall and hadn't seen each other at all.

"No, just me and my parents," she said. Her eyes drifted to somewhere over my shoulder and I half-turned to see if there was someone behind me, but there was no one. She refocused on me and changed the subject. We talked about Italy. She said she'd love to have more time to travel.

The waiter came by to clear our plates, and left more tea and a plate of fortune cookies. Rebecca took a cookie, broke it in half and pulled out the slip of white paper, laughing. "I love reading these things," she said.

"'You will discover the truth about the one you love,'" she quoted. Her smile faded. "I wonder what that could mean." Crumpling the paper in her hand, she put it on the table. "Here, let's do one for you."

She opened a second cookie and read the fortune aloud. "'If you speak honestly, everyone will listen.'" She handed the little piece of paper to me. I stared at it.

Should I speak honestly? Tell Rebecca about the air over her head and my fear that it was a portent of some kind? Of course not. She'd think I was mad. I thought I was crazy and so did Leo.

"Are you all right?" Rebecca asked, looking concerned.

"Yes, I'm fine. Still getting a headache from time to time."

"I really think you should get some medical help," she said. I told her about the doctor visit and the scheduled CT scan.

"Oh good," she said. "It's sensible to be sure that there was no damage done when you were hit by that car. Do you want me to come with you?"

"No, but thanks for offering. I'm going to sneak out at lunchtime and hope it will be as quick as possible. If Alan realizes I'm away from my desk, he'll have a fit."

She laughed. "He does seem a bit scary."

The waiter brought more tea. I took a sip and then put the cup down on the table, thinking of the fortune cookie message. Be honest, it said. My one attempt at honesty had earned me a lecture from my brother. But I thought that Rebecca would be more understanding. At the very least, I owed her a warning.

"There's something I want to talk to you about," I said. I cleared my throat to stop my voice from shaking. "Since the accident, I've been seeing these strange visions, of air moving around over people's heads. Well, not all people. Just a few."

Rebecca tilted her head to one side. "Visions? Goodness, Kate, I'm so glad you're getting a scan tomorrow. But who has this air moving over them? People you know, or strangers on the street?"

"Both," I said. "Strangers and..." My voice croaked to a stop. I drank some more tea. "And friends."

She stared at me. "Do you mean me?"

I nodded. She reached up and moved her hand across the top of her head. "Is it there now?"

"Yes."

"What does it mean?"

I couldn't tell her that Francesca was dead.

"I don't know. It could be nothing, or it could mean you're going to, I don't know, fall in love or find some money."

I tried to laugh, but Rebecca's face was like stone.

"That's really weird, Kate. How many others?"

"Just a few. A man on the Tube, a little girl in a park. A friend of my Dad's."

I hurried on, before she could ask me any more questions. "Anyway, I'll know more after the test tomorrow. Maybe I have a swelling or something that's messing up my vision. My aunt had something like it once. Well, vertigo, I think it was, and she saw everything double for weeks." I was rambling, unsure how to stop talking.

To my surprise, Rebecca smiled. "You've always been a little eccentric, Kate. We relied on you to make life interesting and you usually did. Do you remember when we all shrink-wrapped every single object in Sheila's room, including her bed?"

"You remember that?"

"Of course. And that time when we covered the whole whiteboard in the lecture theater with sticky notes and Professor Ormond didn't know what to do with them."

I smiled at her, grateful for the reminder of the fun we'd had. My college years had been a good time for me. Away from home and the constant reminders of my little brother, I'd relaxed and enjoyed all that university life had to offer.

When I turned my attention back to Rebecca, she was still recounting details of our pranks; she seemed to be ignoring what I had told her about the moving air. In spite of my anxiety for her, I smiled. She had a flair for telling stories. Even though I knew she was embellishing, her recounting of our student exploits was funny. We were still laughing when the waiter came back with the bill. I offered to pay, but Rebecca grabbed the check and put her credit card down on it.

"My treat. I feel badly about not being able to make the movie this evening."

"That's all right. I hope you have a good time with Edward."

"Edward? Oh, right. I'm sure I will."

"What are you going to do? Dinner?" I knew I was pressing, but I was desperate to learn more about the boyfriend.

"Probably. We'll decide later."

"Rebecca, I want you to be careful. I don't know what the moving air means but I have a feeling it's not something good."

She blinked a few times. "Why do you say that?"

I crumbled a fortune cookie into tiny pieces on my plate. "I saw the air around someone who died a few days later," I said. "But I also saw it over the head of a little girl. She nearly drowned, but I was able to save her."

Rebecca signed the receipt and waved over the waiter to pick it up.

"Are you going to save me?" she asked. I flinched at her tone. This was ridiculous. I had no idea what the aura meant. I should have kept quiet until I knew more. Pushing her chair back, she stood up. "I hope the scan goes well tomorrow," she said. "Maybe they'll work out what's causing these bizarre visions of moving air. Let me know, won't you?"

I didn't blame her for being upset with me. I would be too, if someone had dumped that on me. I stood up, picked up my coat from the back of the chair and put it on.

Rebecca suddenly smiled. She gave me a hug. "Don't worry about me. I'll be fine. How about doing our theater trip next Saturday? I'll get the tickets and call you with the time and where to meet?"

"Yes, definitely," I said, although Saturday was far away and the air was moving fast. I was staring too obviously, I realized. Self-consciously, she smoothed the hair on the crown of her head.

"I must run," she said. "See you soon, sweetie."

CHAPTER EIGHT

At lunchtime on Monday, grabbing my bag and coat, I hurried towards the elevator, glad that my knees had mended well enough for me to move with some speed. Praying that I wouldn't run into Alan, I crossed the lobby and hailed a taxi.

Ten minutes after arriving at the hospital, I was shivering in a changing room, wearing an ugly grey gown that hung almost to my ankles. I felt like a novice nun, a most unlikely vocation for me, a practicing agnostic.

I clutched the gown tightly around me. Hospitals made me nervous, really stomach-clenching, sweaty-palm nervous. A nurse took me into a room dominated by a massive machine that whirred and clicked, like an alien spider crouching over me.

A young technician gave me instructions. He was rather handsome, which motivated me to be brave. I followed his directions carefully, lay still, and managed to smile at his jokes even though I was scared. Not so much about the process, but of the potential result.

In fact all I had to do was lie very still, while the machine moved over me. It was loud, but not as bad as I'd feared. When it was over, the technician gave me a high five.

"Good job. You're a model patient. Wait for a few minutes just outside there," he said, pointing the way to a small waiting area furnished with several tan-colored sofas and end tables piled with magazines and papers. "I just need to check the scan to make sure I got everything."

Trying to ignore the churning in my stomach, I picked up the local newspaper, and flicked through it, not really able to concentrate on stories of celebrity misbehavior and political shenanigans. But on page six, a headline caught my eye. "Tragic death of toddler in park."

Sophie McDonald died after falling into the park's boating pond, the article said. A passerby pulled her from the water and the child was taken to the ER, where she died late on Sunday. The mother was treated for shock and released.

My head began to spin with the memory of what had happened. Sophie had been safe, I thought. The paramedics were there. She should have been all right.

"All good," the technician said, poking his head into the waiting area. "You're free to go. Your doctor will call you with the results."

He turned and disappeared through the double doors into his strange, technological universe. The newspaper fell from my lap to the floor just as a nurse accompanied another patient into the waiting room.

"Are you all right? You look very pale," the nurse said to me. She hurried over with a paper cup of water. "Drink this. Do you feel dizzy?"

I nodded. The waiting room began to swirl around me, a nauseating carousel of tan sofas and beige walls. I gripped the arms of my chair. I couldn't breathe. A whirlpool of brown, churning water was dragging me down and my limbs wouldn't move. I couldn't reach the surface. Panicking, I was taking in gulps of water. I knew I was going to drown.

When the spinning stopped, I was lying on a gurney in a cubicle with white curtains. A nurse took my blood pressure and my temperature and told me to lie still until the doctor arrived. I seemed to be hooked up to a monitor that beeped occasionally. Twisting my head around, I saw green lines scrolling across a screen.

"I'm fine," I protested, but the nurse insisted I stay still.

It seemed to take a long time until a young Indian doctor arrived. He examined my eyes and ears and checked the information on a chart at the foot of the bed.

"How are you feeling?" he asked. "The wound on your head appears to be healing nicely but I wondered how it came to be there?"

I told him that I'd been in a hit and run, and had suffered some injuries to my legs and head.

He clucked sympathetically. "Dear, dear," he said. "I'm very sorry to hear it. The good news is that I see no sign of damage to the head apart from the superficial external wound. I've reviewed your CT scan and everything is clear. Sometimes, just the stress of having the scan can induce symptoms such as vertigo. I think that's what happened here. Do you mind if I check your other injuries? Your legs, you said?"

He gently peeled the sheet to one side and folded my gown back to expose my knees. His fingers were soft on my legs. He murmured to himself before straightening up, pulling the sheet back in place.

"You said you were hit by a car?"

I nodded.

"These injuries don't seem consistent with the impact of a car," he said, with a frown. "Did you have any other injuries? To the hip or shoulder, perhaps? Were you facing the car when it happened, or crossing a street?"

I felt dizzy again, felt the blood draining from my head. The bright lights were dazzling and hurt my eyes. Telling Leo the real story hadn't worked very well. I could only imagine the reaction if I told the truth to the nice young doctor. He was watching the heart monitor and scribbling notes on my chart.

"Don't talk," he said. "Just rest for thirty minutes. Then we'll check on you again."

"I really need to go," I said. "I'm late for work."

"I can't discharge you when your heart rate is so high. I'll be back soon. Stay calm and rest."

A nurse appeared to place a warm coverlet over me. The heaviness of it seemed disproportionate to its fluffy whiteness. Lying still, held captive by the blanket, I tried deep breathing to slow my heart down. My watch and cell phone were with my clothes in a locker in the changing room, so I had no idea whether one minute had passed, or five or ten. The achromatic cubicle was timeless and ephemeral, a space where patients and doctors passed through; a brief interaction and a myriad of outcomes.

Maybe I dozed for a while, maybe the time vortex spun faster than I thought, but the doctor was soon back and he smiled at me when I opened my eyes.

"Very good. All vital signs are normal. Do you have anyone who can come to fetch you?"

"No." The only person who might possibly come was Leo and he was in Italy.

"I could send you home in an ambulance, I suppose," the doctor said, taking off his glasses to clean them with a corner of his white coat. "You must have assistance to get home."

Embarrassed by the attention, his concern, and the thought of using up an ambulance driver's valuable time, I decided to call Josh, hoping that he'd have his cell phone on. I also hoped that Alan wasn't around to prevent him from answering it. The doctor gave me my bag and I found my cell phone. When Josh picked up on one ring, I explained what had happened.

"I'll be right there," he said.

**

It took some time to convince him I was well enough to go back to work, especially as the nurse had told him I should go straight home. In the taxi, Josh was quiet, sensing that I wasn't up to talking. When we reached the office, he helped me out of the cab and put his hand under my elbow to walk me to the elevator.

"Don't want you falling," he said.

Inevitably, the elevator stopped on the second floor and Alan got in. There must be some mathematical equation that calculates the chances of such a thing, but it seemed preordained that I'd bump into the one person in the universe that I wanted to avoid.

"So nice of you to make an appearance, Kate. What was it this time? Shopping, quick jet set to Tuscany?"

"I had a doctor's appointment during my lunch hour. It went longer than I thought it would," I said, my head beginning to ache again. "I'll make up the time this evening, I promise."

"You bet you will," he said. "We're not running a resort here."

"Alan, be nice," said Josh. "Kate was injured and she needed a CT scan. You know she'll get the work done."

Alan just scowled at us. He got off on the next floor. Leaning against the wall of the elevator, I closed my eyes briefly. I felt Josh take my hand in his.

"You okay?" he asked. Without thinking, I moved towards him, resting my head against his shoulder. I felt his arms go around me. For a few seconds, I felt warm and safe, until a loud ping signaled our floor and the doors slid open.

I kept my wits about me for long enough to thank Josh for coming to my aid and wandered off towards my office, thinking of how his arms had felt, how concerned he'd looked. Seated at my desk, I picked up a pencil. It felt alien in my fingers. I had no idea what to do with it. Francesca and Sophie were both dead. They'd both had the moving air around them. My mouth was dry and my headache had come back. Could the strange visual phenomenon predict death? It seemed crazy, but both Francesca and Sophie had died. I couldn't help thinking it.

If so, Rebecca was in great danger.

I texted her but there was no response, which wasn't surprising. It was the middle of a workday and she was probably in a meeting. Seeing Alan stroll past my door, I slipped my phone back into my bag, quickly picking up a pencil again.

Late in the afternoon, I got a text from Josh, asking if I'd have dinner with him that evening. Warmth flooded my neck and chest, and my fingertips tingled. I stood up and stretched, feeling the release in my shoulder muscles. Outside, street lamps and headlights shone in the growing darkness like fairy lights on a Christmas tree.

CHAPTER NINE

The interior of the restaurant was warm and filled with the fragrance of curry spices. The red, flocked wallpaper was bright and cheerful. Bollywood music played a soft accompaniment to the clink of cutlery and murmur of voices.

Josh was waiting for me, sitting at a corner table near the window. He immediately stood up to take my coat. Some of the office staff mocked him for being old-fashioned, but I liked it. He worked as hard as anyone, yet always found time to ask his colleagues how their weekends had been or how their families were doing. Not many people, in my experience, made that effort to interact with their peers.

When we were seated, Josh ordered me a glass of wine. He took a sip of his beer.

"I'm glad you were free this evening," he said. "Alan suggested I have a chat with you. He's unhappy with all the time you've taken off, and being what he calls distracted."

The mellowness I was feeling melted away. So this was a business meeting after all.

"How mad is he?"

"On a scale of one to ten? Maybe eleven."

"Ouch."

Josh broke a pappadum in half and handed me a piece. "He said he's going to let you stay on the Montgomery project but blathered on about this being your last chance. Get this one right or consider yourself out. You know what he's like. Anyway, I've done what he told me to do, and now we can forget about it and enjoy the evening. He's just grandstanding. There's no way he'd let you go."

"I feel as though I've let you down; I'm sorry. I'll work hard on the project from now on. I know how important it is to the company."

Josh took another sip of his beer. "No need to apologize to me. Your work is always first class. But I am worried about you. Since that accident in Italy you've been different. I'm not being critical. I just want to help. If you need medical leave, you'll get it. Even Alan can't object to that."

Crumbling a piece of pappadum, I shook my head. "No, I don't need medical leave. I'm healing quickly. My knees are much better and my head, well, physically, it's fine. Mentally, I'm not so sure, but I promise I'm okay."

"If you want to talk, I'm really happy to listen."

I was saved from answering right away by the arrival of our waiter with dishes of steaming chicken tikka masala, sag aloo and rice. Suddenly I realized how hungry I was and scooped food on to my plate, savoring the aromas.

Having devoured most of his food, Josh put his fork down.

"I wish you'd tell me what's going on," he said.

I looked around the restaurant, at the couples and groups of business people, men with loosened ties and women in business suits with their jackets off, an Indian family laughing together. So normal. I was jealous of them all. There was nothing normal about my life now.

I felt tears welling in my eyes and Josh handed me his napkin. Then he called the waiter over to ask for our bill.

"Why don't we go have a cup of tea at your place, as it's closest?" he suggested. He'd been over a couple of times, walking me home after a company dinner or drinks.

Too tired to argue, I nodded. We walked out of the restaurant into a steady drizzle that soon soaked our shoes and coats. With our collars turned up and heads bowed against the wind, we hurried along the few blocks to my apartment.

"I'll get you a towel," I said to Josh, once we were inside. I gave it to him, then went to my room to change out of my wet clothes into a sweatshirt and jeans. When I got back to the kitchen, Josh had put the kettle on and was measuring tea into a pot. I smiled. He reminded me of Leo, always calm and practical. He'd rubbed his hair dry and it was sticking up slightly, in a way that I couldn't help finding adorable. We took our mugs into the living room, where I sat on the sofa. Josh perched on the edge of the opposite armchair.

"I hope you don't mind," he said. "I took my shoes off and left them by the door. The rest of me will air out gradually."

"Of course not." I looked at his socked feet. Navy blue. Cashmere, I guessed.

"So are you going to tell me what's worrying you?" he asked.

"I'm stressing about all the work time I've missed because of the accident."

It seemed easiest to explain a single, tangible concern than to launch into a description of the weird moving air phenomenon.

Josh put his cup down on the coffee table and came to sit next to me. He took my hand in his squeezing it gently. "Ignore Alan. He's full of pith and vinegar, as my mother would say. He gets over-excited and doesn't know when to stop talking, but you're keeping up with your project deadlines. The work you've done this week is good, really good. He has nothing to complain about."

"There is something else," I began, but a lump in my throat stopped the rest of my words. Josh moved closer and put his arms around me. With my head on his shoulder, I felt warm and protected. Tears spilled out, soaking into his blue shirt that smelled of laundry soap.

After a while, I lifted my head to look at him. "I'm sorry."

"Don't be sorry. Listen, Kate, I really care about you. Not just as a friend. Don't get me wrong, I like being friends, but for me there's more to it."

I didn't answer and the silence built between us like a tangible wall. I could almost hear the clink of bricks, one on top of the other. Letting go of me, he leaned back into the sofa cushions.

"You don't feel the same way, I guess."

"Josh, I do." Again, my throat clogged up and I couldn't speak. Josh smiled, a wonderful smile that made his eyes sparkle, and he wrapped his arms around me again.

"But there is something I need to sort out first," I said.

"We can sort it out together," he said. "Whatever it is."

I eased myself out of his arms and went to the kitchen for a paper towel to dry my eyes. I wanted to tell him everything, about the visions I was having, about Francesca and Sophie. But it sounded so outlandish. I couldn't dump all that on him. I just couldn't open myself up to the risk of ridicule or rejection.

I walked to the window and looked outside. The rain had stopped, and a half-moon shone, partially obscured by the soft edges of a dark cloud. I slid the window up and leaned out, breathing in the scent of rain-soaked slate. Traffic hummed on the main road a few blocks away, and a group of teenagers shouted and laughed in the street below. I should be thrilled, happy, singing with joy. But the timing was all wrong.

He came to stand behind me. "What are you thinking?" he asked.

I leaned into him for a few seconds, then twisted out of his arms and turned to face him. "I just need some time."

"And you can't tell me why?" he asked. When I didn't answer, he frowned, a vertical line between his dark brows. I reached up to smooth it away.

"Is there someone else?" he asked.

"No, no. Nothing like that."

"I don't want to pry. But, if you can trust me with whatever it is, I'll be there for you."

I wanted to tell him. I needed to, if I had any chance of being with him in the way I wanted to be. If I said nothing, then I was telling him a lie.

"I can see when someone is going to die."

To give Josh his due, he didn't laugh. He did look very skeptical.

"What did you say?" he said, his voice a little higher than usual.

"Sit down and I'll tell you everything." I led him back to the sofa.

"You remember that my mother died a few months ago? I went back to Italy for the funeral?"

He nodded. He'd been kind to me, bought me some flowers, left condolence notes on my desk.

"I never knew how she died," he said. "You didn't really talk about it."

"She was killed by a car while she was walking in a pedestrian crossing. The thing is..." I found it hard to form the words. "It was my fault. I'd texted her and she was texting me back. Witnesses said that she checked the road was clear before walking across, but was looking at her phone when a car came out of nowhere. It didn't stop. She never even saw it."

"That doesn't make it your fault, Kate," Josh said.

I plunged on, describing how I'd seen my mother get out of a car on the hill in Tuscany. Josh was silent. I didn't blame him. I wouldn't know what to say either.

"After that, I started to see this strange thing, air rippling around people's heads and shoulders."

I told him about Francesca and Sophie. "They're both dead," I said. "And Rebecca has the same thing. So I think that means she's going to die."

Josh was quiet for a long time when I finished talking. The only sound was the faint rustle of cloth as he jiggled one leg up and down nervously.

"Josh, I don't want to freak you out. It sounds insane, I know."

"Have you told anyone else?"

"My brother. He didn't believe me, thought it was all in my head."

"You really believe that Rebecca is going to die?"

I shrugged. "Based on what happened before, yes, but I don't know when or how."

"So it could be tomorrow or next week or next month? Next year?"

I leaned back and rubbed my eyes. "I've only got two experiences to base this on, but with Francesca, the air was fainter than with Sophie. I saw her several days before she had the stroke. With Sophie, the air was moving faster, and she fell into the pool just minutes later. So I think there is a connection between the movement of the air and the amount of time left. Rebecca's was faint when I first saw it and it's growing more pronounced every time I see her."

Josh shook his head. "I'm sorry. I'm finding this hard to take in."

"You and me both." I laughed, but it came out as a sob.

"I've heard about people who can see energy fields." His voice was calmer. "Sort of light auras around people that change color depending on how they feel."

He must have seen the surprise on my face.

"There was a movie I saw once, I can't remember what it was called," he said. "But it was interesting and I looked up 'aura' on the Internet. It's bizarre, I admit, but then there's all sorts of stuff going on in the universe that we don't understand or even know about."

He walked into the kitchen, opened the fridge and took out a half-full bottle of white wine. Pouring two glasses, he came back and gave me one.

"I need something stronger than tea to handle this," he said with a grin. We sat together on the sofa, holding hands.

"So, you've seen this aura three times..."

"More than that," I said. "But sometimes with strangers, so I don't know what happened to them. I try not to think about it, really."

He nodded. "I can understand that. He took a long swallow of wine and put the glass on the table. Without thinking, I picked it up, placing it on the coaster. He laughed.

"You always were a control freak," he said. "And I mean that in the nicest possible way."

I raised an eyebrow at him, which he answered with a sheepish smile. "It's true. You're so organized and efficient. Everything has to be orderly. Until recently, of course. Now you're a crazy, discombobulated mess. Personally, I find that rather enchanting."

Using my elbow, I jabbed his arm. "Watch it. I don't intend to be like this forever. I'll soon be back to my old ways."

"I like your old ways too," he said. His grin faded and he looked more serious. "If you hadn't seen the aura thingy over Rebecca's head, would you still be worried about her? I mean, she hasn't hinted about being ill, threatened, suicidal?"

I thought about it for a few seconds. "No. Nothing. So no, I wouldn't be concerned."

"Well, perhaps you should try not to worry then," he said. "There's every chance that there's no real meaning to the aura and that the two deaths you've told me about are just coincidences. Besides, Rebecca is a grown-up. I'm sure she's very capable of looking after herself."

I looked up at him. There was something about his tone of voice. "You don't like her?"

"I don't know. I've only met her a couple of times, but she does seem kind of superficial." He stopped when he saw the expression on my face. "Ok, that's judgmental. I'm sorry. I'm sure she's a good person."

"She is, once you get to know her. I think with her being so beautiful, it changes how people relate to her."

"You're beautiful, but you're also kind and thoughtful. You're real."

I took a moment to let Josh's words sink in, like warm honey on my skin. But, seconds later, the old chill was back. I wanted to believe what Josh was saying about the aura being coincidental, but I was sure it wasn't. It was his way of dealing with my bizarre confession.

"The aura's real too, Josh."

He nodded. "I believe you. Just tell me what you want me to do and I'll do it. We'll get it sorted out, I promise."

My eyelids were feeling heavy. I realized I was really tired. I drained my wineglass and leaned back against the cushions. "I'm sorry. I need an early night. Everything still hurts."

"Are you sure you're going to be okay by yourself?" he asked. "I could sleep on the sofa if you don't want to be alone."

I shook my head. "I'm so tired, I'll be asleep before you even reach the bottom of the stairs. Thank you though for listening, and for caring…"

Leaning towards him, I kissed him briefly, on the lips. It was tempting to have him stay, but I knew that I wasn't in control of my emotions. I felt capable of laughing hysterically and bursting into tears, both at the same time. I didn't want to weird him out any more than I already had.

His jacket was still damp when I picked it up. While I watched him pull it on, I wrestled with conflicting desires. To sleep, or to stay up all night, drinking wine and talking with him. He pulled me towards him, stroking my hair back from my face. "Get some sleep. I'll see you tomorrow."I wanted to answer but my throat hurt too much. Tears made my eyes burn as I watched him close the door gently behind him.

CHAPTER TEN

There was a meeting with the Montgomery group on Tuesday morning. Arriving early at the conference room, I took a seat, and watched everyone else file in. Josh sat opposite me.

"You okay?" he asked, while Peter Montgomery and three of his associates took their seats.

I nodded, grateful for his concern.

"Are we ready to begin?" Alan asked. He seemed to be more orange than usual, or maybe it was the lavender polo shirt that exacerbated his skin tone.

"Where's Rebecca?" I asked, looking at Montgomery.

He shrugged, glancing at his assistants with an eyebrow raised in query.

"I don't know," one of them said.

"Is she sick?" I demanded, leaning forward in my chair. I caught a glimpse of a warning glance from Josh and sensed Alan tensing at the end of the table.

"She was away from her desk yesterday?" the man replied, his voice rising into a question of his own, clearly unsure that he needed to respond to me.

"Didn't anyone bother to find out why she's not here today?" I stood up.

"That's enough, Kate. Please sit down." Alan's tone was of barely subdued fury.

Peter Montgomery looked at me. "I don't understand what

business it is of yours," he said, a deep frown forming over his blue eyes.

"Rebecca's my friend. I'm worried about her."

"Your friend? Well, I'm sure there's nothing to be concerned about," he said condescendingly. "People take time off work when they have a cold, or a hangover, or when there's a good sale on at Selfridges. But in Ms. Williams' case, she could very well be out of town at one of our other offices. We have many of them, which she visits regularly. I'll check with my secretary when I get back to my office. Now can we please proceed?"

I thought about it. Rebecca could be away on business, but wouldn't she have answered my text from yesterday? Even if she were really busy?

"I need to make a quick call," I said walking towards the door.

"Kate, please come and sit down," said Alan quietly. I turned to look back. He looked like a python coiled and ready to strike. Josh had one hand over his eyes as though he couldn't bear to watch. The Montgomery money men were reading files, oblivious to it all, or pretending to be, and Montgomery's eyes were cold, his mouth pursed in disapproval.

I walked out, closing the door carefully behind me. My fingers trembled as I pressed the buttons for Rebecca's number. I knew a major confrontation with Alan would come later, but I couldn't worry about that now. The call went to voicemail. I tried again and left a voicemail telling Rebecca to call me right back, then stood motionless, unsure of what to do. Finally I walked back to my office. I'd barely sat down when Alan arrived. He leaned both hands on the desk opposite me, his face flushed with anger.

"What the fuck are you up to?" he demanded. "Peter Montgomery is our biggest client, and you just walked out on him. Now please get back in there and do your job."

"I just need to check in on Rebecca."

"You can do that later."

I hesitated. I felt like I was walking along the rim of a cliff and the ground was subsiding beneath me. If I didn't do as Alan said, this could be the end of my employment at Bradley Cohen. But I was worried sick about Rebecca. I realized that I hadn't heard from her all day Monday. It had been such a crazy day that I hadn't noticed. Now, I felt crushed with guilt. I was supposed to be looking out for her and I didn't even know where she was. But I couldn't lose my job.

I nodded at Alan. "I'm sorry."

"Whatever," Alan said and headed back towards the conference room. I followed him and took my seat. Josh looked relieved to see me and, for his sake, I did my best to focus on the discussion and do my part. The meeting lasted for several hours and then Alan requested we stay for a review meeting after Montgomery and his crew had left. It was mid-afternoon by the time we wrapped up. The conference table was littered with paper plates and remnants of sandwiches, empty cans and cups and a mini-blizzard of rejected notes and drawings. While everyone packed up and left the room, I swept the debris into a wastepaper basket.

"We have people who do that, you know," came a voice from the door. I looked up to see Jack Cohen beaming at me.

He was dressed in a suit and a green bow tie, a matching handkerchief poking out of his breast pocket. The bow tie was a fixture, with a daily change of color.

"How are you, my dear?" he asked.

"I'm fine, thanks, Jack, How are you? Looking very dapper in green today."

Jack smiled widely, sending a battalion of wrinkles marching over his cheeks and forehead. He was in his sixties but fit and wiry. He'd run the London Marathon for the first time the previous year and was in training for the one in New York.

"Good, good," he said. "I heard on the grapevine that you had an accident, and that the road to recovery has been a little bumpy?"

Alan complaining about me, no doubt. I briefly explained that I'd been hit by a car, and apologized for taking time out.

"I'm much better now," I said, half-expecting him to tell me I was fired or on probation. But he just looked at me with concern in his eyes.

"You let me know if there's anything I can do," he said. "Although I won't be around much for the next week or so. I've got an outing planned for later this week, followed by a business trip to Edinburgh early next week."

I pushed the last paper plate into the bin and set it down in the corner. "Well, send me a postcard."

"I might just do that."

I went back to my office to call Rebecca again, but there was still no answer. Josh dropped by to say he was going off-site with Alan. I breathed a sigh of relief. With Alan out for the rest of the afternoon, I'd be able to leave early.

Ben walked past my office, seemed to think of something and came back to my door.

"So, you're spending time with the Montgomery Financial Director outside of the office?" he asked.

"We're just friends," I answered. "There's nothing sinister going on."

Ben's pale moon face crumpled in mock amusement. "Friends? That's fast. No one makes friends that quickly."

"No one would make friends with you that quickly," I retorted. "But, no, we knew each other in college."

That silenced him for a few seconds, but then he started again. "Even so, it's against company policy to socialize with clients," he said. "You might be giving out information on details that we're not ready to commit to yet."

"Rebecca's not going to hold us to anything I tell her in a social setting," I said. "Besides, we don't talk about work."

"Says you," sneered Ben. Although I knew better, I was provoked into arguing back.

"I promise you, this is just about two girls having lunch or a glass of wine together. We're not sharing corporate secrets or planning the overthrow of the male-dominated management regime. The future of Bradley Cohen is not at stake. I think you're over-reacting."

Ben sniffed. "I doubt that Alan sees it that way."

"I'm busy, Ben. If you'll excuse me, I have work to do. And I'm sure you do too."

I called Rebecca's cell several more times and on the third call, got a recorded message saying that her voicemail box was full. The minutes dragged by. Every time I looked at the time in the corner of my computer monitor, I thought the screen had frozen. Finally, when the display showed 5p.m. I packed my briefcase, grabbed my coat and headed for the Tube.

Back at home, I dumped my briefcase in the hall. After putting the kettle on for tea, I changed into jeans and a warm sweater. I thought of calling Josh to ask his advice, but he was probably still out with Alan. I could go over to Rebecca's flat to see if she were there, but she would have answered her phone. Peter Montgomery seemed to think she could be working elsewhere. Still, she had been out of touch for a long time, and that bothered me.

I took my cup to the living room, feeling my anxiety harden into a rock of foreboding that sat like lead in my stomach. Taking a last gulp of tea, I opened my laptop and started searching for the name Williams in Bournemouth. Maybe her parents would know where she was. There were ten listings, fewer than I'd feared, but the first five rang through to voicemail or to voicemail boxes that were full and refusing messages. Maybe nobody checked their landlines nowadays. On the sixth call, a woman answered. I asked for Rebecca.

"Who the hell is Rebecca," she said. "And who are you? Do you know my husband?"

I rang off quickly and kept going, tapping numbers into my iPhone and feeling a little stupid. On the ninth call, a man responded. "Williams household. Who's calling please?"

"Mr. Williams. I'm wondering if Rebecca is there?"

After a short pause, he replied. "No, I'm sorry. Who is this?"

"I'm a friend of Rebecca's. You wouldn't happen to know where she is, would you?"

"Well, she'll be at home, I'd think," he said. "Or maybe still at the office. She does seem to work long hours."

I didn't want to worry him by telling him she hadn't turned up for work. "I lost her cell phone number," I continued. "So I haven't been able to reach her. I'm sorry to bother you."

"Oh, no bother, I can give you her number," he said. I was touched by how trusting he was. Pretending to take note of the number, I thanked him and was about to ring off when he asked "Are you Kate, by any chance?"

"Yes, Kate Benedict," I said, wondering how he could know who I was.

"Rebecca was here on Friday night. She told us she'd bumped into you. You were dorm mates in college, weren't you? She sounded very happy that you are going to be friends again."

"Thank you, Mr Williams," I said. "I'm happy too."

I tried to think of a way to ask him when he'd last heard from Rebecca without alarming him, but he was already saying goodbye. At least I knew that she wasn't in Bournemouth.

Feeling rather morbid, I scanned some Internet news sites for any news of accidents or deaths in the London area, but nothing came up. I tried Rebecca's cell again and when she didn't pick up, I went to get my jacket and scarf. If she were at home, then she might be sick, perhaps sleeping with her phone turned off.

I joined the tail end of the late evening commute on the Tube, got off at Sloane Square, and hurried through the quiet streets to Rebecca's house. Under the amber light of the street lamps, I could see my breath curling away in the cold air. An elderly lady walked past with a little dog on a leash. It was wearing a red jacket and matching red socks.

The bell for Rebecca's apartment was lit and clearly marked. I pushed it several times, but there was no answer. Stepping back from the entry on to the pavement, I looked up at her windows. They were dark; the curtains were open and no lights were on, so it seemed obvious that she was away, perhaps on business, or perhaps at her boyfriend's place. Now I was standing here in the cold, I felt rather silly. Of course, she could be with her boyfriend. She had seen him on Sunday evening, which was why she had cancelled our movie plans. If he was available for a couple of days, then maybe she had just decided to call in sick. I tried to ignore my hurt feelings. Surely she would have responded to my texts.

A taxi circled the square and pulled up a few yards away. I waited. Perhaps it was Rebecca coming home. The back door opened. A young couple paid the driver before making their way to the house next door. Defeated, I turned to walk back to the Tube station.

I had a thought, turned back, and walked up the black and white tiled pathway. The two men who lived in the flat on the second floor, what were their names? Nick and Gary? They might know where Rebecca was. I glanced up to confirm that their lights were on, a lambent glow behind gold-colored curtains. I pressed the button labeled Nick Carpenter. After a few seconds a voice came over the intercom.

"Yes? Who is it?" His voice was smooth and warm, like cafe latte.

"My name is Kate," I answered. "We met about a week ago. I'm a friend of Rebecca's."

After a pause, Nick replied. "What can I do for you, Kate?"

"I'm worried about her." I hated talking into the brass speaker plate. "Can I speak to you inside?"

CHAPTER ELEVEN

There was a long silence, before I heard the door click open. Stepping into the elegant entryway, I waited, unsure whether Nick would come down to meet me. After a minute or so, he appeared at the top of the gently-lit stairs and waved me up. He was dressed in jeans and a white T-shirt, with bare feet. Music leaked from the open door of his apartment. I recognized the percussive piano notes of Thelonius Monk.

"Thank you," I said, a little breathless from hurrying up the stairs. "I haven't heard from Rebecca since Sunday and she hasn't been to the office for two days. I'm worried that she might be ill..."

I stopped, gripping the banister. Nick had an aura. It was faint but there.

"Have you seen her?" I finished, but my thoughts were on what Nick's aura could mean. What danger could there be to two people in the same building? Poisoning, toxic air, what was the name of that gas? Carbon monoxide. Or a building collapse? I realized my hand was hurting from grasping the smooth wood rail so tightly and I let go, feeling unsteady on my feet.

Nick cocked his head to one side. "Not since Friday actually. We chatted for a minute or two while we picked up our mail downstairs. I didn't see her over the weekend because Gary and I were away until Sunday evening. We went to Brussels on the Eurostar, did some shopping, ate some amazing food and lots and lots of chocolate." He shrugged. "Sorry, that's all irrelevant, I know. So that was it. I didn't see her this morning because Gary and I overslept.

We just flew out of here in a rush to get to work."

"She's not answering her phone or responding to texts," I said, "and she didn't answer when I rang the bell just now."

Nick shrugged. "Then she's probably away. Business, pleasure..." His voice trailed away. "I don't know what to say, Kate. It's not unreasonable that an adult woman would be out of touch for a day or two. A little romantic liaison maybe?"

"There are no lights on in her flat."

He gave me a look that made me smile in spite of the anxiety. "I said romantic. Candles, firelight? Get it?"

"Okay, I know," I said. "But I still don't think it's that. She wouldn't miss work."

Or would she? I couldn't be sure of that. This was probably a major overreaction. Still, having come this far, it would be good to know that she was all right.

"Can I go up and knock on the door?" I asked. "If she's there with someone, she might answer even if it's only to say 'go away'. Once I know she's all right, I can stop worrying."

Nick nodded. "Of course. I'll come with you."

Gary appeared behind him. "What's going on?"

"We're just going to check on Rebecca," Nick replied. I stared at Gary, but there was no aura. Goosebumps came up on my arms. What did Nick and Rebecca have in common that they would have auras, yet Gary didn't?

Gary scowled and turned away. I got the impression he didn't like me, but couldn't think why not. We had never actually spoken to each other.

Nick led the way up the stairs to the next floor and then along the carpeted hallway. I hesitated before knocking on the door. As if by mutual agreement we both stood stock still, barely breathing, listening for any sound from inside. After half a minute, I looked at him and he nodded. I knocked again. This time I heard a rustling sound near the door followed by a loud and plaintive meow.

"Caspian!" Nick exclaimed. "Rebecca wouldn't go away and leave the cat alone. She always asks me to check on him if she plans on being out late or is away on business."

The cat, hearing our voices, began yowling and scratching the inside of the door.

"Oh, poor baby," said Nick. "He sounds hungry."

"And angry," I added.

"Wait here. I have a key. I'll be right back." Nick disappeared, silent on bare feet. I leaned my forehead against the door, murmuring to the cat, who now sounded desperate to get out. Impatiently, I waited for Nick to reappear, which he did after a few minutes, bounding up the stairs, holding the key aloft.

"I'm coming, precious kitty," he called as he put the key in the lock.

"Be careful. Make sure he doesn't make a dash for freedom."

As he pushed the door open just a few inches, I knelt down to block the cat's exit. A cannonball of soft grey fur shot into my hands.

"It's okay," I cooed as I picked him up.

"Oh yuck, his litter tray needs cleaning out," said Nick, poking his head through the door. I cradled a wriggling Caspian in my arms while Nick pushed the door open and felt around inside to find a light switch. Clutching the cat tightly, I followed him in and closed the front door behind me. The central heating was running. The air was hot and fetid. A sweet and cloying odor caught in my throat and made me gag. I bent to release Caspian, who fled up the hallway towards the bedroom. The motion of bending over made my stomach heave. I thought I might be sick.

Nick's face was ashen. "What on earth is that?"

I put my hand over my nose and mouth, taking short sharp breaths. A sense of impending disaster weighed on me like a giant hand pressing down on my shoulders.

Nick walked towards the living room, flipping switches as he went, releasing bright light into every corner. I dragged myself a few paces behind him, terrified of what we would find. The silence was overpowering, a physical entity as strong as the smell. My head began to ache again.

Nick stopped at the entry to the living room, reaching in to turn on another light, and I saw him framed in the doorway, motionless. It seemed that minutes had passed before he spoke although I knew it was only seconds.

"Oh God, no," he said.

Feeling detached from my own body, I watched myself take the few steps towards the door, watched Nick move aside to let me in. Both of us standing together, side by side, wordless, still.

Rebecca lay on her back in a pool of broken glass, the remains of the shattered coffee table. White roses, thrown from their ruined vase, rested all around her, the tips of the petals turning yellow. Blossoms of rusty black patterned the white carpet and Rebecca's cream sweater. All color was drained from the scene, like an old black and white photograph, apart from the red of Rebecca's hair, still as vibrant as ever. An empty wine bottle lay close by and the stem of a broken wine glass rested in her hand. The air around her head was perfectly still. The aura had gone.

A bloody print down the front of the white sofa. I imagined her fingers grappling for a hold. That detail hit my stomach like a fist. Rebecca had been hurt but hadn't died immediately. How awful to lie there, feeling your life slipping away and not able to save yourself.

"Oh, Rebecca," I whispered.

"I'm calling the police," said Nick. His voice came as a shock in the silence. I heard the tapping on the cellphone and then him calmly saying that there had been an accident and to please send someone. He gave the address and put his phone back in his pocket.

"They'll be here in a few minutes," he said. "I can't look at this any more. I'm going to make sure Caspian has food."

I stood alone, paralyzed and numb, then sank to the floor, dizzy, while the room spun around me. Acid rose into my throat. I scrambled to my feet and ran to the bathroom, where I vomited several times. I remained there, curled up on the tile floor until I heard Nick tap on the door.

"Kate, the police are here," he said quietly. "Can you come out? I hate talking to people in uniforms."

I went to the sink and washed my face and hands and took several gulps of cold water. Noticing that the door of cabinet was slightly open, I peeked in to see that one shelf was empty. The bottle of aftershave and tubes of shaving cream had gone. That was odd. I wondered if the boyfriend had moved out.

Wiping my hands on a fluffy pink towel, I took a deep breath before leaving the bathroom. Two officers were with Nick in the living room, one of them in a corner talking on his radio. The other one introduced himself, but my mind was too full to absorb his name. I thought I might be sick again and stayed close to the door.

When the second policeman had finished his call, he came over and murmured something to his colleague, then turned to me.

"Sergeant Wilson," he said holding out a hand to shake mine. "DCI Clarke and the medical examiner will be here soon.

Meanwhile, we need to ask you a few questions."

"Why do you need a detective?" asked Nick. "It's obviously an accident."

"It's routine," replied Wilson.

He peered at me. "Are you okay? We should go into the hall. It's cooler out there. You too, sir," he added, glancing at Nick.

I moved on leaden legs out through the front door and across the landing to lean against the banister. Nick crouched down by the wall and Wilson took a notebook and pencil from a pocket and ran through a list of basic questions: names, addresses, relationship to the deceased.

Deceased I thought. He had never known Rebecca as a person, a living being. She was just a dead body to be accounted for in his files. The mention of death reminded me of Nick's aura, and I lifted my eyes to look at him. The aura was distinct but the air was moving slowly. What did it mean? I started feeling sick again.

"Miss Benedict?" Wilson was looking at me.

"Sorry."

"How did you get into the apartment?" Wilson asked. Nick explained that he had a key because he looked after the cat. Wilson looked around. "Where is it?"

"What?"

"The cat."

"He ran into the bedroom when we got here," replied Nick. "I took his food bowl and some water in there for him when we got here. Poor thing was starving and probably scared." He paused. "Do you think he knew his owner was dead? A dog would know, I think, but maybe not a cat..." he trailed off when he saw the expression on Wilson's face.

"What time did you get here?" Wilson asked.

Nick looked at me. "About eight?"

I nodded. Wilson checked his watch and wrote something in his notes.

There were voices on the stairway, but Wilson continued to jot in his notebook, the sound of his pencil scratching on the paper loud on the quiet landing.

A few minutes later, two men appeared at the top of the stairs. One, a tall thin man with a balding head, carrying a leather case, the other, young, good-looking with blonde hair and a nice suit. The younger one introduced himself. "I'm Detective Inspector Clarke," he said. "I'd just like to ask a few questions."

I was surprised at how young he was, maybe in his mid-thirties, and I wondered at his choice of profession, dealing with violence and death on a daily basis.

"We've given the officer all our information," said Nick. "And I really have to go. Gary will be wondering where I am."

"A couple more minutes," Clarke said in a tone that brooked no argument.

He looked at me. "When did you last see or hear from..." He checked a piece of paper in his hand. "From Miss Williams?"

"Sunday lunchtime. We had lunch together. At a Chinese restaurant."

"And you didn't come back here with her afterwards?"

"No. We left the restaurant at about two. I went straight home."

Clarke nodded, wrote some notes and turned his attention to Nick.

"And you sir? Where were you this weekend?"

Nick described his weekend trip to Brussels, keeping the details short and precise and not even mentioning the chocolate.

"So you wouldn't have known if Miss Williams had any visitors over the weekend?"

"Sorry, but no."

"She was supposed to be meeting her boyfriend on Sunday evening," I said. "We'd made plans to go see a movie, but then she canceled that. We had lunch together instead."

"Did she tell you what time she was planning to meet him, or where?"

"No." I shook my head. I was confused by his questions. "But this was just an accident, wasn't it?"

Clarke didn't answer. He looked at Nick. "You didn't see anyone arriving or leaving on Sunday evening?"

"No, I've seen her boyfriend a few times, coming and going but, as I said, we were away this weekend." He paused, frowned, straightened the cuffs on his shirt.

"Good." Clarke scribbled something down in his notebook. "I'll need you to give detailed descriptions of the man and we will draw up an identikit picture."

"There's a photo of the boyfriend in Rebecca's room," I said. "His name is Edward."

"You've met him?" Clarke asked.

"No, Rebecca just told me his name."

"Do you have a second name, any idea where he works?" Clarke asked.

"Nothing on the second name, but she said he works in technology and travels a lot. Can I go get the photo?"

Clarke spoke to Wilson. "Please go with Miss Benedict."

I followed the police officer back into the apartment and down the hallway. When we entered the room, he gave me a pair of latex gloves. "Put these on, please," he said. I noticed that he was already wearing some.

I picked up the photo of Rebecca and the dark-haired young man with his arm around her shoulders, looked at it briefly and turned it face down in my hands. It was too painful to see the picture of my friend, alive and smiling. After following Wilson back up the hall, I held the picture out for Inspector Clarke to see. Clarke gestured for me to show it to Nick.

"This is the boyfriend?" he asked.

"No, it's not," said Nick. "The boyfriend is taller and older. This is Rebecca's brother."

"Her brother?" I exclaimed. "But she told me her only relatives were her parents."

"Her only living relatives, maybe," said Nick. "Her brother - I think his name was Andrew - was killed in a climbing accident about two years ago, not long after I moved in here. She was heartbroken. That's the first time I looked after Caspian for her, when she went home for the funeral. She was gone for a week or so."

I swallowed down the hurt I felt that Rebecca hadn't chosen to share this with me. But then, I reflected, I hadn't told Rebecca about Toby, hadn't really even talked much about my mother's death. Funny how you could spend time with someone and not say anything very meaningful.

Clarke cleared his throat to get our attention. "Is there anything else that you think might be helpful for me to know at this point?" he asked.

I hesitated. I should tell him about the missing toiletries in the cabinet, but that meant admitting that I'd been poking around. He looked at me closely. "You're really pale. Are you okay?"

Not really. I felt exhausted and sad, but I said I was all right. Against my better judgment, I told him about seeing the aftershave and shaving cream a week ago, and then noticing they weren't there any longer.

Clarke winced. "You used the bathroom this evening?"

"I was being sick," I said, and he nodded.

"Understandable," he said as he wrote something in his notebook. "We'll need you to come to the station for fingerprints. And you too, please, Mr. Carpenter."

"Do you think Rebecca was murdered?" asked Nick. He was as pale as I felt.

Clarke shook his head. "I don't think anything yet." He looked up from his notebook. "Were the lights on when you arrived?"

"No," said Nick. "We turned them all on. That means it was probably daylight when she died, doesn't it?"

"How long has she been dead?" I asked.

"I'll know more when the medical examiner has finished," Clarke said. "Meanwhile, is there anything else that you can tell me?"

"I was supposed to be looking out for her."

I didn't realize I'd even said the words out loud until Clarke cocked his head to one side. "Looking out for her? Had she indicated that she felt she was in danger? Was she depressed? Or sick?"

I felt the blood rushing to my cheeks and neck, and I touched my throat nervously. I couldn't tell him about the aura.

"No, nothing like that," I said, which was the truth.

The silence stretched out between us, Clarke waiting for me to clarify my comment in some way. I had said more than enough, though, and I leaned back against the wall, hoping he would leave me alone.

For the first time, Clarke smiled, a minuscule lifting of the corners of his mouth. He was really quite attractive, I thought. His eyes were the color of malachite. He looked good in his pristine white shirt and dark green tie.

"Thank you for your help, both of you. Officer Wilson will finish up here."

He turned away to answer his cell phone, which was buzzing in his hand. Wilson came over and asked Nick if he'd go to the station to help work up an identikit picture of the boyfriend.

"Yes, I can do that tomorrow," Nick said. He stared up at the ceiling. "I could do with a ciggy, but I gave up smoking three months ago."

"I'm trying to pack it in," said Wilson. He tapped his arm. "Got the patch but it doesn't really help. Now I just eat more. French fries, donuts. Damned if you do, damned if you don't, it seems to me. Lung cancer or heart attack, I'm not sure what difference it makes, really. One of them's going to get me."

Pulled from my thoughts by Wilson's comments on dying, I looked at him intently. There was no aura over his head.

"You'll be fine," I said, without thinking.

"Glad to hear it," he said with a grin.

Clarke finished his call and talked to Wilson. "We need to contact the parents to let them know about their daughter," he said. "Can you make the necessary calls to locate them, please?"

"Will you do it, sir, be the one to tell them?"

Clarke nodded wearily. "Yes, just get me their contact information."

"I've got that," I said to Wilson, and his face lit up briefly. One less task to do. I gave him the number I had dialed earlier, feeling a stab of grief for poor Mr. Williams and his wife.

Wilson wandered back into the apartment, radio in hand, and Clarke was on his phone again.

"So, the police seem to be taking this pretty seriously," Nick said, pushing himself away from the banisters and coming to lean against the wall next to me. "It looked to me as though she had a couple of glasses of wine too many and tripped into the coffee table. But the way they're talking in there, they seem to think there's been foul play."

I didn't respond. My head hurt, I still felt sick, and indescribably depressed. Voices and the sound of footsteps drew Nick back to the banisters to look over into the stairwell. A few seconds later, three men appeared at the top of the stairs, all in plain clothes and carrying an assortment of boxes and bags.

After finishing his call, Clarke came back to where Nick and I stood.

"Come into the station on Buckingham Palace Road tomorrow to do your fingerprints, and to sign statements please. Meanwhile, if you think of anything that might help us trace the boyfriend, please call me on this number."

He gave each of us a card with his name and a cell phone number on it.

"What about Caspian?" asked Nick. "Can I take him downstairs? He can't stay here alone."

Clarke nodded. "Of course. Wilson will accompany you. Don't touch anything."

"I'll help you get him," I said, following him back into the apartment. I didn't really want to go back inside, but I wasn't sure what else to do.

Wilson was in the hallway and Nick told him about the cat. He came with us to the bedroom, and waited while we coaxed Caspian out from under the bed. Nick picked him up, and gave me a kiss on the cheek. "Stay in touch," he said before leaving.

For a few seconds, I stood by the bed, unsure what to do next. "Do you need a ride home, miss?" asked Wilson. "I'm going back to the Yard but I'm happy to make a detour."

"Thanks, but it's okay. I need some fresh air," I said. Staying in motion seemed important, anything to put off the moment when I'd be alone with my thoughts. Rebecca was dead. She'd had an aura, as had Sophie and Francesca. And now Nick was in danger.

It was late by the time I reached my apartment. Kicking off my boots, I slipped out of my jacket, got into bed with my clothes on, and pulled the duvet up to my chin. I couldn't stop shaking. My head ached, so I got back up to find my pain medications and swallowed two with a handful of water from the bathroom tap. The vision of Rebecca's inert body kept pushing in on my closed eyes. I burrowed deeper under the covers, leaving the bedside light on like a scared child. I hadn't saved Rebecca even though I knew she was in danger. The guilt felt like bricks piled up on my chest. I should have done more. I should have never let her out of my sight.

CHAPTER TWELVE

Thin grey light seeped around the edges of the curtains, filling the room with an aqueous gloom. The only color came from the red numbers on the digital clock, showing that it was almost nine. I stretched my neck from one side to the other, trying to work out the kinks.

The kitchen beckoned with the promise of hot tea and Marmite on toast. I was hungry, which reminded me that I hadn't eaten the evening before. My cell phone was on the counter next to the kettle. I had missed four calls, three from Josh, and one from a clerk at the police station reminding me to come in to sign my statement. Damn. It had been an effort to walk a few yards from the bedroom; I couldn't imagine dragging myself halfway across London, especially in this weather. The rain was pounding against the windows and thick granite-colored clouds formed a low-slung ceiling over the city.

I took my tea and the phone back to bed, listening to the messages from Josh again. He sounded increasingly worried that I wasn't picking up and asked me to call him back as soon as possible. I started to pull up his number to phone him, but then realized he didn't know about Rebecca's death. I couldn't talk about it yet, knew the words wouldn't come out. So I settled for sending him a text to tell him I was all right and that I'd call him later.

I wasn't sure whether I was sick or suffering from the shock of finding Rebecca. My muscles hurt, my head ached, and I felt exhausted even though I'd slept late. But I had to get up and moving, so I dragged myself off the bed and into the bathroom. I ran the shower as hot as I could bear it and, as the water flowed over my back and shoulders, I examined my knees, which had healed well apart from little collections of scars that had faded to light pink.

I didn't have time to dry my hair so I tied it up in a ponytail, found some clean wool pants, and threw on the sweater I'd been wearing to bed. Not very hygienic, but I didn't have the energy to look for clean clothes. A glance in the mirror proved to be a bad idea. Zombie was the first word that came to mind but I didn't care. I wanted to get the police station trip over and done with and get to work before Alan noticed I was missing, again.

My umbrella did little to shield me from the deluge of rain that had soaked through my coat and boots by the time I reached the police station. It was my first time inside such a bastion of law enforcement and it was cleaner and quieter than I'd imagined it would be. In the entry area, a teenager in a hoodie sat on a plastic chair, his eyes glazed and distant, while a thuggish-looking man in his forties shot poisonous looks at everyone who walked by.

A high counter carrying a "Reception" sign was staffed by a tired-looking woman who picked away at her keyboard. She looked me up on the computer and then directed me to a room down the hall. I walked slowly, noticing the beige lino floor, a popcorn ceiling, and bright neon lights that flickered and buzzed. A faint smell of disinfectant and burned coffee filled the air.

A clerk handed me the statement I had made to Officer Wilson the day before. I skimmed it and signed, then rolled my thumb and fingers over an ink pad and on to a piece of card. It was all done in minutes and I hurried back to the front entrance.

Rubbing at the ink stains on my fingers, I pushed the outer door open with my shoulder and heard a yelp of pain. Mortified, I realized the door had hit someone coming in. That someone was Inspector Clarke.

"Miss Benedict." He greeted me with that smile that lit up his green eyes. "You've done your fingerprints, I see. Thank you."

I regretted not doing my hair or not putting on any make-up, and then felt guilty for worrying about such trivialities when Rebecca was dead.

"Can I have a few minutes?" he asked me. "There's a decent cafe around the corner if you have time."

Nodding, I followed him outside, turning my coat collar up

against the driving rain, worried about being even later to work, but glad of the opportunity to find out more about what had happened to Rebecca.

We settled at a table in a quiet corner with styrofoam cups of coffee, straight black for him and a latte for me. It was warm and humid inside and the windows were opaque with condensation. Taking off his wool coat, Clarke draped it over the back of his chair. I kept mine on, as much because I still felt shivery and chilled as to hide the fact that I was wearing the same sweater I'd been wearing when I saw Clarke at Rebecca's flat the night before.

"Have you found out anything more about how Rebecca died?" I asked.

"I'm supposed to be the one asking the questions," he said with a faint grin. "But not yet. I'm expecting the autopsy report later today."

"Did you find out when she died?"

He took a sip of coffee and pulled his notebook from his jacket pocket. I waited, hoping he would tell me more. Instead, he leaned back in his chair and took another sip of coffee.

"Miss Benedict, I wonder if you could tell me more about your relationship with Miss Williams? How did you know her?"

Surprised by the question, I told him about being friends during college and then not seeing each other until she walked into the conference room at Bradley Cohen.

"And would you count yourself as a good friend?"

"Yes," I said and then thought about it. "Well, not really. We'd only just started seeing each other again and hadn't got much beyond the small talk about jobs, boyfriends, that kind of thing. It had been a few years since I last saw her."

Nodding, he wrote something in his notebook. "And why did you think the photo was of the boyfriend? Did she tell you it was?"

I felt my cheeks burn with embarrassment. "No, she didn't. I just assumed. I didn't know she'd had a brother, or that he was dead. She told me it was just her and her parents. They live in Bournemouth."

Something stuck in my throat. "Did you tell them? About Rebecca?"

Clarke inclined his head in what could have been a nod, or a bow of prayer. I thought of my short conversation with Mr. Williams and tears blurred my vision. He had seemed kind and gentle. How could he and his wife handle the death of their daughter, just a couple of years after losing their son?

"That's a crappy job," I said, wondering how Clarke could do it. He gave a thin smile and nodded. "The worst part. Always."

"Did they know more about Rebecca's boyfriend? His name or where he lives?"

"No." He didn't seem willing to say more. After a long pause, he asked. "Are you doing all right? You're still looking very pale."

I took a slug of coffee and put the cup down on the table.

"Yes, I'm fine. You're treating this as an accident, right?"

He nodded but didn't speak. "So why are you involved?" I asked. "I mean, you're a detective, but it seems that there's nothing to detect."

Clarke smiled. "It's just routine. When I get the coroner's report, I'll close the case, in all likelihood."

He leaned forward slightly, elbows on the table. "Why? Do you have a different view?"

I decided to say what had been on my mind ever since the moment of walking into Rebecca's apartment.

"Well, I suppose I do." My voice shook and I took a gulp of coffee. "It just seems unlikely that she fell. She was a dancer in college and had amazing balance. You could still see it in the way she walked. She had great poise."

He raised an eyebrow. "Accidents happen," he said. "You'd be amazed at the range of accidental deaths I've seen. The most unlikely people dying in the most incredible circumstances."

'I suppose so," I said. I felt disheartened but decided to keep asking questions. "What time did she die? She was supposed to be meeting her boyfriend, don't forget. Maybe he was there when it happened?"

"Initial estimate of time of death is around six on Sunday evening," he said.

That was more than forty-eight hours before Nick and I found her. I shivered.

"Tell me more about this boyfriend," he said. "You never met him?"

"No. All she told me was that his name is Edward and that he travels a lot. That's it. Maybe he'll contact the police when he realizes Rebecca's not answering his calls or texts? I mean, he must get worried at some point and then he'll reach out to someone. Perhaps he'll ask Nick?"

Clarke played with the lid on his cup, bending back the piece of plastic that covered the opening until it broke off in his hand. He looked at it before answering.

"This boyfriend seems to be a bit of a mystery. You said that his shaving cream and aftershave were removed from the bathroom cabinet? If he moved out, he may not expect to hear from her, or be in touch with her in any way."

"Oh, right. I hadn't thought of that."

I paused, unsure whether to share another idea I'd had. "I was wondering about Rebecca's apartment," I said finally. "It's in a very expensive part of London. I know she had a good job, but I was thinking it might be out of her pay range. I mean, we're only three years or so out of college. I'm certainly not making that kind of money. So maybe the boyfriend was paying for it and you could perhaps trace him through a rent check or something." I tailed off, feeling embarrassed that I was making suggestions to a professional.

Clarke nodded, with a hint of smile. "Good thinking, Miss Benedict. I'd thought the same thing. I'll follow up on that."

In the long silence that followed, Clarke shifted in his chair and stuck his legs out in front of him, leaning back as though he was in a comfortable armchair at home.

"Yesterday you said something about looking out for Rebecca," he said. "Can you tell me more? Why did you feel you needed to look out for her?"

I really have to learn to keep my mouth closed, I thought. There was no way I was going to try explain the aura to Inspector Clarke.

"It was that she seemed vulnerable, you know? The boyfriend seemed to have her on a short string. She set her schedule around when he was home."

Clarke's expression indicated that he had expected more but he nodded.

"Ok."

The ensuing silence was broken only by the pattering of rain on the windows. I drank more of my coffee, starting to feel a slight buzz that was so much better than the dog-tired fatigue I'd started the day with. But the increased energy also took the edge off the numbness I'd been feeling since finding Rebecca's body. I took another gulp of coffee to hide my sudden emotion. I'd never see her again. We wouldn't go to the play we'd planned to see. We wouldn't drive around in my Dad's Fiat 500 and flirt with Italian waiters. I wouldn't take her to my favorite museum in Florence or up the Campanile. None of that would happen now.

Clarke handed me a clean and pressed white handkerchief even before I realized I needed it. I blotted the tears from under my eyes.

"You must be a good listener," he said, in an apparent non sequitur. I raised an eyebrow, not sure what he meant.

"I know you haven't seen much of Rebecca, but you've taken the time to consider what she's told you about this rather mysterious boyfriend, to analyze what the missing aftershave might mean. Not many people do that. Most of what we say goes in one ear and out the other. In my job, I'm often asking questions, talking to witnesses, trying to construct a backstory for a victim or a perpetrator and you'd be amazed at how hard it is. We don't communicate with each other very well at all."

I felt my cheeks redden. In my real life, as I thought of it now, the life I'd led before, I'd be as inattentive and unheeding as the people he was describing. It was only because of the aura that I'd been paying attention, listening to the nuances of what Rebecca told me, trying to uncover a clue, a thread that would have helped me to save her.

Clarke straightened up in his chair and glanced at his watch. "I should be going. Are you all right? Do you have far to get home?"

"I'll be fine. I'm going straight to work. Just a few stops on the Tube. It's no big deal."

"Do you live alone?"

"What?"

He laughed. "I'm sorry, That came out wrong. I just want to know if you have anyone who will be with you. Look after you for a few days. Finding a body is enough to throw most people into a tailspin. Do you have somewhere you could go? Family?"

"My brother," I said. "But he's in Italy, for a funeral."

"I'm sorry to hear that. Someone you knew?"

"Yes, a friend of my father's. She died last week of a stroke."

"My condolences," he said. "That and now Miss Williams. That must be hard on you."

And Sophie too, I nearly said out loud.

"Not great," I agreed. I was mired in misery, but he didn't need to hear that.

Two young women walked past our table, both giving Clarke a sidelong glance of appreciation. He didn't look like a detective. In his well-tailored suit and black wingtips, he could have been one of the City finance guys; he had that same air of self-confidence.

He pushed his chair back, slipped on his coat and followed me out, hurrying forward to hold the door open for me. We stood under the awning for a few seconds.

"Thanks for taking the time to talk with me," he said.

We said goodbye to each other. I watched him walk away under the relentless rain. Just as I turned around to head towards the Tube station, I caught sight of Nick in a Burberry coat and scarf, carrying a black umbrella and walking in the direction of the police station.

"Nick!" I called, and he lowered the umbrella.

"Hi, Kate. Just going to the station to do my fingerprints. Have you done yours?"

I nodded but didn't speak. Even in the torrential rain, I could see the aura moving around his head and shoulders.

CHAPTER THIRTEEN

When I walked into the office, Annie waved me over to the reception desk. "Darth Vader's been demanding to know where you are," she whispered, even though there was no one else around. She always called Alan Darth Vader.

"You have five messages, and there's a meeting going on in Josh's office." She handed me the message slips.

"Good luck with DV."

I punched the button for the elevator and used the short ride up to smooth my hair and apply some lipstick. At least I should look as though I was trying.

Alan, Josh and Ben were grouped around Josh's desk, looking at something on his computer. Alan pushed his chair back when he saw me come in. He crossed his arms.

"Good afternoon, Kate," he said. "I don't recall approving flexible hours for the staff. Must have slipped my mind completely."

I didn't have the energy to fight with him.

"Rebecca's dead," I said.

Josh jumped up from his seat. "What?"

"An accident in her apartment."

"Who are we talking about?" asked Alan.

"Rebecca Williams, Montgomery's Financial Director," I said.

Ben's mouth dropped open.

"Jesus Christ. You've got to be kidding." Alan shot a look of disbelief at me. "How do you know?"

"I found her, found the body. After she was missing for two days

I was worried about her and went to her apartment."

"I hope this doesn't mess up our contract with Montgomery," Alan muttered. I glared at him.

"How could you even think like that? God, Alan. I don't think you have any feelings for anyone. She was sitting here in this conference room last week and now she's dead."

Josh came over to me and gave me a hug. "I'm so sorry," he said. "About all of it."

I knew he was apologizing for not believing me when I told him about the aura over Rebecca, but we couldn't say anything more there in the office.

Alan's face went red with the effort, but he managed an apology too. "It's not that I don't care," he said. "She seemed like a very nice person. It's just that we could do without any disruptions."

"I'm sure there'll be no impact on the project," I said. "The contract is signed. Peter Montgomery will find someone else to handle the finances of it all, don't you think?"

"Yes, yes. Probably. Damn."

It wasn't clear how word got out, but it did. In the middle of the afternoon, I locked myself in a cubicle in the bathroom just to get away from the onslaught of questions. Even the team members who hadn't worked on the Montgomery project professed to be shocked and saddened, and pressed for details of how she'd died. I was glad when it was time to go home. I couldn't pay attention to what people said, meetings seemed pointless, project planning was a waste of time. We were insects scurrying around, busy busy, oblivious to the foot that was going to crush us to death at any moment.

***

Josh caught up with me in the lobby to ask if we could go out for dinner. I was too tired for a long evening out, so we settled for a drink at the Hare and Hounds. We found a table near the fire, away from the blare of the television and the draft from the main door. Logs burned in an antique tiled fireplace, the smell of smoke mingling with the odor of beer-sodden carpet. Condensation ran down the wavy glass of the old windows, gathering in pools on the sills.

"I'm so sorry, Kate," Josh said again. "That must have been awful, finding Rebecca."

I just nodded. It was hard to speak.

"And I'm really sorry I didn't believe you. Well, I did, but with some reservations."

"It's all right, Josh. I've had a hard time believing it too."

A group of young men in suits came in, loud, laughing, making jokes about someone's age, celebrating a birthday perhaps.

"Have you seen any more of those auras?" he asked. I told him about Nick's.

"That's very odd," he said, leaning into the straight-backed chair. Covered in red plush and gilt-framed, the chairs looked as though they'd been lifted from the palace at Versailles. But the velvet was stained, and the gilt chipped, showing patches of dull brown paint underneath.

"What do you think?" he asked. "What would Rebecca and Nick have in common apart from living in the same building? Just a coincidence?"

I shook my head. I'd been thinking about it all day. What were the odds that it was pure chance? Small, I thought. There had a to be connection, but I couldn't see what it was. "The boyfriend must have something to do with her death," I said. I told Josh what I knew, which wasn't much. "I think they had a fight on Sunday evening. She fell, or was pushed, and died, and then he moved his stuff out."

Sounds like a plausible scenario," Josh said. "Did she tell you what time she was meeting him?"

"No, she was vague," I said. She'd been vague about almost everything to do with Edward. Apart from his name, I knew nothing about him. Nick had seen him, he'd said, on the stairs a few times, but never talked to him.

"Maybe the boyfriend is the connection between Rebecca and Nick," I said. "But I can't work out how, given that Nick never spoke to him."

We were both quiet, pondering the puzzle. "The thing is that I have to try to help Nick," I said. "I failed Rebecca. I can't let Nick die."

Josh looked startled. "God, Kate, you can't start taking responsibility for whether people live or die. It's impossible. I mean, you hardly know him. How can you protect him?"

I drained my wine. I seemed to be drinking a lot of it nowadays.

"I can't just do nothing," I said. "Should I warn him at least?"

"From personal experience, I'd recommend against it. It sounds, well, incredible. And coming from a near stranger, not something he'd be inclined to believe."

A couple holding tall glasses of something with maraschino cherries in it came to sit at the table next to us. Their umbrella drinks seemed out of place in a rain-soaked London pub, but maybe they were trying to recapture happy memories of some tropical vacation. Regardless, they were so close to us that it made any conversation about the aura impossible. Josh drank the remains of his beer, and we headed to the door.

"Sure you don't want to go out for dinner?" he asked.

I was feeling dead on my feet. I wouldn't be good company.

"Another night?"

"Of course," he said. We walked the short distance to the nearest Tube station and went through the turnstiles together. We were traveling on different lines. My platform was to the left. His was straight ahead. Ignoring the crush of people around us, we stopped, holding each other tightly. When he kissed me, I felt myself clinging to him. It was hard to let go. I wanted to be with him. But what I wanted more than anything was to go back to my old life, the life I'd had before I started seeing these weird visions. Before I'd seen my dead mother on the hill in Tuscany. I didn't know what was happening to me, but I had to work it out, and it wasn't fair to drag Josh into the mess of my current existence. There would be time, later, I told myself. When things were resolved and back to normal.

***

I was thinking about Rebecca while I ran a bath and lit some candles. It was taking some time for me to realize that she really was dead. I expected to receive a text at any moment, asking how my CT scan had gone, suggesting a place for dinner one evening, confirming the time and place for our theater outing on Saturday. The ring of the phone made me jump.

I knew it would be my father. He was the only one who called me on the landline. Juggling the handset and the kettle, I made tea while we talked.

"Are you all right, pet?" Dad asked for the third time. "Leo is worried about you. Have you been to a doctor?"

"I'm fine, Dad, and there's no need for you to worry, honestly. It's been busy at work, that's all. And yes, I had a CT scan and everything is good. What about you? How are you doing? I wish I could be there for the funeral tomorrow. I'm glad Leo is with you."

"It's all right," he said. "Leo told me how busy you are at work. I hope they're treating you well there, and not expecting too much of you after the accident. You need time to heal."

"Everyone's being very nice," I said.

There was a long pause and I heard classical music playing in the background but couldn't place the piece. Beethoven maybe or Mahler. Something dark and heavy, which wasn't a good sign. My father selected music according to his mood.

"Did you tell Leo what happened on the hill. I mean about what you thought you saw. That confusion over what happened?"

"There was no confusion, Dad. I know what I saw."

"I was thinking about coming over for a few days after Francesca's funeral," he continued, ignoring my response. "What do you think? Would that work? I've got some shopping to do anyway."

The shopping wasn't a good cover. He hated shopping and certainly wouldn't fly all the way to England to buy anything. He was coming to check up on me.

"Let me look at my schedule, okay? I'm really busy. But the good news is that the project is going well."

"That's excellent," he said. "Well done." His tone reminded me of when I was little and had fallen off a bike and scraped my knee. While Mum had cleaned out the wound with an antiseptic lotion that stung and brought tears to my eyes, Dad had praised my bike-riding skills, a successful attempt to distract my attention from the injury.

The music swelled in the background and a violin played a heart-wrenching solo that made my pulse quicken.

"Anyway, I'll be there in a few weeks for the long weekend," I reminded him. The company always celebrated the anniversary of its founding by giving everyone a Monday off in mid-November. I planned to go to Florence for the long weekend.

"That's lovely, Katie. I'll look forward to it. I miss you."

Feeling sad for my father, I put the phone down and went to take my bath. Sinking into the scented water, I watched the candle flames flicker and dance.

I felt so helpless. I hadn't tried hard enough to save Rebecca. I ran through my conversations with her, looking for clues, any hint of what might have happened. I had to do something. I'd find Edward. I had a feeling that he held the key to Rebecca's death. I thought about where she might have met him. Work was the most obvious place. I would start with that.

CHAPTER FOURTEEN

The following morning, I climbed the wide marble steps in front of the Montgomery Group's headquarters. It was the first time I'd been there, and it was hard not to be impressed. Befitting a successful real estate development company, the building was spectacular, with a multi-story atrium, glass walkways, and enough plants to populate a small jungle.

I approached the reception desk, where an impeccably coiffed and manicured young woman tapped on a keyboard. A nameplate on the desk said her name was Amanda. She was wearing a headset and talking into a microphone. When she'd finished, she looked up at me.

"Can I help you?"

I wasn't sure how to start, so I plunged in. "I'm a friend of Rebecca Williams. She worked here."

Amanda's face clouded for a second, but it wasn't clear whether in deference to Rebecca's death or confusion as to who she was.

"Yes?" she said after a short pause.

"Anyway, I'm trying to trace a friend of hers. To give him something. His name's Edward and I think he may work here."

Amanda stared at me. "Edward what?"

"I don't know."

With a sigh, she began clicking away at the keyboard. Those long red nails had to be a major deterrent to fast typing, I thought. She looked up.

"Which department does he work in?"

"I don't know."

Another sigh. She held her hands up over the keyboard, like a pianist preparing for the grand finale, and finished with another flurry of tapping and clicking.

"Nothing. We don't have any Edwards in the employee directory?" Her voice tilted upwards as though she was asking a question.

"He may be a consultant or a freelancer. Do you have a list of outside contractors?"

"We have our own IT department?"

I assumed the implicit question was "so why would we need a technology contractor?"

"Well, thank you," I began, and she cut me off.

"There's a Ted Evans who works in IT?"

Ted, Edward. That could be it.

"Can I go see him? Where is his office?"

She shook her head. "No visitors without an appointment? Would you like me to make one for you? Tomorrow perhaps?"

"Don't worry. I'll come back another time," I said. I was far too impatient to wait a day to see him and besides, I didn't want to tip him off. I doubted that Rebecca had mentioned me to her boyfriend but, in case my name had come up, I thought it best to make our first meeting a surprise. I wasn't sure what I was expecting, but I hoped that he'd give away something.

I loitered near the desk, pretending to read a company brochure until a group of Japanese businessmen approached. I wondered what they would make of Amanda with her red nails and Essex accent. Then I heard her speak to them in Japanese. She stood and matched them bow for bow. So much for my reading of the ditzy receptionist. My Dad always warned me against judging people before getting to know them.

Slipping out of the reception area, I chose a hallway and walked along it until I reached a bank of elevators. Unlike the glass ones in the main lobby, these were more traditional enclosed cars. Of course, I had no idea where the IT department was located, but I figured I could work it out.

The doors opened on the first floor to an empty corridor with no one around, so I pressed the button and rode up to the next floor. This time, several people got in, employees with photos and nametags pinned to their lapels.

"I'm looking for the IT department," I said.

"Fifth floor," said a young woman. "Do you have an appointment?"

"Yes." I made a show of looking at my watch. "And I'm a little late."

I rushed out as soon as the doors opened. The corridor took me past glass-fronted offices with nameplates on the doors, and several huge rooms full of computers with flashing lights. At the other end, a knot of people had just come out of a conference room. One of them was tall, with brown hair, in his early forties, and dressed in dark pants and a crisp white shirt, bearing a faint resemblance to the man Nick had described. I loitered, pretending to read something on a notice board on the wall. My heart was jumping around in my chest. If this was Rebecca's boyfriend, what would I say? Would he know that she was dead?

The group wandered past me, arguing about something to do with back-up systems. The brown-haired man was in the middle, and I couldn't read his nametag. While I debated whether to follow him, a door opened behind me and an older woman came out. "Can I help you?"

"I'm looking for Ted Stevens."

"Ted? Sure, he's in his office. Four doors down on the left."

The door was open. I tapped on it before stepping inside.

"Yes?"

The speaker was pink-faced, with thinning mahogany-colored hair that looked dyed. He looked at me in such surprise that I thought perhaps he didn't get many visitors.

"I'm sorry, wrong office," I said.

"Who're you looking for?" He put his sandwich down.

A name jumped into my head. "Phil Collins?"

It didn't seem to register. He just shrugged. "I don't know him," he said. "Maybe down on level 3. There are a bunch of new programmers working there."

I glanced at the nameplate on the door just to be certain this was the right office.

"Thanks, Ted," I said.

He nodded. "No problem."

I trudged back to the elevator. So much for that idea. It had been a long shot, but it seemed that Edward, whoever he was, didn't work for the Montgomery Group.

CHAPTER FIFTEEN

I ran through other possibilities while I traveled to the office. The Tube was almost empty at this time of day, leaving me alone with only my own reflection in the dark glass opposite for company.

Not for the first time, I thought about the phenomenon that was the Tube, with its trains that sped along narrow tunnels barely wide enough to accommodate them, carrying subterranean travelers that seemed, for the most part, oblivious to the fact that we were hundreds of feet underground. I'd heard the urban myths about mysterious walled-off stations, giant rats, and the numerous ghosts that wander the platforms at night. Shivering, I shrank into the corner of the seat, perversely wishing the carriage was chock full of ill-tempered commuters.

By the time I reached my station, I was glad to ride the escalator up to ground level. When I got to my office, Josh was loitering near the door.

"I'm so glad you're here," he said. "Alan's on the war path, asking where you are. Are you all right?"

At the end of the hallway, Alan's voice signaled his imminent appearance. I said I was fine. Slipping into the conference room, we took seats at the table, where I lined my pen up next to my notebook, hoping to make a good impression on Alan. I fixed a bright smile on my face as he opened the door and strode in, flanked by Ben and a couple of other team members who were consulting on the Montgomery project.

Taking a seat at the head of the table, Alan aimed a death glare at me. Ben shot me a look of malicious glee and ran his finger over his throat. In response, I lifted my middle finger just above the edge of the table. It was gratifying to see him flush and look away.

"Happy you could join us, Kate," Alan said. "Are you ready to discuss this presentation?"

I nodded, unable to speak. My hand shook as I turned a page in my notebook. Josh darted a curious glance at me, and Ben shrugged his shoulders as if expressing despair. I coughed and forced out a few words. "Yes, I'm ready."

Alan rubbed his hands together. "Great. Let's get started."

I stared at him while he talked about permits and timetables, foundations and landscaping, unable to digest his words, because all of my attention was on the air that trembled over his head.

The meeting seemed to drag on interminably. I made a few comments, but let Josh and Ben do most of the talking. I knew that Alan would be less than impressed by my contribution, but his opinion seemed irrelevant right then. The aura over him meant he was going to die.

My mouth was dry. My hands wouldn't stop shaking, so I put my pen down and pinned my hands between my knees, trying to look interested. The conference room with its expensive furniture and tasteful prints, filled with the fragrance of coffee, seemed unreal, as though I were sitting on a stage, acting a bit part in a play. And I had no idea what the ending would be. I could hardly take my eyes off Alan's face; he was so blissfully unaware of his impending fate. If he knew, would he act differently? Would he be nicer to the people who worked for him? Would he even waste his time going over a business presentation?

More importantly, what was I going to do? I felt that I had to warn him, but didn't know how. It would sound insane, whatever I said. "Hey, Alan, had a medical check up recently?" Or "Look both ways before you cross the road this weekend."

"Something tickling your funny bone?" Alan asked, looking at me.

"Sorry?" I replied with a guilty start. I couldn't believe that I had smiled at my own thoughts. "Oh no, sorry. I was just concentrating."

He shook his head in mock sadness. "You were my star, Kate, until recently. The clients loved you. You were so full of energy and..." He cast around for a word. "And enthusiasm. Now you look like you're dragging yourself in here and can't wait to get out. What happened, for Christ's sake?"

Josh intervened. "Kate's been through a lot," he said. "Her mother died and now Rebecca's dead. She just needs some time."

"You're a dangerous person to know, Kate," said Alan. "Everyone around you dies, it seems."

More than you know, I thought, but remained silent under the heat of his gaze.

"Well, then, let's wrap this up," he said. "Josh, you can make those changes we discussed. I'm leaving early today, going up to Silverstone."

"Silverstone?" I echoed. "To watch a race?"

"No, to be in one," said Alan, pushing his chair back and standing up. He tucked his polo shirt, yellow today, more tightly into his belt.

"Sounds great, what are you racing?" asked Ben.

"A Ducati Desmosedici." Alan had a huge, goofy grin on his face. "Jack won two places at some charity auction. Tomorrow morning, we have training and then we race in the afternoon."

"I'm jealous," said Ben. "The Ducati is fantastic. What does it have? 800cc and a top speed of 220? Brilliant. I wish I could come and watch you."

"Sounds dangerous," said Josh. I felt the hair stand up on the back of my neck. The aura was presaging Alan's death and he was going to be racing motorbikes the next day.

"Not a good idea for both the company directors to be doing something so risky at the same time," I said, trying to keep my voice calm.

Ben raised his eyebrows in surprise and immediately looked at Alan to see his reaction. Alan's brow was furrowed and his cheeks were red, both sure signs that he was angry. "Not a good idea for you to pass judgment on what your bosses do in their spare time," he growled.

"I didn't mean to make a judgment. I just meant that it would be awful for the company if anything happened to you, or to Jack. Motorbike racing sounds scary, that's all. People come off those things all the time."

Josh shot me a warning look, but I had to keep going, to make Alan aware of how dangerous the race would be, maybe convince him not to go after all.

"Are your kids going to watch?" I asked.

"No, it's a school day."

"Probably just as well."

"What's that supposed to mean?"

"Well, you know if anything were to happen, you wouldn't want your little boys to see it. That would be really hard on them."

"Nothing is going to happen," Alan snapped.

"We need to get this presentation finished," said Josh. He stood up, came around the conference table and put his hand under my elbow to pull me to my feet. "And we need to do it right now."

CHAPTER SIXTEEN

Josh led me to the employee lounge, asked me to sit down on the sofa, and poured a cup of coffee. He pulled a chair over so he could look at me.

"Kate, are you all right? I mean, I know you're going through a rough patch, with Rebecca, the aura visions, and all that. I'm worried about you."

I listened to what he was saying, but kept my eyes fixed on the ficus in its pot next to the sofa. I thought that if I looked at Josh directly, I might start crying. A few of the leaves were turning brown at the ends. I wanted to prune them off and mist the plant with water. I had inherited my Dad's love of gardening but not, I thought wryly, all of his skill. Earlier in the year, I had bought and nurtured a lemon thyme plant, keeping it on the kitchen windowsill and turning it carefully each day so that it could absorb as much sunlight as possible. When it was particularly cold outside, I took it off the sill to protect its delicate leaves. One night I forgot and the following morning, the plant had died, its fragrant green leaves pooled on the counter.

"What was going on with Alan?" Josh continued. "Why would you try to stop him doing something fun? He's already watching you closely, you know, so picking a fight with him seemed a bit perverse."

I shifted my gaze to Josh's face, feeling tears spring to my eyes when I saw his look of genuine concern. "It's dangerous, what he is going to do," I said. "You said so yourself."

"Yes, but I didn't tell him not to go. Honestly, that's not our job. He's an adult. If he wants to hurl his aging body around a track at two hundred miles an hour, that's up to him. I'll bet he'll hardly be able to walk afterwards."

"But what if he's killed?"

Josh stared at me for a few moments. "I don't understand why you'd think that way. People do crazy things every day and, yes, some get hurt or killed, but not that many statistically. My cousin goes sky-diving every weekend. He's been doing it for years. It's a high-risk sport but he loves it. Says it gets him through the drudgery of Monday to Friday. It doesn't make a lot of sense to think that Alan will get hurt. That's a bit morbid."

I bowed my head. Of course it sounded morbid and, a week ago, I wouldn't have given Alan's weekend a microsecond's thought. Now I was worrying about his kids growing up without their father.

"Besides, you don't even like him!" Josh added. I looked up to see him grinning.

"I don't really, but that doesn't mean I shouldn't warn him."

"Warn him? Oh Christ, don't tell me he has one of those aura things too?"

"Yes."

He shifted on the green upholstered chair and leaned forward slightly, the grin replaced with a look of serious concentration.

"Kate, I want to believe you, I really do. But don't you think it's weird? I mean, you keep seeing this aura over people. Perhaps it means something else and has nothing to do with dying. Do I have one?"

"No."

He waved his hand around his head for a few seconds. "That's a relief, at least until we know what they mean. But maybe it's not predicting death?"

"It is, Josh. I wish it wasn't, but think about it. Rebecca, Sophie, Francesca."

The silence in the room was almost absolute, marred only by the soft hiss of the radiators.

Josh stood up and walked to the window and back. "So you believe that Alan is going to die? That's really what the aura means?"

"What do you think? It seems obvious to me."

Josh moved back to the window and leaned up against the

windowsill. Behind him the rain ran down the windowpane, obscuring the view beyond.

"So what do I do about Alan? Do I tell him?"

"No way," said Josh. "I think that would be the end of your employment here. He'd think you were making it up, or doing it to spite him. I don't think you should say anything."

"Say anything to who?"

Ben was at the door and I wondered how much he'd heard.

"I have to go," I said. I was lost and bewildered. I knew something I couldn't tell for fear of being censured or fired. The Trojan princess, Cassandra, had foreseen the destruction of Troy, but her warnings had gone unheeded. Her family and friends thought she was insane. She'd even predicted her own death, and it had come to pass as she'd said it would. She was murdered by Clytemnestra.

"Where are you going?" Josh asked, as I moved towards the door.

"To my desk."

"Are you two fighting?" asked Ben.

Josh ignored him. I glared at him then turned back towards Josh. The gap between us physically was only a few yards. I could cover the space in three or four steps. But I felt like an abyss was opening up between us. The vertical line between his brows was pronounced and his jaw was tense. I couldn't blame him.

"Well, I'll see you soon," I said, hoping that he would move towards me, or say something to make me stay. But he remained where he was, perched on the windowsill. Ben still stood at the door, grinning. What pleasure he got out of seeing confrontation between others I didn't know, but I pushed past him and went to my desk.

***

I didn't see Josh again until it was time to leave. He waved at me when I walked past his office, but he carried on talking with Laura and Ben. On the Tube, I sat next to a man with fuzzy air moving around his head, and I closed my eyes for the rest of the journey. I never wanted to see another aura again.

The rain had stopped by the time I came out of the station. I wandered slowly, kicking at leaves that clumped together in damp piles. The lit windows of the houses I passed seemed to taunt me. I imagined families and friends gathered together inside. When a couple passed by me, longing, like a physical pain in my chest, stabbed at me. Normal life was a vague memory. Like a player sidelined with an injury, I watched but couldn't participate, and wondered if I ever would again.

After dragging myself up the four flights of stairs, I opened the door to my flat, and was struck by how quiet it was. I wished I was out somewhere in a noisy bar or restaurant where my thoughts wouldn't have space to run around in my head quite as much.

I poured a glass of sauvignon blanc, carried the bottle and glass into the living room, and kicked off my shoes.

Sipping my wine, I turned on the television for some company. My cell phone lay on the coffee table in front of me. After a few minutes, I picked it up. Alan's number was speed-dialed in, as was everyone's at the firm. Alan encouraged out of office hours communication, as he called it, which really meant that he expected us all to put in free overtime. Taking a deep breath, I pressed his number and waited while the phone rang twice and clicked to voicemail. I didn't leave a message. I wasn't clear on what I would have said if we had been connected.

I turned on a lamp, grateful for its warm yellow light. There was nothing more to be done, I decided. I couldn't take responsibility for Alan or anyone else. Pushing myself to my feet, I went to the kitchen to contemplate dinner. My refrigerator, usually well-stocked, was empty. I hadn't found the energy to go shopping. But I boiled some penne pasta, added some olive oil, herbs, and grated cheese. It looked appetizing, but the first mouthful made me gag. It tasted like cardboard, and I realized I wasn't hungry anyway. Instead, I poured another glass of wine and took it back to the living room. Just then, my phone trilled, the sound of Pachelbel's Canon filling the room.

"This is Kate."

"Kate, Alan. You called?"

"Er, yes." I put my glass down on the table, and stood up. I thought better when I was standing. "Are you driving or are you already at Silverstone?"

"Driving, but in the wrong bloody direction." Alan's voice echoed a little and I pictured him in his Jaguar, talking on the hands-free speaker.

"Why are you driving in the wrong direction?"

"My son fell off his horse and broke his arm. He's fine, but Tish is insisting I go home to be with them all."

"I'm really sorry about the accident," I said, my head light with relief that Alan was going home. "But I'm glad he's okay. So does that mean you'll miss your motorbike race?"

"Yep. Jack's already called a friend of his to take my spot. Bloody idiot. Not Jack, I mean this wanker who's driving like a snail in front of me." Alan uttered a string of swear words and I held the phone away from my ear. I felt a prickle on the back of my neck. I'd been worried about the racing, but maybe that wasn't where the risk lay. Alan was out on the road, in a bad mood. What if he crashed his car on the way home?

"Well, I'd better let you concentrate on driving," I said. "One accident in the family is enough for tonight, right?"

A sound somewhere between a growl and a snort came over the phone. "Wait," he said. "What were you calling about?"

I should have come up with a viable excuse before making the call, I realized, thinking fast. "I had some ideas about the Montgomery project and wanted to pass them by you. We have another presentation early on Monday morning, so I didn't want to wait until then. Sorry, I shouldn't be disturbing you when you're out of the office. We can talk on Monday."

"No, I'm glad to hear that you've been giving it some thought," said Alan. "That's the old Kate I've been missing recently. So, what's the idea?"

I considered pressing the end call button to pretend that we had been disconnected. But, knowing Alan, he'd just ring right back.

"Glass panels," I said.

"Glass panels?"

"You know, like the custom ones that we used for the RBS building?"

"The ones from Germany? They're friggin' expensive."

"Yes, but we'd only need a couple for the design I have in mind. In the reception area."

"Ok," he said after a pause. "But I need detailed drawings, dimensions, and pricing before the Montgomery meeting on Monday. Get it done and bring it to me first thing Monday morning. I'm going to take the day off tomorrow anyway, and spend it with the family."

He sounded as happy as if he'd been invited to spend the day with the Spanish Inquisition.

Perfect, I thought, as he disconnected the call. Now I had a boatload of work to do, with no way of knowing if Alan was safe or not.

CHAPTER SEVENTEEN

I worked on the glass panel design for most of Saturday morning, and decided it was good enough. I called Nick several times, but only got his voicemail, and couldn't think of a single good excuse to call Alan to see if he was safe. Still, I surmised that if anything had happened to him, I'd hear about it.

Josh texted me to say he'd gone to Gloucestershire for the weekend to see his parents. Leo was still in Italy, due to fly back on Sunday morning. My fear for Nick and concern for Alan at least kept thoughts of Rebecca at bay for a while, but the prospect of the dreary, solitary weekend almost paralyzed me with despair. I drank endless cups of tea and thought about my friend's death.

I wondered when her funeral would be. Several times I picked up my phone to call Rebecca's parents, but I couldn't bring myself to disturb them. The people at Montgomery Group would be sure to know something, though. I could ask them at the meeting scheduled on Monday.

In pajamas, socks, and an old sweater of Leo's, I sat down on the sofa and stared at the coffee table, running my fingers along its lustrous cherrywood surface. If Rebecca's coffee table had been made of wood, she might not be dead. I shuddered at the memory of all that glass.

I conjured the scene again in my mind. Rebecca on her back amidst the glass shards, the blood dried into the carpet, the bloody handprint on the front of the sofa. There was something I'd noticed when we first entered the room, but now I couldn't remember what it was.

Pulling a sketchpad and pencil out of a drawer in the coffee table, I drew a rough outline of Rebecca's living room, with rectangles for the sofas and the table. With a shaking hand, I sketched an outline of the body, arms flung out to either side, one hand touching the sofa. The shattered vase and the white flowers, wilted and brown. I was a visual thinker. Seeing details on paper helped me to concentrate.

What was it that I'd seen that night? Something that made me doubt the theory that this was a simple accident. What I'd said to Clarke I really believed. Rebecca had been a dancer, a talented ballerina. She'd organized a dance recital the first term at University, and I'd been amazed by her grace and strength. She'd outperformed all the other dancers on the stage with ease. She moved with a poise that made me feel ungainly and clumsy. That was it, I thought. She wasn't clumsy. Every movement seemed to be choreographed. She was aware of her own gracefulness, I knew, and it was part of her appeal. The idea that she'd fallen into her own coffee table seemed so unlikely, in spite of what Inspector Clarke thought.

I stared at the drawing. There was no rug to trip over; the white carpet ran all the way to the baseboards. There'd been no sign of anything else, no bag or stool in the way, no magazines or papers on the floor that she might have slipped on.

And then there was the boyfriend. Did they have a fight? Did he push her, deliberately or accidentally, and then run away? The more I thought about it, the more I was convinced that Rebecca hadn't just stumbled into the table.

I stared at the diagram for several minutes. I remembered the gold bracelet of her watch against the whiteness of her wrist. It didn't seem that robbery was involved. I couldn't really recall if anything had been missing.

Turning the paper around, I realized that I'd drawn Rebecca's right arm in the wrong place, so I erased it and redrew it. Still something was wrong. Then I remembered. A wine glass in her right hand, broken, the stem pointing up to the ceiling, a jagged spike, and the rest of the glass in splinters. And a bottle of wine lying on its side a few feet away, near the fireplace. It was a Cabernet, like the one we'd drunk the night I had gone for dinner. Perhaps even the same bottle because we'd only had one glass each. Rebecca wasn't a big drinker; she told me she was careful with her calorie intake and I knew she was proud of her willowy figure.

Suddenly, I had a hundred questions. I knew that Inspector Clarke would have some of the answers, but would he talk to me? His goodbye at the cafe was pretty final, as though he didn't intend to see me again. But I remembered he'd given me a card with a phone number on it. I found it in my purse, and made the call. Thankfully, I heard his voicemail click on. Leaving a message seemed easier than actually speaking with him. I left my name and cell number, saying I had a couple of questions, and would he please call me back. And then I went back to the sofa and wondered what to do for the rest of the weekend. I missed Josh. It didn't seem right to disturb him while he was at his parents' house, though. I had a feeling he'd gone away to avoid having to see me, or to avoid having to make excuses not to see me.

My newfound gift could hardly have been more badly timed. Josh and I had been friends almost from my first day at Bradley Cohen, and, for me, the attraction had been instantaneous. He hadn't shown any romantic interest in me though, even though we spent a lot of time together. When I confided in Laura, one of the senior architects, she said she'd heard that he'd broken up with a long-term girlfriend just after graduating from university. He didn't talk about her and it was obvious he wasn't ready to date anyone new.

Until now.

I pulled Leo's outsize sweater tighter around me. This was ridiculous. There must be something I could do instead of cocooning myself in misery and self-pity.

***

I knew I was taking a risk and that the Williams' family might refuse to see me, but it was worth doing. I wanted to see if they knew anything that might help locate Rebecca's boyfriend, or provide some kind of clue as to why Nick was in danger.

The train to Bournemouth was fairly empty on a Saturday afternoon. I took a seat by a window. Just as the train was about to pull out, a group of young men in hoodies got into the carriage. They turned on rap music at full volume, and passed a cigarette around, ignoring all the No Smoking signs. When another passenger, a middle-aged man, nervously asked them to turn down the music, they responded with jeers and threatening gestures. He retreated into a window seat near me. We exchanged sympathetic looks.

Fortunately, the youths got off at the next stop, leaving us in peace. I spent the rest of the journey watching the suburbs pass by. Train tracks rarely ran through the prettier parts of any city, I thought. The view from the window was of the backs of terraced brick houses, washing lines, garden sheds, neglected yards with broken fences and piles of rubbish. Further out were the Industrial parks, low-slung prefab buildings, acres of deserted parking lots, grey and dismal under the clouds.

Finally, leaving the suburbs behind, we rode through neatly-hedged green fields dotted with sheep, past grey stone churches with pretty spires and stained glass windows, presiding over ancient graveyards.

Finally we pulled into the station at Bournemouth. When I went outside to find a taxi the rain of the past weeks had stopped; an anemic sun hung uncertainly in the pale blue sky.

The Williams' house was a semidetached brick two story, identical to all the other houses on the street. Each one had a small parking area in front, and a glossy white Volvo sat in front of number 26. The curtains were drawn. I hesitated before ringing the bell. This seemed like a huge intrusion on a grieving family, but now I'd come this far, I had to go through with it. I rang and waited. A curtain moved at a window. A man in his fifties with grey hair and glasses opened the front door.

"Yes?"

"I'm Kate, Rebecca's friend. I'm so sorry to disturb you..." I didn't finish my sentence before he stepped aside and waved me in. "Come in, come in. Rebecca talked about you when she visited us last weekend. She seemed excited that you two had reconnected. Please, take a seat. I'm Terry, by the way."

He gestured towards the sofa. The living room was crowded with a large floral sofa and several armchairs. A huge flat panel television in one corner seemed out of place amidst the slightly shabby furniture.

"I'll get Janice," Terry said. "She'll want to meet you."

He disappeared for a few minutes; I looked around the room. Photos of Rebecca and her brother filled the surfaces of several side tables. My throat started to close up, just thinking of the parents, bereaved twice.

When Rebecca's mother came in, I stood up to shake her hand.

Her eyes were puffy, and her grey curls were disheveled. I wondered if she'd once had red hair like her daughter.

"Put the kettle on, dear," she said to her husband, who obediently disappeared again.

Janice sat down and patted the cushion next to her. I sat next to her, unsure what to say. All the words I'd rehearsed on the train down dissipated like ash in the cold light of such grief. "I'm so sorry," I managed finally. She bowed her head. Tears dripped onto her tan slacks, leaving dark spots on the fabric. Unsure, I put my hand over hers. We sat in silence until Terry came back with a tray of china cups and a teapot with pink flowers on it.

"Thank you for seeing me," I said. "I just wanted to tell you how sorry I am, and to see if there is anything I can do to help."

"You were the one that found her, weren't you?" Janice asked.

"Yes, and Nick, her neighbor. Have you met him?"

No," said Terry. "She moved into that new flat about two years ago, but we never visited. I mean, we would have liked to, but I think Rebecca was too busy. She always said she liked coming here when she had some free time. We'll have to go up, at some point, I suppose, to get her things, but the police said we have to wait a bit longer."

"We are so proud of her," said Janice, holding a handkerchief to her eyes. "She got such a good job. She bought that television for us, you know." She pointed at the big TV, like a black hole in the flowered wallpaper.

"And the car," added Terry. "The old Rover I'd had for years just about fell apart, and she insisted on getting us a new one. She said it was her way of repaying us for putting her through college."

I nodded and sipped my tea. The visit had already answered one question, which was whether Rebecca came from a wealthy family, one that could subsidize the rent on her luxury apartment.

"Did you meet her boyfriend?" I asked. "Did she ever bring him down here?"

They looked at each other, Janice lifting a shoulder in a faint shrug.

"No, we didn't. I got the feeling we weren't good enough for him, if you know what I mean? We put out the invitation, but he never came. And then last weekend she said she was going to break up with him."

"Break up with Edward?"

"Yes. In fact, that's when she talked about you, dear. She said she'd started thinking about her relationship and decided it wasn't right for her. She said she wanted to be more like you, although, to be honest, I wasn't sure what that meant."

I didn't know what it meant either.

"So Rebecca was here last weekend?" I asked.

"Yes, she came home on Friday night," Janice said. "She stayed the night and went back on Saturday morning. I thought she seemed a bit distracted, didn't you, Terry? I wanted her to stay longer, but she said she had to get back. I never imagined it would be the last time I'd see her..." Janice's words tailed off.

"Did she ever tell you Edward's second name?" I asked. "Or show you a photo?"

"No. We didn't talk about him much when she came down," Terry said. "I think she was just being independent, you know, keeping her London life and home life separate. She lived in a way that we couldn't really imagine, in the city, all those nice clothes she started wearing. It was very different from what we're used to."

"Designer bags," added Janice. "She was obsessed with designer handbags. She gave me a couple that she said she didn't like any more, but I can't use them. Would you like them, Kate?"

"Thank you, but I really.... "

"Never mind the bags, Janice," said Terry. "More tea, Kate?"

"No, thank you. May I ask when the funeral will be?" I asked. "I know some of Rebecca's work colleagues would like to attend. And I'll be there, of course."

Terry looked at Janice before answering. "We don't have a date yet, lass. The police haven't released the body from the autopsy."

Janice began to sob loudly.

"Sorry, love. But that's the fact. Until then, we can't plan anything."

"Why did they need to do an autopsy?" wailed Janice. "Cutting her up like that. It's cruel."

"Best not to think about it," said Terry.

"It's quite normal," I said, trying to soothe Janice. "When my grandfather died in a nursing home a couple of years ago, they needed to do an autopsy just to verify cause of death. I'm sure it won't take long."

I wondered what the delay could be.

"Have you talked to Inspector Clarke?" I asked.

Terry nodded. "Just on the phone a couple of times. Seems like a nice enough young man. A bit cold and professional in my opinion, but I suppose that's the way it is. He's just doing his job. He said they were doing a toxicology assessment, because it seemed that Rebecca had been drinking at the time of the accident."

"Rubbish," said Janice. "She never drank enough to be drunk or incapable. She was a dancer, you know," she said, looking at me.

"I know," I said. "And a good one. I watched her dance in college."

"Well, she looked after her health and her figure," continued Janice. "She disapproved of drinking too much. It's ridiculous that the police think she was drunk enough to fall over her own coffee table."

Toxicology assessment, I thought. Clarke hadn't mentioned that. In the long silence that followed, I tried to think of something to say.

"Nick is looking after Caspian," I managed, finally. "I was wondering if that's all right with you? I'm sure we could get him down here if you wanted him?"

Janice stood up and moved slowly to the other side of the room, where she picked up a photo in a silver frame. "Rebecca sent us this just a month or so ago."

It was a shot of Rebecca holding Caspian, his grey fur contrasting with her mass of red hair. "He's a good-looking animal," commented Terry. "But Janice is allergic to cats. I don't think we can take him."

"That's all right. I'll let Nick know. I'm sure he'll be happy to keep him."

For as long as Nick is alive, I thought.

We sat quietly in the gathering gloom. Through the window, I saw dark clouds move across the sky, deleting all the blue, erasing the sun as though it had never existed.

CHAPTER EIGHTEEN

On Monday morning, Alan called out to me when I walked past his office. With a surge of relief, I saw that the moving air over his head had disappeared. Whatever danger he had faced was gone, and he, completely oblivious, was his usual cantankerous self, demanding to see my drawings without even saying good morning. I was glad that his plans had changed through no intervention of my own; it meant that events could alter a person's fate without him even knowing.

That made me wonder if I'd ever had an aura. Had there been a time when I'd avoided a fatal encounter and not even realized it?

"Good," Alan said, once he'd skimmed the papers I gave him. That was high praise from him, and I hurried out of his office before he could say anything else. Downstairs, Josh was already at his desk. He waved me over when he saw me. For a brief instant, I imagined a discreet hug or a kiss, but his words quickly burst that bubble.

"You had a busy weekend," he said. I wondered what he meant.

"Oh, the glass panels?" I asked finally.

"You didn't mention those to me or Ben," he said, unrolling some blueprints and spreading them on his desk. "Alan just told me about them this morning. He said he couldn't wait to see what you'd come up with."

"The idea just popped into my head," I said.

"So you called Alan to share it?" he asked, eyebrows raised. We were supposed to be collaborating on the project and this looked as though I was going over Josh's head to the boss.

"I called him because of the aura and I thought he was in danger," I whispered, although there was no one else around. "Then when I got through to him, I had to come up with a reason, so I invented one."

I flopped down in the visitor chair, angry at having to justify myself, but understanding why Josh was upset. He leaned forward, elbows on the desk between us.

"The aura thing," he said. "It doesn't seem to be working, because Alan is fine as far as I can see."

"His aura has gone. He didn't race; that must have been where the danger lay. He had to go home because his son was hurt. So the risk passed, and the aura went away."

"If it was ever there."

"What's that supposed to mean?" I asked, feeling the heat rising into my cheeks. "Of course it was there. I saw it."

"You saw it. No one else can see it. You must admit it's a bit hard to believe. It comes, it goes, and only you know about it."

I stood up, feeling my knees tremble. I hated conflict with anyone, and most especially with Josh, but he was being unreasonable.

"You can't see gravity, but that doesn't mean it doesn't exist," I said, and stalked out of the room.

I went to the kitchen to get a cup of coffee, irritated to see that my hand was shaking. I leaned against the counter to drink my coffee, feeling my heart rate gradually slow down. Jack came into the kitchen, wearing a red bow tie.

"How are you, my dear?" he asked.

"I'm fine, thanks," I said, getting an extra mug from the cabinet. "How was Silverstone? Did you enjoy it?"

"Fantastic. I've never gone that fast on two wheels before. What an experience! Alan really didn't know what he was missing."

"I bet he didn't," I said, thinking that neither of them had any idea what the day at the racetrack might have been like.

"I thought you were supposed to be going to Edinburgh," I said, handing him a cup of tea. He rarely drank coffee.

"Tomorrow," he said. "I just have a few things to clear up here today. How are things with you?"

"We're busy with the Montgomery project," I said. "We have another meeting today even though...." I trailed off. I'd been surprised that it was all business as usual with the Montgomery

Group in spite of Rebecca's death.

"Ah yes," said Jack. "Sad, very sad. Miss Williams was an intelligent young woman."

"I didn't realize you'd met her?"

Jack pursed his lips. "I meet all our clients, Kate. I handle the contracts and the money. Boring stuff, compared to the real work that goes on here, I know. But someone has to do it. And this project is a big one, even by our standards. Lots of paperwork."

He stirred two sugars into his tea before dumping the spoon in the sink. "Alan told me that you were the one who found Miss Williams? You were friends?"

"Yes. We were friends in college, lost touch and met up when she came to a Montgomery project meeting. I was enjoying getting to know her again..."

"Yes, Alan mentioned to me this morning that you'd been spending time together. When did you last see her?"

"Sunday lunchtime. We were supposed to be going out to see a movie on Sunday evening, but something came up, so we had lunch instead. I had no idea that I'd never seen her again."

He tore off some kitchen towel and gave it to me.

"It's too bad she cancelled on you. Did she say why?"

I shook my head, blotting my eyes and cheeks, trying not to smear my mascara. "I think she was seeing her boyfriend."

Jack nodded. "Well, love takes precedence, I suppose. I'm sorry, Kate. This must all be very hard on you." He glanced at his watch. "I shouldn't keep you from your work. I'll bring you some Edinburgh rock back. Look after yourself."

I carried my coffee to my desk, hearing snippets of the usual morning conversations floating in from the hallway. I turned on my computer, pulled my panel designs from my briefcase and spread them out on the desk. But I was too distracted to work.

The significance of what had happened with Alan gradually sank into my brain. It meant that even though auras presaged death, something could happen to avert the danger, whatever it was. With growing panic, I realized that, if it was possible to change the outcome, then the burden on me to warn or assist was huge. I wasn't just a bystander, seeing auras with no chance of saving anyone. I could intervene. I had to. My headache bloomed, pushing against my temples with sickening intensity. How could I save Nick?

I felt like screaming. I had no idea what might cause his

premature death. An accident? Illness? There were so many ways to die; I couldn't be his bodyguard.

He answered when I called, although the connection was faint and crackly.

"Nick, it's Kate."

"Hi Kate. I'm in an elevator. Bad line. Everything okay?"

"Yes, yes," I said, relieved to hear his voice. "Er, I was just wondering how Caspian's doing?"

There was a pause and then. "He's fine."

"Good. Just wanted to let you know that Rebecca's parents are hoping you'll keep him."

"Of course. I love the little chap."

"Great. Well, I'll let you go. Have a good day."

The line crackled and faded "...bye."

Feeling like an idiot, I put my phone away, and stared at the printouts on my desk. What was I supposed to do about Nick? I couldn't let him die, but I hardly knew him and it would be impossible to watch over him. What I could do was warn him, tell him about the aura, explain what it meant. I'd have to see him in person. I sent him a text, asking if we could meet for a drink after work.

I gazed at the screensaver on my computer, a photo of my Dad's house in Tuscany, a beautiful yellow stucco villa surrounded by colorful gardens and dark green cypress trees. Leo had texted me earlier to say that Francesca's funeral had been well attended, Dad was doing pretty well, and Paolo was keeping him company. I missed them all. I wished I was there with them.

After finishing what I needed to do for the meeting, I walked to the conference room, hoping I might have a chance to chat with Josh, but he arrived with Alan just seconds before the Montgomery team came in.

Soon, the conference room was crowded, full of stale air and an undercurrent of despondency, at least on the Bradley Cohen side. Montgomery behaved as usual, asking questions, checking that his assistants were taking notes, and occasionally looking at his cell phone and sending texts. I wondered if he felt guilty about his lack of concern when Rebecca first no-showed for work, but no one talked about her, and there was no empty chair at the table. Alan had brought in Laura and Jim for extra input.

As soon as the meeting drew to a close, I gathered up my

sketches and pens, and followed Montgomery to the elevator.

"Mr. Montgomery?"

He swung around. "Yes?"

"I was friends with Rebecca. I just wanted to say I'm sorry. There's no date for the funeral yet, but I could let you know when I hear something."

"Why would I need to know that?" he asked, jabbing at the elevator button.

"I thought you would want to go," I said, surprised by his attitude. "Or at least perhaps some of her colleagues would."

His shoulders seemed to relax. "Of course, of course," he said. "Please let me know what you find out. I remember now that Rebecca mentioned you two were friends. Very sad. She was a valued asset."

Valued asset? It sounded cold. I wondered what Alan would say about me.

"Do you have a card?" Montgomery asked. "I'm sure we all exchanged cards at our first meeting, but here's mine. Feel free to call me if you need anything."

I fumbled in my purse for my wallet, where I always kept a few business cards, but couldn't find one.

"Here," he said, handing me a second card of his own. "Write your cell number on this." He took it back, looked at my number scrawled on it. "That way we can coordinate for the funeral."

When the elevator arrived, he got in. "You coming?"

I shook my head. I was shocked by his indifference to Rebecca's death and didn't want to talk to him more than necessary. I took the stairs.

CHAPTER NINETEEN

My cell phone rang just as I reached the bottom stair; I moved to a quieter corner of the lobby to take the call. It was Inspector Clarke. He began with an apology.

"Sorry it took me so long to get back to you," he said. "Do you have time to grab a coffee?"

After agreeing to meet at a small cafe just a few blocks away, I hurried back upstairs to get my coat and scarf. I had a sinking feeling that I was pushing Alan to the limit by leaving the office yet again. Clarke was already at a table when I got there.

"Thanks for seeing me," I said.

"Not a problem. I got you a coffee. I hope it's what you wanted. How are you doing?"

How was I doing? I couldn't begin to answer that question. Every night, I dreamed about Rebecca, strange disjointed dreams that left me sweating and breathless. We'd been together in a car, driving in circles around the Campanile in Florence. Swimming in a deep blue pool with eerie black shapes lurking at the bottom. Climbing an infinite number of stairs to the top of a massive building that looked out over a city that wasn't London. In all of them, Rebecca was smiling, laughing, talking. Every time I woke up, I lay still for a minute, waiting for the images to fade, bracing myself for reality to seep back in.

But Rebecca's death was just one layer in my own personal Russian nesting doll of misery. The auras, Francesca, Sophie, the conflict at the office. There was no respite.

Clarke said, "So, you left me a message and said you had some questions?"

"Yes, I was drawing some pictures of the scene at her flat, the way I remembered it. There were a couple of things I noticed that I wanted to check with you. The main anomaly was the wineglass."

Clarke's eyes narrowed, green lasers pointing at me. "Go on."

"There was a broken glass in Rebecca's hand," I said. "If you're falling, you wouldn't keep hold of something in your hand would you? You'd let go of it. Or if not during the fall, then afterwards. If she was trying to get up, she wouldn't hold on to the glass."

The detective leaned back in his chair. "What makes you think she was trying to get up?"

"The bloody handprint on the front of the sofa," I said. "As though she'd tried to grab at the sofa to pull herself up. That means she didn't die instantly when she hit the table."

"Anything else?"

"Only that I truly believe someone else was there with Rebecca. I don't believe it was an accident."

Clarke was quiet for a long time. "I'm going to bring you up to date with the details we know," he said. "First of all, you may be right. It's possible that the wineglass and the bottle were placed there after she fell."

His words fell like stones into the surging torrent of my thoughts, adding to the tumult of emotions eddying around in my head. Edward, if he was the killer, was a cold-blooded bastard.

"So you do believe it was murder," I said. I was relieved that the police were starting to investigate. At the same time, I was horrified. Accidents happen, and it would have been impossible for me to protect Rebecca twenty-four hours a day. But murder should have been preventable. I'd known enough to fear that the boyfriend was a danger, but not enough to stop him from killing Rebecca. I really hadn't taken the aura prediction seriously enough. My hand shook when I picked up my coffee, so I put the cup back down on the red formica table.

"What else did you find out?" I asked.

"The autopsy..." he stopped when he saw me flinch. "The examination showed that Rebecca had bruises on both wrists as though someone had held them tightly -- very tightly, in fact."

"Oh my God," I breathed. "Her boyfriend? They must have had a fight."

"We don't know who was there," said Clarke. "And we can't jump to conclusions that it was this boyfriend."

"But who else could it have been? There was no sign of forced entry at the door. Rebecca must have known the person and let him in."

"Or her."

"Her?"

"We have to look at all the options," he said. "But for now, let's pursue the idea of this boyfriend. I have a question for you. Is there any chance that the boyfriend knows who you are?"

I was confused. "We've never met, I told you that."

"But would Rebecca have talked to him about you?"

A feeling like cold water sloshed around in my stomach. "I don't know. Why? Am I in danger?"

Clarke shook his head. "I don't think so, to be honest, but I'd rather address the possibility than ignore it. If he has any reason to think that you know who he is, he might conceivably consider you as a threat."

I took a minute to digest that.

"I see," was all I managed to say. "So this changes everything? You're officially looking for a murderer now?"

"Possibly. There are shades of grey, especially with a situation like this one. She wasn't stabbed or strangled, so it's not a clear-cut case of unlawful killing. No evidence of premeditation. We have a long way to go before we know what we're looking at."

"And you're heading the investigation?"

He nodded. "I am."

"Good."

He grinned. "Good?"

"Well, first, I'm glad that you're in charge. I mean, I trust you, you know. And secondly, I've thought all along that this wasn't an accident, so I'm relieved that it's going to be properly investigated. Whoever did this to her needs to be found and punished."

"I'll do my best," he said. "I was wondering about her job at the Montgomery Group. What did that entail?"

"Her title was Financial Director. She was really good at math, so it makes sense she'd end up doing something with finance."

"It sounds like a high-level job for a young woman just a few years out of college," Clarke said, spinning his empty cup on the table in front of him.

"I think she was director for just one unit of the Montgomery Group," I said. "The New Development Group, or something like that. Still a good position for her, but perhaps not quite as high level as it sounds. I'm sure someone at the company could give you more details."

"Do you want another coffee?" Clarke stood up. "I'm going for a refill."

I nodded. I hadn't even tasted the first one, hadn't realized I'd finished it.

When he came back, Clarke was silent for a while. I heard the clink of cups from the counter and a radio spitting out rap music. The cafe was empty apart from us.

"I've been thinking about what you said about watching out for Rebecca," he said finally. "Did you have a reason to think she was in danger? I know you said not, but in the light of our new findings, I'd really like to know what it was that made you believe there was a threat of some kind."

I was aware of him watching me closely. His green eyes rested on my face and his body was motionless. His stillness was calming, and seemed to invite my confidence. I wanted to tell him about the aura, about the deaths, about the danger to Nick. I ran my finger around the rim of my coffee cup. I felt my lips part, the words starting to form and then I closed my mouth. I couldn't tell him any of it.

"I can't really remember what I said. I was upset, you know, about finding her body. I didn't have any reason to think that she was in danger. The only thing that ever crossed my mind was that she was secretive about the boyfriend. Also, that when she talked about him, she didn't seem happy."

Clarke took a swallow of his coffee, his eyes still on mine as he drank.

"I wish you could tell me the truth, Kate," he said, putting the cup back in its saucer. "It might help me work out what happened to your friend."

It's not fair, I thought. Even if I were to tell him about the aura, and even if he believed me, which he wouldn't, what good would it do? I had a useless ability to see that someone would die, but had no idea of where, when, or how. What was the point? Anger welled inside me. I felt my hands curl into fists. Clarke noticed, his eyes flicking from my hands to my face and back again. What did he see?

Guilt? Did he think I was involved somehow? I felt the rage ebb away, replaced by fatigue and despair. I wanted to cry, but I wouldn't do that under the scrutiny of those inquisitive green eyes.

"Tell me again what time you left the restaurant," he said. "What was it? Indian?"

"Chinese. I left at about two o clock."

"And where did you go after that?"

"Back home."

"Did anyone see you? Was anyone with you?"

"Am I a suspect?"

He seemed to take forever to answer. "I'm just doing my job," he said. "And you are hiding something, I'm sure of it."

"I'm not," I said, even though it wasn't true. "And I want to find whoever did this just as much as you. In fact, I went to the Montgomery Group building to see if I could find Edward, the boyfriend."

Clarke's eyebrows shot up. "And?"

"Well, I thought it was possible that Rebecca would have met her boyfriend through work. I knew it was a long shot, but worth a try. She said he works in technology. I found one employee who works in the IT department. His name is Ted Stevens. But there's no way he's Rebecca's boyfriend, believe me."

Clarke leaned forward across the table. "Kate, it's not your job to go looking for people. Leave that to me. You have no idea how this man might react if you do find him."

Chastened, I nodded, loosening the scarf around my neck. Either the little cafe was overheated or I was.

He pushed his cup away, leaned forward, palms flat on the table.

"I'm sorry about Rebecca. I'm sorry you found her body. I know how traumatic that can be. The best thing I can do now is find out who was with her when she died. If you know anything at all that would help me with that, I'd like to know." He paused, leaned back. "Remember you told me about Rebecca being a dancer? That was information I couldn't have known, but it made me understand that an accidental fall was possible, but perhaps less likely. So please think about it and call me if you know anything else that might help."

He pushed his chair back and stood up, put on his coat and scarf. "I'll look forward to hearing from you." He walked out, jangling the bell over the door.

CHAPTER TWENTY

The bar Nick had suggested was an upscale cocktail place in Mayfair that specialized in martinis. Mirrors behind the bar reflected shelves of bottles with colorful, arty labels and trays of inverted martini glasses. The crowd was young, around my own age, but I felt old and out of place among the well-dressed, upper class patrons. A brief silence greeted the arrival of a celebrity, a minor Royal who frequently graced the pages of the tabloids, and then the volume immediately rose again.

Nick arrived, debonair in a long black wool coat unbuttoned over a pink striped shirt. Several women watched admiringly as he walked past. I stared too, but not for the same reason; his aura was still there, moving fast around his dark glossy hair. Taking the stool next to me, he ordered two vodka martinis, and we touched glasses. I drank wine more often than cocktails; the sharp taste of the liquor took my breath away

"So, how are you doing?" he asked. "God, it's been a tough week. I can't get over finding Rebecca like that. Poor girl."

"Have the police been in touch with you? Asking for more information?"

"Yeah, that detective, what's his name? Clarke. Good-looking guy." He laughed. "He called me, said he had some questions and could we meet. But I've been swamped with work and haven't had time yet. Tomorrow I plan to do it, although I can't work out why. It was obviously an accident."

"It wasn't. At least, that's not what they think now. Rebecca had a lot of bruising on her wrists, as though someone had held her very tightly. And they think that someone, presumably the boyfriend, put the broken wineglass in her hand after she fell. To make it look as though she'd been drinking."

Nick put his glass down and stared at me. "No way. Murder?"

"Well, I don't know for sure, but that's what Inspector Clarke told me. So they are looking for this Edward person. Your picture ID of him will be helpful."

Nick groaned. "Oh shit. I completely forgot to do that today. They said it would take a couple of hours. I meant to go, but I've been swamped at work. Did I tell you about the shoot I'm setting up for...? never mind. I'll find time soon."

He checked his watch. "I don't want to be rude, but I can't stay long. Gary's waiting for me and we have dinner plans." He smiled. "And he'd be very jealous if he knew I was out drinking with a pretty girl."

"But I thought you were..." I stopped, and he laughed.

"Bi, sweetheart. Either way works for me."

I grinned at him. His laughter was infectious.

"Ah, I can see how that would make Gary a little insecure."

"Gary makes insecurity into a career. If it were an Olympic sport, he'd win the gold medal. But I love him, and mostly I avoid doing anything to feed his anxieties. But he is pretty easy to wind up."

He took a swallow of his martini.

"What about you? Boyfriend? Girlfriend?"

I shook my head, feeling the faint buzz of the alcohol "Not right now."

"So what was it you wanted to talk about? I got the impression there was something particular, not just a drink to chat over the lurid details of a murder? Do you think Rebecca's folks are really happy for me to keep Caspian? I'd give him to them if they want him."

"Her mother's allergic," I said. "So they'd be grateful if you continued to look after him."

Nick looked relieved. It was endearing that he really cared about the cat.

"I'll thank them when I see them at the funeral. Is there a date yet?"

"Not yet."

I took a big gulp of my martini; it was time to talk to Nick about the aura.

"There's something I need to tell you," I began. I described the moving air and what I thought it meant.

"Rebecca had one, before she died." I said. "And you have one, Nick. Which means that you're in danger from something. Maybe connected to Rebecca's murder, maybe something completely different. An accident. perhaps. But I want you to be careful."

Nick drained his glass, leaned over and took my hands in his.

"They say the good-looking guys are always gay, and the beautiful girls are always crazy. Good to see you're fueling the myth. Really, Kate? Auras that predict death?"

He gave an exaggerated shiver. "Thank you, I think, for the warning. Now I really have to go."

"Nick, I'm sorry."

Ignoring me, he stood up, put a couple of banknotes on the bar, and pulled on his coat.

"I'll see you at the funeral," he said. "And I mean Rebecca's, not mine."

I stayed at the bar for awhile after he'd gone, hearing the chatter and laughter of the crowds behind me. When an older man in a business suit took Nick's vacated stool and leered at me, I finished my drink and left.

On the way home, I noticed auras over the head of one man on the street and another on the train, but I willed myself to ignore them. I'd seen quite a few in the last week in London, on the Tube and in restaurants. I'd become adept at not noticing them and, after a while, succeeded in passing by without a second thought. Like homeless people. Everyone knew they were there, but didn't really see them.

CHAPTER TWENTY-ONE

When I arrived at Leo's house on Friday evening, the street was bathed in a soft, warm light that made the red brick houses glow. When I rang the bell, Leo appeared with an apron on and tongs in one hand. He gave me a peck on the cheek, and I followed him through the kitchen to the small garden beyond. The smoky fragrance of grilled meat permeated the air. The weather had surprised everyone yet again by turning warm, very unusual for this late in October.

"Where are the boys?" I asked.

"At the soccer field, playing with some friends. It's the first time it hasn't been raining for weeks, so they're making the most of it. They have to be back by seven." He glanced at his watch. "Ten minutes."

We exchanged news about work, and Leo told me about their week in Italy.

"How's Dad doing?" I asked.

"Francesca's death hit him pretty hard," he replied, turning sausages with the tongs. "I know you had reservations about her, but it was nice for him to have her company. I think he's going to be lonely, although Paolo will spend more time there. Dad's talking about writing a book on gardening."

"That's a wonderful idea," I said, wrestling with the corkscrew and one of the bottles. "Maybe I could offer to take photos for the book. I'd love an excuse to brush up my camera skills again. I'm planning on going out to see Dad in a couple of weeks. My big project at work will be finished by then."

The thought of the project reminded me of Rebecca. I felt my throat clogging up. I finally got the cork out of the bottle and poured two glasses of wine.

"Cheers," I said as we clinked glasses. The front door banged, and the house resounded with the din of feet on the wood floors and the raised voices of the two boys. Leo checked the time. "Right on the dot," he said. "Not even one minute late."

He went to the kitchen door. "If your shoes are muddy, take them off," he yelled. "And wash your hands!"

He came back and took a seat at the wrought iron table next to me. "They're good kids," he said. "Aidan's half-term report was really excellent. His grades went up. Gabe's not so much. He's a bit of a dreamer. He likes to draw, like you."

"Well, he's only ten," I said. "Plenty of time to work out what he wants to do. I seem to remember Dad saying that you were a late bloomer and look where you ended up!"

Leo smiled, but shook his head. "I think I'd wish for something more for the boys. Academia can be frustrating. So much pressure to publish. I'd like to see them go into engineering or something useful where they can make the world a better place. You're helping, being an architect, designing green buildings and making sure we don't let big construction put too many blots on the landscape."

"Not as green as I'd hoped," I said, and took a sip of wine. "Money always wins out over good intentions. It costs more to build green, and not everyone is convinced of the value. A lot of people just don't care about the long term. But I don't want to talk about work on a Friday night."

I'd already decided not to tell Leo about Rebecca. He didn't know her, and I had no intention of having the guilt conversation again. I intended to put all of it aside for now, intent on enjoying the weekend with the three favorite men in my life. Well, three of the four, I thought, but Josh had been distant ever since our discussion about the glass panels. On Friday evening, I'd lingered late in the office, hoping he'd come by and suggest a drink or dinner, but he'd left with Ben, Jim, and a few others. A boys' night out, which wasn't that unusual, but I thought he would have at least dropped by to say goodnight.

"Why don't you tell me more about the lady you've been seeing?" I said. "What was her name?"

"Olivia." A smile settled on Leo's face, tilting the corners of his mouth upward and crinkling his eyes. I felt a burst of happiness. I so wanted him to settle with a new partner, someone who wouldn't mind sharing the upbringing of the boys.

"I'll tell you all about her after dinner. She's planning on coming for lunch tomorrow."

"Perfect. I'll look forward to meeting her."

I stood up, glass in hand to review the status of the sausages on the grill. One of them slid through the grate on to the hot coals, and I grabbed at it instinctively, burning my fingers. I sucked on them, feeling the sting of burned skin.

"Hi Aunt Kate!" Gabe ran out of the kitchen to give me a hug. "Look at what I got in Italy." He proudly showed off his soccer shirt emblazoned with the number three and the name Chiellini.

"Juventus is rubbish," called Aidan from the kitchen. "I support Fiorentina like Grandpa." He walked into the garden in socked feet, carrying a soda bottle.

"Hello Auntie Kate," he said, with a small wave. At fourteen years old, he'd decided that hugs were strictly off limits.

I felt my knees turn to water. My wine glass slipped from my fingers. A thousand tiny shards of glass glinted on the stone patio, and the red wine flowed into the cracks between the paving stones.

CHAPTER TWENTY-TWO

I found myself sitting on a chair, with Gabe holding my hand. Leo was sweeping up the glass with a dustpan and brush.

"Are you all right, Aunt Kate?" asked Gabe, his little fingers closed tightly over mine.

I straightened up and looked for Aidan. "Where's your brother?" I asked.

"He didn't have shoes on, so I sent him inside to get some, just in case I miss any pieces," said Leo. "Gabe, go grab another glass from the kitchen, and tell Aidan to bring the salad and the potatoes from the fridge. Dinner's ready."

Gabe released Kate's hand and sauntered into the house.

"Are you okay?" asked Leo. "Do you feel sick?"

I blinked a few times. Everything was as it had been before. The barbecue grill, the table laid for dinner, the long stretch of green grass strewn with daisies and littered with frisbees, footballs and a broken trampoline. But I saw them as though through a shattered lens, the images distorted and at odd angles.

"I'm fine," I said. "I forgot to eat lunch, and it made me a bit light-headed. I'm sorry about the glass and the mess."

"Don't be daft. It's nothing. I was just worried about you."

Both boys reappeared, carrying bowls and a clean glass for me. When Leo'd finished sweeping, they helped themselves to food and sat down. I sat next to Aidan, keeping my eyes on Gabe and Leo on the other side of the table. I didn't want to see the aura that floated over Aidan's head. I needed time to absorb the shock of it. My thoughts drifted back to when he was born.

Back then, of course, Leo and Marie had been happily married, struggling on the pitiful salary that Leo was earning as a teaching assistant. I had overheard some talk of Aidan being a mistake, but there was no hint of that in the joyful celebrations of his birth. I still had a photo of the whole family crammed into the small birthing room at the hospital in Harlesden, smiling against a backdrop of flowers, balloons and baby presents, with my father proudly holding his first grandchild.

"Aunt Kate? Can you pass the salad?" Gabe said. Then he went back to relating the details of his week in Italy, mostly focused on the Fiorentina-Juventus game that Grandpa had taken them to. The original reason for their visit, Francesca's funeral, seemed to be forgotten, and I was glad for that. They'd enjoyed spending time with their grandfather, with dinners at Ricci's, the local trattoria where they were always sure of a cheery reception and delicious spaghetti bolognese. It made me homesick for the long weekends I had spent with my parents in Italy, always a welcome reprieve from work and the grey London weather. Life had always seemed simpler there, less fraught with everyday problems. But my mother's sudden death had made me realize that the complexities of the human existence reached everywhere.

When the boys had finished eating, they started clearing plates away. I stood up to help, but Leo put his hand on my arm and told me to sit. "They're good at cleaning up, and I want you to rest. Considering you missed lunch, you haven't eaten much. Are you sure you're feeling okay?"

For a fleeting moment, I considered telling Leo about the aura over Aidan, but I couldn't bring myself to do that. It would be devastating. I needed time to think through how to handle it, and how to protect my nephew.

Was he sick with some yet undiagnosed disease? Would there be an accident; a driver not yet drunk, but who would soon down a few beers, get in his car and plough across a pedestrian crossing just as Aidan walked on to it? Would he be an innocent victim of violence, from a bomb, or a random mugging?

I shivered. The catalog of ways to die seemed infinite in its scope. It was incredible that anyone survived long enough to die peacefully of old age, content with a life well-lived. A picture of Toby flashed through my mind. I remembered his chubby arms and plump pink toes, his carnation-colored lips and long dark eyelashes. I recalled with great clarity these individual parts of my little brother, but my only image of him as a small human being was taken from the many photos of him in frames and albums at my parents' house. He would be eighteen years old now, but he had lived for just thirty-eight months. Leo was waving a hand in front of my face.

"Hello, Katie? Are you feeling all right?"

I settled for one of the many lies that had been coming to my lips so readily in the past two weeks.

"Yes, really, I'm okay. Maybe I'm coming down with a bug, but I feel good now, honestly."

We sat in the gathering darkness, Leo relaxed and talkative, relating stories about his students and the work he was doing on his latest math textbook. When he talked about Olivia, his voice softening, I realized he truly liked her, maybe even loved her. At any other time, I would have interrupted him, asking for more details, but I found it hard to talk. Instead, I concentrated on what he was saying, refusing to let my mind stray from the well-lit path of his words into the tangled shrubs and shadows of fear that lay in wait for me.

The darkness hid the aura when Aidan came out to tell us he and Gabe were going to bed. I was grateful not to see it. I said goodnight as calmly as I could, hoping Leo couldn't see the tears on my cheeks.

It was impossible to sleep that night. I lay on my back on the daybed in Leo's study, watching the flickering shadows cast on the ceiling by a streetlamp outside the window. Alone in the room, all my fears and forebodings crowded in on me like a multitude of nightmarish figures pawing at me for attention. Pulling the sheet up to my throat, I closed my eyes, desperately trying to go to sleep. Eventually, giving up, I got out of bed and tiptoed across the hallway to the bedroom the two boys shared. Gabe would only sleep with a nightlight on; its soft reassuring glow fell across the boys' sleeping figures. Aidan sprawled across his bed with his arms wrapped around a pillow and one leg dangling over the side. He was snoring gently. Gabe, as usual, slept on his stomach. I wondered how he managed to breath with his face squashed into his pillow.

Leaning over Aidan, I put a hand on his forehead. It was cool and dry. I passed my hand through the space over his head, wondering if I could feel the aura in some way, but sensed nothing. He stirred and I pulled my hand back, hoping he wouldn't wake up. I didn't want to scare him. Turning back towards the door, I stepped on something hard and pointed that pricked the sole of my foot and made me gasp. I picked up a piece of Lego, as Aidan shot up in bed, his eyes open, but not really seeing yet.

"What?" he said, his voice thick with sleep. Gabe stirred, but didn't wake up. I headed for the door.

"Aunt Kate?"

I turned back. "Sshh, it's okay. Go back to sleep," I whispered.

"What are you doing up?"

"Couldn't sleep. Don't worry. See you in the morning."

I left the room and pulled the door almost closed behind me. My heart pounded in my chest while I lay back on the narrow bed, thinking sleep wouldn't come that night. But exhaustion must have won the battle because I woke up to the fragrances of coffee and bacon and the murmur of voices in the kitchen. I pulled on my jeans and a sweatshirt and ran a brush through my hair.

"Morning!" I tried to keep my voice light, although the aura hung ominously over Aidan's head. Was it my imagination or did it look more distinct? I poured some coffee while I watched Leo frying bacon and making toast.

"Are you feeling better this morning, Aunt Kate?" Aidan asked through a mouthful of cereal.

"Yes, good, thank you."

"Were you sleepwalking when you came into our room?"

I sensed Leo turning away from the stove to look at me.

"Sleepwalking?" he asked.

"Aunt Kate scared me to death," said Aidan, but he was smiling. "I woke up and there she was, looming over me like a ghost or something. Lucky Gabe didn't wake up or he'd have screamed the place down."

"I'm sorry. I didn't mean to wake you," I said, dreading Leo's next question.

"What were you doing in their room?"

"I thought I heard one of them call out," I said, shocked at how adept I was becoming at lying. "I just went in to check on them."

"Oh." Leo started forking bacon from the frying pan on to a plate.

Over breakfast, the boys decided to go to the park to try out the rocket launcher I had given them. "We can skateboard over there," said Gabe, jumping up from the table to go find his board.

I felt my heart rate go up. So many dangers lay in wait for Aidan. "I'll come with you." Leo raised his eyebrows at me.

"Are you going to skateboard too?" he asked with a grin.

"No, I'll jog," I answered. I glanced at Aidan. "If it's all right for me to come? I'd like to see you launch a rocket or two."

"Yeah, of course," he said, carrying his plate to the sink and heading up the stairs.

"Well, I intend to sit here, read the paper and drink coffee," said Leo. "Ah, peace and quiet. Wonderful. Off you go then. You'd better be ready quickly because they won't wait for you."

Several hours later, I got back to the house, cold and wet. The skies had opened up just minutes after we arrived at the park, but that did nothing to deter Aidan and Gabe. The rocket launcher had attracted a small group of boys who all wanted to have a turn while I'd sat on a wall to watch, feeling the rain creep in through every seam of my clothes.

I had planned to return to London late on Saturday afternoon, but the situation with Aidan changed my mind. I asked Leo If I could stay another night. He seemed happy, if a little perplexed.

"I can't think why you want to hang out here in the suburbs with me and the boys. You must have an exciting Saturday night lined up in the glamorous city, surely?"

"Not really," I replied. "Why don't we cook a big Italian feast for dinner tonight? I can go shopping and get what we need. Or we could go out for curry?"

Leo opted for Italian. I checked that Aidan was planning to stay in and watch television before I set off for the supermarket. I knew I couldn't stay forever to keep an eye on him, but I couldn't stand the thought of leaving him alone, exposed to whatever danger lay in wait. While I chopped vegetables, I sounded out Leo on Aidan's health.

"Everything okay?" I asked. "He looks a little pale."

"Really? I hadn't noticed, but he's always pale. He inherited his mother's coloring."

"Maybe a check-up would be a good idea anyway," I suggested. "Just to be sure."

Leo grunted. I knew he wouldn't do it. A few minutes later, Aidan came in. "Ryan just texted me and wants me to go over to his house to do our Latin homework together. I'll be back in time for dinner."

"Ok," said Leo. "Labor omnia vincit."

"Huh?"

"Hard work conquers all," replied Leo. "So hop to it."

"Are you going by yourself? How far is it?" I asked.

"Just a ten-minute walk, over by Merton College." Aidan pulled on his shoes and tied the laces.

"You have to cross Iffley Road?" I asked.

"Well, yes, but I do that to go to school every day. No big deal." He gave me a funny look.

"Be careful. Look both ways," I said. I wished I'd been able to restrain myself.

When the front door had slammed behind him, Leo put down his knife and looked at me.

"What's going on? You're acting like some over-protective mother hen. Aidan's a good kid and he's sensible. I don't want to smother him. He's learning independence, and that's the way it should be."

"I know. It's just hard to see them growing up so fast. And hard not to worry about them, don't you think?"

"I'm obviously finding it less difficult than you are. This all seems a bit sudden on your part too. You've always cared about the boys, I know that, but you've never worried about them before. I think it's misplaced concern, to be honest, and I'd rather you stick to the fun-to-be-with aunt role. We're doing just fine as we are."

A wave of anger rolled over me, quickly followed by a more temperate swell of compassion for Leo. I resented the comment about my role in the boys' life; I had tried hard to visit as often as possible after their mother had walked out, and always spent Christmas with them. Both boys emailed to let me know what they were doing at school or called me with a good result on an exam. But Leo had shouldered the burden of single parent without complaint and with obvious success. I knew that he fed the boys, did the laundry, helped with their homework, went to as many soccer games and school concerts as he could and still managed to hold a prestigious position at Oxford. He was working on a textbook in the evenings. It made my life seem shallow by comparison. My old life, at least. This new existence, with the ability to see disaster before it struck its victims, was complex and messy. I felt like Atlas, carrying the weight of the world on my back.

I felt tears spring to my eyes and looked down at the carrots I'd been washing so that Leo wouldn't notice. My throat had closed up. I couldn't speak. From the loud thud of the knife on his chopping board, I could tell he thought I was sulking.

"I'm sorry, Leo," I said when I couldn't stand the silence any longer. "I don't mean to butt in. You're doing a wonderful job of looking after the boys and it's not my place. Sometimes, I suppose, I can't help myself." I attempted a smile. "It drives my friends nuts too."

Putting the knife down, Leo wiped his hands on a tea towel. "You've always had a bit of a control thing going on," he said. "Ever since you were a kid..." his words trailed off and he bit his lower lip. "Anyway, it's okay. I know you care about the boys, and me. That's what counts."

Nodding, I carried on preparing the vegetables. Gabe wandered in and took a bag of chips from the snack cupboard. "Only a few," warned Leo. "We're eating in an hour."

"Okay," said Gabe, taking a handful of chips. "When's Aidan coming back?"

"In time for dinner."

Gabe strolled out of the kitchen. A few seconds later, I heard the television go on in the living room.

The kitchen soon filled with the rich aroma of simmering chicken cacciatore. Leo went to the fridge and pulled out a bag of fresh basil. "I should just get a plant and put it on the windowsill," he said, pulling the bag open. "Buying it this way costs a fortune."

I watched as he snipped some of the tender leaves into the pan. The aroma of the basil floated towards me. My chest tightened. That smell always reminded me of Toby, the day he died.

CHAPTER TWENTY-THREE

We were playing in the pool at Mrs. Parry's house, me, my brother Toby, and his little friend, George. George's mother sat in a blue deckchair, watching us all. The two boys, with red swim bands on their arms, stood in the shallow end, splashing each other. I sat on the edge at the deep end, swinging my legs in the water, enjoying the silky chill on my sunburned skin. I rested my hands on the textured deck tile, feeling the indentations pressing against my palms. It was going to be a perfect summer. No homework, and Kyle, a boy in my class, had asked me to go to a movie with him. He was so cute. I could hardly wait.

Next to me, a pile of basil lay wilting in the heat. The boys had picked it earlier from Mrs. Parry's vegetable patch. They told me it was what dragons liked to eat.

The jangle of a telephone came through the open French doors. Mrs. Parry glanced that way, but ignored it. The ringing stopped, started again, and this time she clambered out of the deck chair, pulling her robe on over her swimsuit.

"Come out for a few minutes," she called to the boys. "Sit on the edge with Kate until I come back. Kate, keep an eye on them both. I'll be right back."

Both boys obediently waded to the side and climbed the stone steps. They knew that if they didn't get out, George's mother would ban them from the pool for a week. She was very strict about safety and sunscreen, and not getting in the water right after eating.

Toby padded along the rim of the pool, yanking up his blue

swimming shorts. George went up a couple of steps and then stopped, looking back to the green alligator inflatable he'd been playing with. It wasn't an alligator. It was a dragon, according to the boys. I'd pointed out that it didn't have wings and they'd explained that a dragon can fold his wings away when he doesn't need them. Or when he was taking a dip in the pool.

Toby sat down next to me, pressing his wet arm against mine.

"Eew, you're cold and wet, move further away," I said. He grinned and nestled even closer to me.

"Come on, George," I called. He'd gone back into the water to retrieve the dragon. Holding the inflatable, he clambered up the steps.

A puff of wind made the dragon wriggle in George's arms. Another, and it was gone, landing in the pool upside down and floating into the middle, out of George's reach. The boy stood looking at the toy for a few seconds and then scampered back to the shallow end of the pool, and down the steps.

"Leave it, George," I called. "Come out of the water until your Mum gets back." Either he didn't hear me or he chose not to, and I stood up.

"Stay there," I told Toby. "I'm going to get George out."

Little horror, I thought, the hot tiles burning the soles of my feet. He and Toby were best friends and went to Pre-K together. They were inseparable. The night before, George had slept over at our house, and I'd helped them set up a tent in Toby's room, then read them a story by flashlight. George could be sweet, but he was a little spoiled and often defiant.

"George," I said when I reached the top of the steps. "Come here, right now." He grinned at me. I was just a ten-year-old girl. He had no desire to do what I wanted.

Hands on my hips, like I'd seen my Mum do when she was cross, I told him again to get out. Maybe the stance did it, because he plodded across the pool, grasping the alligator. I went down a few steps to take his hand. I didn't want him slipping and hurting himself while I was in charge. We climbed up the steps together and turned back towards the deep end.

There was no sign of Toby. Both his armbands lay on the pool rim, bright red against the creamy stone. I glanced around the garden. Had he gone over to the rope swing? Still holding George's hand, I pulled him behind me. The alligator flew out of his arms into the pool again, and he began to cry, pulling his hand away from mine. I stopped, saw him run back towards the steps and yelled at him to come back. I had to find Toby, but George was about to get in the water again. The alligator was in the middle of the pool where it was far too deep for him.

For a few seconds, I stood, undecided, then the sun bounced off a ripple at the far end of the pool. My heart lurched. Shouting to George to stand still, I ran, seeing through the reflections on the bright surface, a glimpse of darker blue against the sky blue of the water. I jumped in feet first and then swam down, taking deep breaths. I wasn't a strong swimmer. Hated getting water in my eyes. Nervously, I opened them and felt the sting of chlorine. Toby was lying on the bottom bobbing slightly in the movement of the water. With a surge of frantic energy, I reached him, grabbed his arm and then swam up. It just took a few kicks of my feet until my head reached the surface and I took a breath.

I pulled Toby up, got his face out of the water. His eyes were closed. "Wake up, Toby. Wake up!"

"Get your mother," I screamed at George, who was standing on the steps, water up to his ankles. I reached up for the pool rim and held Toby up with the other arm. His head flopped forward, his face in the water again. Crying, letting go of the rim, I trod water, panicking, supporting Toby's head with both hands. George hadn't moved.

Everything after that was a blur; a vague memory of the siren of an ambulance, men in dark suits rushing to the pool side. Mrs. Parry crying. My mother, weeping, my dad standing stiff and unmoving, bright sun shining on the tiny white casket, the wilted clump of basil I threw into the grave.

CHAPTER TWENTY-FOUR

I finished washing the chopping boards and knives and wiped down the surface next to the sink. Leo was humming loudly as he collected knives and forks. When he was in a particularly good mood he'd sing, belting out songs that had the boys rolling their eyes. His repertoire consisted mostly of music from before he was born, like Stairway to Heaven and Supertramp's Dreamer, and what he lacked in talent he made up for in volume.

I glanced at my watch again. Aidan was supposed to be back at seven. It was two minutes past. I began scrubbing the sink, wanting to stay busy, to keep my mind off the aura that hung over my nephew's head. Another glance at my watch. It was five past seven.

"Aidan's late," I said.

Leo stopped humming and looked at the digital clock on the stove. "He'll be back in a minute."

He carried the handful of utensils into the dining alcove in the living room. The brief warmth of the previous day had been chased away by grey clouds and a light drizzle. I opened a window to air out the kitchen, and heard the evensong of birds and in the distance, the wail of a police siren. My stomach churned. I did my best to ignore it. A police car in the neighborhood didn't mean anything, but I checked the time again.

Leo came back in to collect napkins.

"Shouldn't Aidan be back by now? Maybe you should call his friend's house to see where he is?" I asked.

My brother shrugged. "It's not like him to be late, but let's give him another few minutes. They were probably engrossed in all that Latin."

Fifteen minutes later, with dinner ready and staying warm in the oven, Leo began to look concerned. "I'll call Ryan's mother."

I heard him talking in the hallway. When he came back he was frowning. "Aidan left their house nearly forty minutes ago. He should have been back by now. I'm going to drive that way."

"I'll come with you," I said. Leo didn't argue. He told Gabe to stay home in case Aidan came back by a different route. Once we were in the Land Rover, Leo shifted fast through the gears, speeding along the tranquil residential street. Neither of us spoke. Leo's anxiety had dissolved my last shreds of confidence that all was well, and I felt sick to my stomach. He braked to take a right hand turn and came to a screeching stop. The road was closed ahead, filled with emergency vehicles. Blue lights turned on top of an ambulance, behind several police cars that were parked to block the road.

"Oh my God," I said, fumbling to undo my seat belt.

"Maybe you should wait here," said Leo, already opening his door. He headed towards a group of people who were watching as two paramedics wheeled an empty gurney from the ambulance. I scrambled out of my seat to catch up with him. Beyond the police vehicles was a car, or what was left of it. Its front end was planted in a telegraph pole, the windscreen shattered and the airbags deployed.

"Car hit a pedestrian and then swerved out of control," I heard a man telling Leo. I felt the ground under my feet soften like quicksand, threatening to swallow me. My feet stopped moving, my legs were like columns of cement, and I was incapable of any forward motion.

"Was the pedestrian badly hurt?" asked Leo. His voice was remarkably steady, I thought, although it seemed to be coming from far away.

"I dunno. But I'd guess that's a body under that blanket over there." The man pointed past the telegraph pole where I glimpsed a grey cloth on the ground, surrounded by several uniformed police officers.

Leo glanced back at me. His face was ashen.

"Go back to the car, Kate," he said. "I have to find someone official to talk to."

"I'll wait here. You go." I watched him move away, pushing past the onlookers to get closer to the policemen. The streetlights flickered on, casting long shadows across the road. The red and blue lights threw patterns on the asphalt and faces grew indistinct in the twilight. Fear had coiled my stomach into an impenetrable knot. I found it hard to breathe. Waiting alone in the dusky light, I began to shiver and leaned over, hands on my knees, hoping to fend off the nausea that was building inside.

"Are you all right, miss?"

I looked up to see a policeman standing over me.

"Just worried sick," I said. "My nephew is missing and this is the way he would have walked home from his friend's house."

I looked towards the grey blanket.

"Your nephew? Tall lanky kid with blonde hair?"

The pavement shifted and I felt the blood draining from my face.

CHAPTER TWENTY-FIVE

"Hey, you're okay. Take some deep breaths."

I opened my eyes, saw disembodied hazy faces floating in the darkness.

"Do you want to sit up?" It was Leo's voice. When his face came into focus, I saw that he was smiling. Why was he smiling? Aidan was dead. I must be dreaming, I thought, closing my eyes again, shutting out the pain.

"Aunty Kate? Can you stand up? I'm hungry and I want to go home."

Minutes later, I was in the back seat of the Land Rover. Aidan was in front, sitting next to his Dad, telling us how he saw the accident and was nearly struck by the car.

"If it hadn't gone into the pole, it would have kept going over the curb and hit me," he said. "A man came out of a house nearby. He called the police and said I should stay to be a witness. It wasn't the driver's fault. The lady just stepped out right in front of the car and the driver tried to swerve, but he still hit her."

When Aidan stopped talking, Leo put out his hand and patted his son's knee. He drove slowly, but we soon reached the house, where he turned off the engine and the three of us sat in silence for a minute. My breathing had returned to normal, but my hands were still trembling. Although I peered through the seats to look at Aidan, I could see only saw his arm and shoulder. I couldn't tell if the aura had gone or not.

"I'll go make sure Gabe is all right," I said, pushing the door open. "He'll be worried."

In fact, Gabe didn't appear to notice we'd been gone. He was engrossed in a television show and managed a quick greeting before his eyes drifted back to the screen. I checked on the food in the oven. Although I'd stopped shaking, my thoughts were rampaging wildly. By his own account, Aidan had narrowly missed being hit by the out of control car. If the aura was presaging that accident, and he had survived it, then the aura would be gone. He would be out of danger. When I heard Leo and Aidan come into the kitchen, I braced myself to look at Aidan. Setting the dish carefully on the counter, I took off the oven mitts and turned around.

Leo had his arm around Aidan's shoulders and was ruffling his blonde hair. "You did the right thing to stay, son. You're probably feeling a bit of shock, seeing someone run over. I'm sorry you had to go through that." He let go as Aidan tried to wriggle out of his grasp.

"I'm fine," said Aidan. "Can I go watch television with Gabe?"

I leaned against the counter so that my legs would hold me up better. The aura was still there, faint but definitely present. How could that be? I was sure it would have disappeared, that this had been a close shave but a disaster averted. The temporary hope I'd harbored ran away like sand through my fingers, and I felt a heavy, dark weight pushing down on me.

Leo pulled out a couple of wine glasses and uncorked a Montalcino that he knew I liked.

"We deserve this," he said. "It was rough for a while not knowing what had happened to Aidan."

Taking the glass from his hand, I sat on a counter stool. "He was lucky."

Leo took the stool next to me and swiveled it to look at me. "You doing all right? You sort of fell apart back there."

"I was scared," I said. "I'm sorry I got all wobbly on you, but I didn't know what to think. You must have felt the same way, though? Afraid that he'd been hit by the car?"

"Of course I did. But I suppose I'm good at taking things one step at a time and not panicking." He paused and took a gulp of wine. "We'd better eat that food before we drink any more. Can you dish some up for the boys? We'll let them eat in the living room."

I went through the motions of putting food on plates and carrying them in to the boys, but my mind was on Aidan. I warned them not to spill on the sofa, but knew that Leo wouldn't really care if they did. Some things were way down his list of things to worry about.

While Leo and I ate, I had an idea. "How about if I get a cell phone for Aidan? I can add a line to my plan. At least this evening he would have been able to call you to tell you what had happened."

Leo shook his head, swallowing his food before answering. "I don't want him to have a phone yet. He'll spend hours texting his friends and he'd never think to use it for anything as practical as a call to me. It would be a waste of money."

"But a phone is a good safety device," I insisted. "Just a precaution in case he ever needs to get hold of you urgently."

Leo put down his knife and fork and looked at me.

"So, are you going to tell me what's bothering you? You've been fretting about Aidan ever since you got here, and didn't want to let him out of your sight. Now you're talking about safety and urgent calls. I don't get it."

"I just have a bad feeling," I stopped when I saw the look on Leo's face.

"A bad feeling about what?"

"I don't know, just a feeling."

Leo stood up to carry his plate to the sink.

"Are you going to explain that?"

"I can't," I replied. I wound a thread of hair around my finger, tighter and tighter until the blood stopped flowing and my finger turned numb.

"Can't or don't want to?"

"It's complicated."

"Try me. I'm a smart guy." Leo's tone was cold.

"Aidan has the moving air over his head. Like Francesca."

"Jeez, Kate. I thought we discussed that and agreed it was a mirage or something."

"We didn't agree, Leo. The aura predicts death. My friend Rebecca had one and she died."

Leo held up his hand. "Hold on. Someone you know died? Since I last saw you?"

"Two people. That little girl I thought I'd saved from drowning, and a friend. It's crazy, I know."

"Crazy? It's fucking lunacy," he replied. I winced as though he had slapped my face. He never swore and I couldn't remember the last time he'd lost his temper with me.

"So you are telling me that you can see this air rippling over

Aidan's head," he continued, "and that makes you think he's going to die? Of what?"

"I don't know," I whispered. "Don't shout. The boys will hear you."

"Right," he said, coming back to sit down next to me. "Tell me what you do know."

I told him about Rebecca and Sophie, and then about Alan and how his aura had disappeared.

"So the outcome can be changed?" Leo asked, keeping his voice low.

"Yes. With Alan, I didn't do anything. Something came up at home and that changed everything he'd planned to do that weekend. The danger passed. His aura disappeared."

Leo took another big gulp of wine. "So what do you think is going to happen to Aidan? Christ, I can't believe we're having this conversation. This is my boy we're talking about. I couldn't... if anything happened to him..."

I reached out and put my hand over his. "I'm sorry."

"When? I mean, how long?"

I took a deep breath. It was surreal, talking like this. "The aura is very faint and that does seem to have some significance. I think the clearer it is, the sooner the event is likely to happen. But, honestly, Leo, I don't know anything for certain. This is all new and overwhelming. I've had, what, four experiences. Not enough to be sure of anything."

Leo was watching me. He seemed to be battling a potent mix of anger and disbelief.

"Kate, I'm a mathematician. I deal in facts, numbers, reality. This is, I don't know, a phantasma. It's not real."

"You think I'm delusional, that none of this has actually happened?" I heard my voice rising, a knife edge of hysteria cutting through my self-control. "Why would I make something like this up, Leo? I hate it. I hate seeing that something bad is going to happen to someone. I wish I couldn't."

"You okay, Aunty Kate?" It was Gabe, who had come in with the two empty plates. He put them in the sink and stared at me, his eyes wide. "Are you two arguing?"

"No, we're not," said Leo. "But we do need to carry on a private conversation, please."

"Can I get some ice cream first? Before you go back to arguing?"

Without waiting for an answer, he hurried to the freezer and took out a pint of ice cream. Grabbing two spoons from the drawer, he rushed out of the kitchen.

I blinked several times, feeling hot, heavy tears in my eyes.

"So what am I supposed to do?" Leo asked. "Believe you and accept that Aidan is in danger, or ignore everything you've said and suggest you get some medical help? What kind of choice is that, Kate? I don't want to believe you. How could I?"

His shoulders slumped. "Fuck it," he said. He finished the rest of his wine.

The tears fell down my cheeks and I watched them fall, unhindered, on to the granite countertop.

CHAPTER TWENTY-SIX

I left Leo's early on Sunday, after a breakfast eaten mostly in silence. He seemed incapable of looking at me and I couldn't find any words to bridge the chasm that had opened between us. Kissing Aidan on the forehead, I'd told him to be good. Seeing the aura made me feel nauseous.

On Sunday afternoon, I went to the mobile phone store to buy a cell phone. It was a fairly simple model, but it had a keyboard for texting and I set it up on a basic calling plan. I packaged it and addressed it to Aidan. I knew Leo wouldn't approve, but I had to do something.

By Sunday evening, I was pacing my apartment, feeling lonely and afraid. Leo and I had never argued before, and I felt the withdrawal of his love and support, like breath had been sucked from my lungs. I hadn't heard from Josh either, although I didn't blame him for staying away.

I hated these auras. And I still had to think about Nick. On an impulse, I decided to go see him. Perhaps I could convince him to take my warning seriously. Maybe not, but at least I had to try.

The journey was easy, the Tube fairly empty, but it was an uncomfortable feeling to be back outside Rebecca's apartment. The unlit windows made me shiver. I rang the doorbell for Nick's flat. It was Gary who answered.

"It's Kate Benedict. I'd like to talk to Nick, please?"

"Nick's out." Gary's tone was brusque.

"Can I come up and talk to you?" I asked. When the front door buzzed, I pushed it open, jogging up the stairs to Gary's flat before he could change his mind. He opened the apartment door.

"What do you want?"

"Can I come in?"

He hesitated before pulling the door open. The layout of the flat was just like Rebecca's, but this one was furnished in chrome and black leather with burnt orange walls.

"Would you like a drink? Coffee, wine? Martini?"

"Wine, please."

While Gary was making our drinks, Caspian appeared, rubbed himself against my leg, and then sprinted away up the hall. I loved the way cats did that, acting on impulses we didn't see or understand.

Gary handed me a glass and sat on the sofa opposite me. "So, to what do I owe the pleasure?"

His short dark hair was gelled into bristles that seemed to reflect his personality. Either he was just a prickly person or he really didn't like me for some reason.

"How's Nick doing?" I asked. "Has he handled the murder inquiry okay?"

Gary shrugged. "I suppose so. He was really upset about Rebecca. He never stops talking about her."

"You weren't friends with Rebecca?"

"Not like Nick, no. He used to go up there often, to play with the cat or whatever. He and Rebecca spent a lot of time together."

So Gary was jealous of Rebecca, I realized. I remembered what Nick had said about being bisexual. Was it possible he was having an affair with Rebecca? But if he were, what about Edward? I found it hard to imagine that Rebecca was two-timing her boyfriend, or that Nick was, for that matter.

I sipped my wine. Gary was drinking something golden and strong smelling; Scotch, I guessed.

"So are you going to tell me what it was you wanted? Nick will be back soon. He's working late, again." He gave a theatrical sigh.

"Listen, Gary. I'm going to tell you something that will sound weird, but please hear me out."

He smirked. "I'm good with weird. Bring it on."

"I can see auras around people that predict death," I said, deciding subtlety was not the right approach with him. "And Nick has one, an aura. Rebecca had it too, and a couple of other people I know who have since died."

"You're a dangerous woman to know, Kate," he said, knocking back his drink. "Hold on, I'll be back."

He went to the kitchen and came back with a bottle of Glenmorangie. He poured himself another generous shot.

"So these auras," he said. "What do they look like?"

"Clear air rippling around the head and shoulders. The faster the ripples, the closer the danger."

"And you don't know what will kill someone or when?"

I shook my head.

"Well, that sucks," he said. "I mean that's kind of like telling me I'll win the lottery but only if I pick the right numbers. What's the point of being able to foresee something if you don't know the place or time, or how? As fortune-tellers go, Kate, you're pretty lame."

"I agree with you," I said. I wanted to slap him, but mustered a smile instead. "It does suck. However, we may be able do something to help Nick."

I explained how the aura had disappeared after Alan changed his plans. "So it's possible to change the outcome," I said. "I'm hoping we can pinpoint some areas of potential danger. Do you have any trips coming up, for example?"

"There's the bungee jump scheduled for Saturday," said Gary. "And the scuba dive on Sunday."

"You're kidding, right?"

"What do you think? No, there are no dangerous weekend pursuits, no travel planned. We're too busy right now."

"What about changing his routine? Taking a different route to work? Maybe he could skip work for a while?"

"I could make him stay in the house for a month," Gary said. "That would eliminate accidents with cars and buses I suppose, and random violence on the street."

"Yes," I said, thinking he was actually taking me seriously, but then he laughed.

"That's not going to happen," he said. "Besides, who's to say that the danger isn't a heart attack, or an airplane crashing through the roof, or a gas explosion. Or he could just die of boredom from being cooped up here for days on end."

He drained his glass and poured another measure of liquor into it.

"And let's not forget that Rebecca was killed in her own home, where she should have been safe. So, on balance, I don't think locking Nick in the apartment is a good idea."

The hair on the back of my neck prickled at Gary's words. Not being safe at home. Was Aidan safe even when Leo was there looking out for him? I leaned back on the leather couch, which creaked and sighed when I moved.

"Any health issues he's not attending to? Anything you can think of?"

Gary drained his glass and put it down on the coffee table. "Listen, I appreciate your concern, but..." He shrugged. "Did you talk to Nick about this?"

"I did. But he didn't take it very seriously. He laughed at me, in fact."

"I can't blame him for that."

I got to my feet and put my half-finished glass down.

"Thanks for listening, anyway," I said. "Are you coming to Rebecca's funeral?"

"I doubt it. I'm sure Nick will go."

He walked me to the door and glanced along the hall towards the stairs that led to Rebecca's flat.

"I heard some new renters have applied to move in up there," Gary said. "A married couple. Hope they don't believe in ghosts. I wouldn't want to live in a place where someone died. But it will be good to have a couple there, you know what I mean?"

"Not a young woman who takes up too much of Nick's time?"

"Something like that."

***

I thought about it for several hours before calling Inspector Clarke. I had no evidence, nothing more than a feeling, but I felt I had to share it. Gary was jealous of Nick. Was he jealous enough to have confronted Rebecca?

Did Nick know? Was he protecting Gary? He seemed to be making up excuses for not getting to the police station to work on the identity picture. Was he stalling for time? Were the visitor sightings just made up to distract the police? I reached Clarke's voicemail and told him I had some information. When he rang back thirty minutes later, I recounted my conversation with Gary. As always, Clarke was non-committal. I didn't know if he thought it was useful or extraneous. But that was up to him.

Just before I hung up, I remembered what Rebecca's parents had said about the toxicology tests and asked Clarke if he had the results yet.

"The initial report shows no alcohol in her system at all," he said.

"So someone did plant the wine glass and bottle to make it look as though she'd been drinking?"

"That appears to be the case," he said. "And while I have you on the line, can you remind me where you were on that Sunday evening?"

"I've already told you," I said. "I left the restaurant at about two in the afternoon and went home. I was by myself in my apartment until Monday morning. I don't have an alibi, but I didn't kill Rebecca. What possible motive could I have?"

Clarke's question unnerved me. For him to even think that I had something to do with Rebecca's death made me nauseous. I knew he thought I was hiding something. I was, but I couldn't tell him about the aura over Rebecca. Maybe I would tell him if I had to. Perhaps then, he'd realize I was a nutcase but I wasn't a murderer. This aura sighting ability was ruining my life in so many ways.

"Thanks for the information about Gary," he said, ending a long silence. "I'll follow up."

I boiled the kettle but forgot to make the tea, went to my bedroom to find a sweater and then couldn't recall why I'd gone there. I turned on the television and remembered I'd left the water running for a bath. I felt as though I was losing my mind.

All at once, I had a cogent thought and grabbed my laptop. I pulled up the British Airways site and found an available seat on a flight leaving late the following day. The price, on such short notice, was prohibitive, but I bought the ticket anyway. I had to go back to Florence, back to the hill where this had all started. Maybe if I did that, something would change. The aura sightings would go away. My life would return to some semblance of normality.

I sat on the sofa until the early hours of the morning, then got up and packed a carry-on case. I dressed for work, and got to the office early, intent on finishing some important drawings for Josh before I left. As soon as they were done, I went to find him. Finding his office empty, I wandered the corridors looking for him, until Laura told me that he and Alan were out on a site visit and wouldn't be back until late afternoon. Disappointed to miss him, but glad to avoid Alan, I wrote notes to both of them explaining that I would be away for a few days. I knew Alan would probably fire me, but my job was a minor casualty in this escalating battle. I took the Dockland Light Rail out to City airport, feeling as though I was running out on Nick and Aidan.

CHAPTER TWENTY-SEVEN

Four hours later, I walked down the airplane steps at the Florence airport. My heart rate slowed as I took a few deep breaths. The smell of fuel and warm asphalt accompanied me as I followed the other passengers to the air-conditioned terminal building. Cigarette smoke mingled with perfume and aftershave and the scent of leather and grease. The Italian language flowed around me and through me, transporting me away from London and the office.

Dad was waiting for me in his old Fiat and I threw my bag on the back seat before folding myself into the tiny car. He looked well, better than I had expected. He drove quickly, changing down through the gears until we reached the freeway. Even at this hour, the A-1 was filled with cars. He weaved in and out of both lanes, driving like a true Italian. When someone honked at him, he leaned on his horn and muttered under his breath. It was only when we reached our exit that I was able to breathe normally again.

"Trattoria Lucinda?" he asked, already taking the left hand turn towards my favorite local restaurant. There the owner gave me a big hug and led us to a table on the covered patio. It was warm and full of noise: cicadas, children and the chatter of Italians enjoying their evening. My father kept the conversation light. I was grateful for that. Mostly he talked about the book he was writing on Italian gardens. He told me he was planning a trip in the spring to Villa Taranto near Stresa.

"The gardens are beautiful," he said, while I dug into my pasta amatriciana. "They were created by a Scotsman in the nineteen-thirties. I've been looking at photos of the dahlia collection, which is stunning. So many colors. There is one I like especially. It made me think of you, sort of an ivory, creamy color."

"Thanks Dad, plain vanilla, is that what you're saying?" I smiled to soften the words, but wondered about his choice. Was that really how I came across to people?

"Don't be daft," he replied. "I was thinking elegant, refined, calm."

"Thank you," I said, surprised and happy.

By the time we got home, I was tired and ready to go to bed. It was comforting to sleep in the bedroom I'd used ever since I was a kid. It looked as it always had. Above the yellow-painted walls, the vaulted ceiling was decorated with pale blue and yellow flowers. A fan hung from a black iron rod screwed into a plaster rosette and a wire looped along the ceiling and down the wall to a switch set in an ornate brass plate. A previous owner had added electricity to the house back in the nineteen-forties, running wires up the walls rather than break into the three hundred year old plaster. The wires were covered with white silk that had yellowed with age and had become as much a part of the décor as the old ceiling frescoes and terracotta floor tiles.

Opening the French windows, I stepped out on to the balcony. The sky was clear and with stars but I couldn't see the gardens in the darkness. Living in London, I was used to constant light, from street lamps, traffic, billboards. Here, once the sun set, it was dark apart from a few lights that twinkled on the other side of the valley. The cool night air raised goosebumps on my arms and I stepped back inside, and pulled the heavy damask drapes.

***

"I'm going for a walk," I told Dad the next morning. We'd made toast and coffee and were sitting in companionable silence while he read *la Repubblica*. His Italian was almost perfect. Mine was good, just a little rusty.

"I'll come with you," he said, putting the newspaper down.

"I'd rather go by myself, Dad. I won't be long and then we can do something together. I just want to walk up the hill to look at the view."

He looked at me with concern.

"I'll be fine, I promise." I gave him a kiss on the cheek. Just a quick walk and then we can go to the market and buy something good for dinner tonight."

It was a pleasant day, with just a hint of a chill in the air. Sky blue, dry, not hot like the last time I'd come up the hill with my father. My loafers crunched on the white gravel. I heard the muted hum of traffic on the A-1 in the distance. Out of breath when I reached the top, I put a hand on my side to quell a cramp. My legs felt heavy from the exertion of the uphill climb. When did I get so out of shape? Since the run in the park when I saw Sophie, I hadn't been out again. Physical exercise had fallen to the bottom of my list.

Winding through old olive groves, the gravel road had originally provided access to a small farmhouse nestled just on the other side of the hill. The owner had long since died or moved, and the farmhouse was derelict. The olive trees were abandoned and untended, with small green olives hanging from their unpruned branches. At harvest time, the villagers would come up to gather a bucket or two, but for the most part the fruits would be left to shrivel on their stems.

I walked to the spot where my mother had got out of the car and talked to me. Closing my eyes, I remembered the moment when we'd hugged, tasted again the saltiness of the tears I had shed, and imagined I could smell my mother's perfume. I knelt down, feeling the sharp points of gravel digging into the tender skin on my knees.

"I'm with Toby now." That's what she had said.

My throat closed up and my chest ached. "Toby," I whispered. "I'm so sorry. I miss you every day. If you can do anything to help me, please do it. I can't take this any more."

I wrapped my arms tightly around myself and rocked back and forth, memories of Toby mingling with thoughts of my mother. I missed them both so much. A crow cawed loudly. I opened my eyes, alarm trickling down my spine. The bird screeched again, flapped up to a higher branch, and folded its wings. In the sudden silence, I heard footsteps. Just a few yards away, passing through the shadow of an ancient olive tree was a figure dressed in black, a hood concealing its face. I jumped to my feet, ready to run.

The apparition kept coming, emerging into the sunlight. I saw that it was a nun. My heart pounded. Was this another visitation like the one from my mother?

"Mi_dispiace," the nun called out in Italian. "I'm sorry. I didn't mean to frighten you. I didn't expect anyone else to be up here."

She came up to me and took my hand. "Sono Chiara. E lei?"

"My name's Kate."

Hearing my Italian, she smiled.

"Thank goodness. I don't speak English. Will you come and sit with me?"

She led me to the grassy area under the trees, set a basket on the ground and took out a bottle of water. "Here, have some of this."

The water was cool and fresh. I felt my heartbeat slowing back to normal.

"I'm with the convent down in the village and I came to pick some herbs," she said. "We make tea with the wild chamomile that grows up here."

The nun was in her sixties maybe, with dark brown eyes that twinkled under untended eyebrows. Her skin was peachy and soft and she seemed unaffected by her walk up the steep hill, in spite of her heavy black robe and head covering.

She waited until I had finished drinking. "Do you want to tell me what it is that distresses you so much?"

I shook my head. The nun was real, but I still felt dizzy and discombobulated.

"I just need to rest for a minute or two," I said.

Sister Chiara patted my hand. "I'll go pick my herbs and you rest here. Then we can walk down together."

She picked up the basket, walked a little further up the gravel road, and disappeared over the crest of the hill. I lay back, smelling the warm, crushed grass, listening to the busy drone of insects in the trees. Although I was exhausted enough to fall asleep, I forced myself to stay awake, to think about the sequence of events that had brought me back to this place. My mind jumped from one thing to another, like a rock skimming the surface of a lake. I thought of Aidan, but tried to push away the fear of what might happen to him, of Rebecca who was dead, and of Sophie, drowned like my brother Toby. My mother's words echoed in my head. "Toby wants you to be happy."

A susurrus of cloth pulled me back to the present. Opening my eyes, I saw that Sister Chiara had returned and was settling herself on the grass a few feet away, pulling her robe down over dark stockings and heavy black lace-up shoes. The basket at her side was filled to the brim with small white flowers that looked like daisies. The distinctive scent of chamomile filled the warm air under the tree.

"How are you feeling, dear?" the nun asked. Her voice was like her skin, soft and smooth.

Sitting up, I crossed my legs in front of me. "Better, thanks," I said. "I think the water helped. I hadn't realized how steep that hill is."

The Sister's eyes were dark and penetrating. "I think it was more than the climb that upset you," she said.

The thick, olive-laden branches above us cast filigreed shadows on the grass. I traced the pattern with my finger.

"I've been having some problems recently," I said. The words came out almost against my will. I had no intention of confessing all to this nun, however kindly and caring she seemed to be. While I was passionate about churches, I was less than enthusiastic about the religions they represented. An afternoon spent contemplating architectural details or gazing at an ancient fresco on a wall was my idea of heaven, and I knew the history of all the major churches in Tuscany. But I had never connected with a formal religion, with priests and confessionals. Everything I knew about nuns came from The Sound of Music.

"You can see things you don't want to see?" Sister Chiara spoke very softly.

I stared at her. "What?"

"Are you having, let me think how to explain it, visions?"

"How on earth did you know?" I pulled my knees up and wrapped my arms around my legs, holding tight to myself, disconcerted by the nun's insight.

Sister Chiara shook her head. "I'm not sure. I can just tell when I look at someone what it is that burdens them. I've been able to do it since I was a child. Ultimately, that is what made me go into the convent. I found it hard to be out in public, seeing so many people weighed down by their affliction, whether it was sorrow, or pain, or guilt. Life in the convent is sufficiently secluded that I don't have to face it every day. And of course, not everyone has a burden that I can discern." She paused and sighed. "If I could help, perhaps I would have chosen to stay outside in the world and put my gift to some use. But all I can do is see. So I choose to pray for those souls instead."

"I'm sorry," I said, meaning it. The nun's obvious pain at being unable to help in a more concrete way reflected my own.

"Maybe I should join a convent too," I joked. Sister Chiara

smiled.

I picked a few blades of grass and shredded them into tiny pieces, trying to gather my thoughts, which were as splintered as the fragments of green in my hand.

"When did it start?" Sister Chiara asked.

"About six weeks ago. It took me a while to realize what was happening. I can see auras that predict death. The first time was here at my Dad's house. I saw the air rippling over Francesca's head. I didn't know what it meant at the time, but she died a week later."

"Francesca Brunetti?"

"Yes, did you know her?"

"Only slightly. Her cousin belongs to my order and Signora Brunetti visited the convent occasionally to bring fruit from her garden. She carried a heavy burden, with the loss of her son and her husband. May she rest in peace." The nun made the sign of the cross over her chest.

"Did anything specific happen that may have triggered this ability to see auras?" she asked.

"I saw my mother right there." I pointed at the place on the road where the car had stopped. "I talked to her and she hugged me."

"I'm not sure why that would... "

"Because she had been dead for six months when I saw her," I said.

"Ah."

"Right."

"And her death was a great loss to you."

"Yes. I miss her so much. We all do."

Sister Chiara turned her face up to the sky, as though sunbathing. After a long silence, she looked back at me. "Was there someone else? Another loss?"

I hesitated, unnerved by the nun's ability to laser in on the very thing I'd been thinking about as I lay under the old tree.

"My little brother, Toby," I said finally. "He died when he was very small. I was too young at the time to truly understand the sorrow my mother had to endure. I mean, we all mourned him, but it was worst for my mother. I remember that she cried a lot of the time. She gave up working on her cookbooks. When I saw her..."

I paused, clearing the lump that had caught in my throat. "When I saw her, she told me she is with Toby now and that he needs her." A tear slid down my cheek. It tasted bitter in my mouth.

"And why do you think you are responsible for Toby's death?"

I shifted uncomfortably on the grass. "Because it was my fault. He drowned when I was supposed to be watching him."

"Did your parents blame you?"

"No, but they wouldn't, would they? Not out loud at least."

"And you were how old when it happened?"

"Ten."

Sister Chiara closed her eyes. The only sound was of the cicadas.

"Unlike me, you can intervene, can you not?" she asked, opening her eyes.

"I don't know," I replied. "There was one where the aura went away, but it wasn't my doing. He just changed his plans with no input from me. But my nephew has an aura and I don't know if I can save him. It's torture. I can't exactly go round telling people they are going to die."

I was about to say more when Sister Chiara put her hands down on the grass and pushed herself to her feet.

"Shall we start walking down? My Mother Superior will be wondering where I am."

"But I was hoping you could help me!"

Sister Chiara didn't reply. She smoothed out the creases in her robe with her hands, picked up the basket and turned towards the road.

I got up, feeling the blood prickle back into my feet and legs. Collecting the empty water bottle, I went after the nun, angry at the sudden lack of interest in my story. When we were halfway down the hill, Sister Chiara stopped suddenly, her sensible shoes sliding on the loose stones. Gesturing to me to follow her, we walked away from the road, in among the olive trees, passing around ancient specimens with twisted, scabrous trunks. The foliage was so dense that no birds nested here. It was eerily quiet and my breath sounded in my ears like the hiss of a steam engine. The nun came to a halt where the ground fell away in a steep rock-strewn drop to rolling fields beneath.

"Have you ever seen this?" she asked, pointing down the side of the hill to a house that stood alone at the end of a long driveway. The house itself was unremarkable, but to one side of it lay a large and complex maze, its winding grass alleyways bordered by manicured cypress trees. From our viewpoint, it was easy to see the intricate network of paths with multiple dead ends. I gasped in surprise. Who would build and maintain such an elaborate structure?

Reaching for Sister Chiara's hand, I squeezed it, my chest filled with inexplicable emotion. I knew something of the history of mazes, from the legend of the Minoan labyrinth in Crete, to the proliferation of mazes and their images during the Renaissance. I had once walked the labyrinth on the floor of Chartres cathedral on a field trip from college. I surveyed the one below me. A multicursal maze of this kind, with its many choices of path and direction, represented a puzzle that must be solved in order for the maze walker to find a way out.

We gazed at the labyrinth for some time while I tried to work out in my mind which path would lead to the exit. Each time I came to a dead end.

"We should go," said the Sister. She turned back towards the gravel road, swinging the basket, which sent out puffs of chamomile-scented air. I followed her reluctantly, wishing I had been able to look at the maze for longer. Sister Chiara walked quickly and with energy; I had to lengthen my stride to keep up. At the bottom of the hill, she turned right, away from the village. That was the way home for me too and we continued walking in silence. I had a hundred questions streaming through my head but didn't know which one to ask. I suspected that Sister Chiara wouldn't answer any of them.

We passed a group of women who were returning from the market carrying canvas shopping bags that overflowed with fennel, radicchio and peppers. The women looked curiously at us, and murmured respectful greetings. An aura shimmered over the gray hair of the oldest in the group. I flinched when I saw it, as much because it reminded me that my 'gift' was still working as out of concern for the elderly nonna. Sister Chiara glanced at me and gave a slight nod of her head in acknowledgement, but said nothing.

A hundred yards further along the road, Sister Chiara stopped at an arched green door set into a white stucco wall. Only a simple iron cross hanging at the top of the arch indicated that the convent lay on the other side. Beside the door hung a bell, its verdigris patina suggesting many years of service, but Chiara didn't use it. She dug a key out of a pocket in her robe and unlocked the door, pushing it open. I glimpsed orderly paths running through trimmed lawns, which were flanked with pots of red and white flowers. Beyond the grass was a two-story stone building with a terracotta tile roof.

I'd known that there was a convent attached to the village but had never thought about it before. It was strange to think that there was a whole community tucked away behind the walls just a few hundred yards from my father's house. Most people only see what they expect to see, blissfully unaware of the hidden secrets that lie under the exposed surface of daily life. I craned my neck to see more of the building, but Sister Chiara stepped through the gate, blocking the view. For a moment, it appeared that she would walk away without speaking, but she turned to look at me, held out her hand and patted my arm.

"Sister Chiara, what should I do?" I asked, sensing that I was about to be dismissed. "Can't you give me some advice?"

"You don't need my help, my dear. The solution lies within you."

I stared at her. Her words sounded more New Age than Catholic. As if guessing what I was thinking, she laughed.

"Oh, I could tell you that this is God's way of testing you or that this is your cross to bear, but you don't want to hear that and it wouldn't help. The solution is in your own hands, or more accurately, your heart. I hope you will tell me when you find it."

"How will I reach you?" I asked, suddenly panicked at the thought of not seeing her again.

"Just come and ring the bell. I will be here." She leaned forward and kissed me on one cheek and then the other. "Alla prossima," she said. "I will be thinking of you until we meet again."

CHAPTER TWENTY-EIGHT

"I was getting worried about you." My father had to shout over the roar of the coffee grinder. "Are you all right?"

"Yes, I'm fine," I replied, taking espresso cups down from the cupboard. "I'm sorry I took so long. I think we missed the market."

"I don't mind about the market. How did you do? Did you go up to the top of the hill?"

He turned off the grinder and looked at me with concern. "Paolo's here. He wanted to see you. I hope you don't mind?"

I got a third cup down and gave it to my father. "Of course not. I love Paolo."

"Did anything happen?" Dad asked. "You look a little pale. I shouldn't have let you go up there by yourself."

I watched the espresso flow like molten bronze into the tiny cups. Dad put the cups on a tray and handed it to me, then brandished a white paper bag.

"Pistachio biscotti, your favorite," he said, following me outside.

Entering the garden was like stepping into an Impressionist painting; the white and yellow flowers, the muted blues and greys of the table and chairs, and Paolo in his blue striped shirt and the white hat whenever the sun shone. I saw it all at a distance, like a visitor in a gallery. My thoughts were still full of Sister Chiara and of the maze.

"Ciao Katerina," Paolo said, standing up from his seat at the patio table. "Com'e stai?" He waited until I had set the tray down, and gave me a kiss on each cheek.

"How are your knees?" he asked. "I hope they healed quickly and there are no scars?"

I lifted one knee for his inspection. "Good as new."

When we had sat down, I tilted my face up to the sun, hoping to empty my mind of the frenzied thoughts that filled it.

"Why is the sun in London either weak and pale or glaring and uncomfortable, yet here it feels nurturing and benign?" I asked of no one in particular.

"It's the Tuscan air," said Paolo proudly. He had been born in Florence and had come back after years away studying medicine in Milan and London, swearing that he would never leave again.

While he sipped his espresso, I caught him exchanging looks with my father.

"Katerina, your father is worried about you," he said, "and I want to offer my help. If you will permit me?"

"This is an ambush, then?" I said. "Two against one?"

"Kate..." my father began.

"It's all right, I was joking. I'm sorry because I don't mean to worry you, Dad, not with everything you're already going through. I wish I could tell you that I'm doing fine, but I'm not. Not really."

"That's what Leo said. He said you'd been up to Oxford last weekend and had been behaving a little erratically, I think was the word. He wanted me to talk to you."

"Did he tell you about Aidan?"

My father put his cup down on the saucer.

"What about Aidan?" he asked.

Paolo leaned forward slightly, resting his elbows on the table's blue tile surface. It appeared that Leo hadn't shared the details about the aura with Dad. And I wasn't ready to tell him yet either.

"Aidan witnessed a really bad traffic accident," I said.

Dad's face relaxed, and Paolo sat back in his chair.

"Yes, that was awful. Poor kid," Dad said. "Leo told me, but Aidan didn't want to talk about it. He did tell me you bought him a cell phone after that incident, so he could stay in touch. That was nice of you."

I felt myself blushing. "Yeah. Well, it would have been good if he'd been able to call Leo to let him know why he was so late getting home. Most teenagers have a phone nowadays."

"So back to the erratic behavior," said Dad. "What's going on, Katie?"

"Do you know Sister Chiara from the convent?" I asked Paolo. He frowned and tugged on his chin, giving it some thought.

"Possibly," he replied. "I've met the Mother Superior and a few of the Sisters because I've assisted with some medical emergencies there over the years. Should I know her?"

"Dad, you've met her at a couple of community events, I think. Anyway, I saw her at the top of the hill today," I said. "We walked down together."

I saw Dad and Paolo glance at each other. Paolo's shoulders shifted upwards in a shrug.

"Bit of a non sequitur there," Dad said.

"She can see things," I ventured. "She can tell when someone is suffering from a burden, as she calls it, like sadness or guilt, or pain."

I paused, gauging the reaction of the two men. Dad looked confused but Paolo nodded as though he understood.

"Go on," he said encouragingly.

"Well, I can see things too." I ignored my father's startled expression and plunged on, telling them about the aura, starting with Francesca and Sophie and ending with Rebecca. I didn't mention Aidan. When I stopped talking, both men were silent. Dad was drumming his fingertips on the tabletop, while Paolo sat with his eyes closed.

A butterfly with amethyst wings settled briefly on the table, exploring the surface with velvety black antennae before flying away to land on a white dahlia at the edge of the patio.

Opening his eyes, Paolo took his hat off, running his fingers through his close-cropped grey hair. "I have heard of this before," he said.

I felt relief flow through my chest like a stream of warm water. At least he didn't think I was mad. Not so sure about Dad though. His brow was creased in a tight frown and the finger drumming had intensified. I let the silence stretch out, unsure of what to say next. It was Paolo who broke it.

"This is related in some way to what happened on the hill then."

I nodded.

"The car accident?" asked Dad. "You mean the injuries caused some other... damage?"

I sighed.

Paolo shook his head emphatically. "No, the injuries were

superficial. I refer to Katerina's seeing her mother that day."

He held his hand up as Dad began to protest.

"Katerina, you believe you saw your mother and she spoke to you, isn't that right?"

I nodded, my eyes on my father, who leaned back in his chair as though distancing himself from the conversation.

"What did she tell you?" Paolo asked.

I told him what my mother had said about being with Toby. My father clenched his hands in his lap and I leaned over to touch his arm. "I'm sorry, Dad. This is hard, but I want to share it with you because then maybe it will go away. I really want it to go away."

He took my hand in his and squeezed it hard. "What happened to Toby wasn't your fault," he said. "You always took the burden of it on yourself. It broke my heart twice over, to see the impact it had on you."

His voice broke.

"The ability to see these auras is linked in some way to your emotions about Toby and your mother, I think," said Paolo. "If what your father says is correct and you feel guilty about your brother's death, that could be the key."

"I don't understand," I said.

"Neither do I, really. This is out of my field." Paolo spread his hands, palms up.

"Are you sure it's not physical?" asked Dad. "I hate to bring it up, but maybe something to do with the brain?"

He shuddered as he spoke.

"Don't worry about that," I told him, even more glad now that I'd seen the doctor. "I had a CT scan, which was totally normal. The doctor couldn't find a single thing to explain this in medical terms."

He looked relieved for a second, but then his face scrunched up again in worry. "So now what?"

"I don't know," I said. "I thought that maybe coming back here would help me sort things out. I was hoping for some kind of epiphany up on the hill, I suppose, but nothing happened."

"You met Sister Chiara," Paolo said.

A large white cloud with bruised purple edges moved in front of the sun as I thought about my encounter with the nun. She'd seemed special. She'd known about my ability to see auras and she had a 'gift' of her own. I was sure I had been meant to meet her, yet our conversation had been inconclusive.

"Do you know the house that has the maze?" I asked him. "You can see it from the hill."

"Yes, I do. It was the brainchild of Professore Bertagli, who created it some years ago as a project to occupy himself after his wife died. He is a professor of the medieval period at the university and had some knowledge of maze designs. It was quite an event, I remember. He rented one of those digging machines to clear out all the flowerbeds and lawns. He flattened the place, and then used white paint to mark the paths. I saw it once after it was finished because he called me to the house to bandage his hand. He'd cut it pruning the hedges. The maze is quite impressive, although I'm not sure I see the point of it."

I wasn't sure I could see the point either, but I knew that Sister Chiara had shown it to me for a reason. "Do you think he would let me in to see it? I'd love to walk through it."

Paolo nodded, smiling widely, obviously eager to help. "I don't see why not. I will call Professore Bertagli."

***

It was late afternoon when my father and I arrived at Professore Bertagli's house. Dark clouds had swept over the hills, threatening rain and bringing with them a sudden drop in temperature. Dad had insisted I put on a cardigan. Paolo waited for us at the gate, joining us for the walk up the long driveway towards the house.

"The Professore was happy for you to come, but he is somewhat reclusive," he said, "so don't expect too much from him."

A dog loped towards us, barking frantically, a straggle-haired grey and white mountain dog with pointed teeth bared in defense of its territory. Dad put his hand on my arm, protective.

"Botticelli!"

At its master's call, the dog stopped in its tracks and sat down, panting, its tongue hanging out of one side of its mouth. A hound from a bad dream transformed instantly into a sweet pet. I wished my nightmare could so easily metamorphose into something benign.

I'd imagined that Professore Bertagli would be older, frail and bookish. Instead he had the look of a farmer, barrel-chested and wide-shouldered, with large hands. His black hair stood up from his head like the bristles of a brush. His welcome was polite but distant; he expressed no interest in why I wanted to see the maze. After walking us all around the side of the house to the maze entrance, he gave me a small silver whistle. I looked at it in surprise.

"If you get lost, blow the whistle and I will find you," he explained.

"Are you sure you don't want us to come with you?" asked my father, looking nervous. We had discussed on the walk over that I would do this alone. Paolo had already confirmed with Professore Bertagli that he and Dad could do a tour of his greenhouse and its precious collection of exotic orchids while I was in the maze.

"No, go enjoy your plant tour," I said.

With some trepidation, I stepped on to the entry path. The cypress walls were tall, about ten feet high, and thick enough that I couldn't see through them. They exuded a faintly astringent smell, like cat pee. After I had walked a few yards, the path curved right. When I glanced back I couldn't see the entrance. I felt a momentary panic, but shook it off and forged ahead.

The first intersection came up quickly; I hesitated. Thinking back to what I had seen from the hillside earlier in the day, I turned left, heading deeper into the center. Then I went left again, keeping count of my turns in my head. A few drops of rain fell. I buttoned up my thin cardigan. The sky, visible only as a narrow strip above the towering cypresses, had turned the color of charcoal.

A dead end loomed in front of me. With hedges on three sides, I had no choice but to retrace my steps back to the last turn. I thought of how Ariadne had given Theseus a silk thread to help him find his way out of the labyrinth. At least no savage and hungry Minotaur waited at the center to tear me to pieces, but somehow the thought didn't make me feel much better.

After a while, I fell into a rhythm of reaching a dead end, backtracking, taking a new path. The motion and the repetition was soothing, like a slow dance. I lost all sense of time, but felt that I was moving in the right direction.

Thunder rumbled over the hills and a lightning bolt filled the air with the scent of ozone. Seconds later, the clouds burst, releasing torrents of rain that soaked through my clothes and chilled my skin. The violent change in the weather disoriented me. After a couple more turns, I realized that I was completely lost. I had no idea if I was still heading towards the center, and was even less sure of how to reach the exit. Another thunderclap broke overhead, echoing off the side of the hill, grumbling away into the distance. Seconds later, lightning flashed again. Its white incandescence rendered the cypress hedges black. The storm was directly overhead, and I felt a small worm of fear crawling through my stomach.

I took a few steps along the path, my ears ringing with the sound of thunder, my vision blurred from the lightning. Another dead end. Disconsolate, I turned around. After a few more minutes of taking wrong turns, I put the whistle to my lips.

***

We left Professore Bertagli's house in silence. I sheltered under Paolo's umbrella even though I was already drenched. My father had hugged me tightly when I'd emerged from the maze in the company of the Professore, but he seemed at a loss for words and I couldn't find any either.

I tried to push my frustration and confusion to one side so that I could think clearly. Sister Chiara had shown me the maze for a reason but nothing had come of it. The maze had first tried to swallow me and then had spat me out like a scrap of bad food. My hopes for some sort of revelation drained away with the rain water into the overflowing gutters that gurgled a noisy accompaniment to the walk home.

CHAPTER TWENTY-NINE

"I'm glad you came, but I'm still worried about you," Dad said, backing his car out of the driveway.

I felt terrible. Dad had been through so much; he didn't need the burden of my problems on top of all that. I put my hand over his. He had to keep a hand on the gear stick to stop it from shifting out of reverse suddenly. Although the Fiat was ancient, he loved it.

We were on the A-1 when a clap of thunder shook the car. The storm that had started while I was in the maze had raged all night, dashing rain at the windows and sporadically illuminating the rooms with fierce white light.

The windscreen wipers were losing the fight against the deluge of rain, and the taillights of the cars ahead appeared only as red smudges. I peered out of the passenger window. The sky, mottled black and purple, hung low over the hills on the north side of Florence. I pulled out my phone to look for the flight details on the CityJet site. There were no delay or cancellation notifications. I wasn't sure whether to be relieved or not. I didn't like flying in bad weather, and this was as bad as I'd seen it for a long time.

In spite of the stop and go traffic, we soon pulled up in front of the terminal.

"Call me if the flight is cancelled," Dad said. "I'll come back for you. Otherwise, I'll see you at Christmas. He leaned over and gave me a kiss on the cheek. "Take care of yourself, promise?"

I pulled off a big smile. "No need to worry. I'm okay. I love you, Dad."

Grabbing my carry-on from the back seat, I headed into the terminal. Seeing very few people around, I realized I was late. I hurried through check-in and security to reach the gate. Passengers were thronging through the open doors with the usual Italian disregard for queuing, so I waited at the back of the crowd and checked my seat number.

When I looked up, I saw an aura over the grey-haired lady in front of me. For a minute, I panicked. Was the plane going to crash? I scanned everyone else in line, trying not to be caught staring. Everyone was busy looking for boarding passes, or checking seat numbers. There were no other auras, and for the first time ever, my aura vision made me happy. It was nice to be sure that we weren't all going down. I felt badly for the lady, but my defense mechanism quickly locked into place and I let the thought go. I knew I couldn't worry about every aura I saw.

When I got home, on time in spite of the bad weather, there was a message on my answering machine from Terry Williams, saying that Rebecca's body had been released and that the funeral would be on Thursday of the following week. My heart went out to him.

I called Nick to let him know, but Gary answered the call, saying Nick was in bed with flu.

"He's been sick for three days," he said. "No thanks to you and your crazy visions. The stress is getting to him."

"I thought you didn't believe in my visions."

He didn't reply. I asked him to have Nick call me when he was feeling well enough, but had a feeling the message wouldn't be transmitted. While I brushed my teeth, I wondered how ill Nick was. Was it something serious enough to be dangerous?

I was just getting ready for bed when my cell phone rang. It was Inspector Clarke, apologetic for disturbing me late at night.

"We still haven't been able to trace Edward," he said. "And I wanted to check in with you to see if anything new has come to mind?"

We talked for a minute or two and then his next words sent a chill down my spine.

"I heard you were in Italy over the weekend?"

"I went to see my father."

"I hope you had a good trip," he said. "But please let me know next time you leave the country."

"Why? Am I a suspect?"

"Not exactly, Kate, but there's something going on that I don't understand. Everything in my gut tells me that there's something you're not revealing."

If I told you, you'd have me locked up, I thought.

"There's nothing. I've told you everything I know. Did you follow up on my message about Gary?"

He hesitated before speaking. "We're working on it."

No wonder Gary was hostile on the phone. I wondered if he knew it was me who'd put his name in front of the detective.

Just before getting into bed, I texted Aidan. I'd been in touch with him regularly, and he was good about responding. Usually nothing more than a short exchange, but it was enough to reassure me that he was all right. When I saw his short g'night message, I turned out the light.

CHAPTER THIRTY

To my immense relief, Alan wasn't in the office the next morning. But neither was Josh; Annie told me they were both out visiting a client for the day. I was sad to miss Josh. I wanted to tell him about my encounter with Sister Chiara and the walk through the maze. Still, as the office was quiet, I managed to catch up on my work, feeling proud of how productive I was being. At the end of the day, I texted Josh, asking him to come for dinner. Then I stopped at the local market to buy enough food for two.

While unpacking the groceries, remembering that Leo was at a university dinner that evening, I sent a text to Aidan asking what he and Gabe were doing while their Dad was out.

"We just ate pizza. Watching a Transformers movie on tv," Aidan texted back. We sent messages back and forth for a couple of minutes, and Aidan told me that his Dad would be back at eleven. I felt nervous and couldn't settle. I wasn't sure if it was anxiety for the boys, even though they often spent a few hours alone in the house, or nervous anticipation about seeing Josh. I tidied up the flat, which was already spotless, and put some white wine in the fridge.

But by eight o clock, when I still hadn't heard from Josh, I resigned myself to an evening home alone. I sent another message to Aidan asking if the movie was any good. It was Gabe who answered. "Aidan's got stomachache. He's in the bathroom."

"How bad is it?" I wrote back.

"He's throwing up. It's gross."

"Can you call your Dad?"

"No. His phone is off."

"What about Mrs. Wright?" She was the next-door neighbor who doted on the boys and had babysat them when they were younger.

"She's at bingo and she doesn't have a cellphone," Gabe texted.

It only took a few seconds for me to decide to go to Oxford. Aidan could have food poisoning or it could just be a bug of some kind, but he needed someone there with him while he was sick. I threw a few things into a bag and called the taxi service I usually used. It took them ten minutes to find a cab willing to take me all the way to Oxford, but I was soon sitting in the back seat, calling Gabe to find out how his brother was doing. For a while, Gabe didn't answer, which made my anxiety level shoot up, but finally he picked up.

"Aidan says he has real bad pains in his side," Gabe reported. "And he's all sort of sweaty and hot. He's still throwing up too."

"Ask him to press on the lower right side of his abdomen," I said.

"His what?"

"Stomach," I amended. "Just ask him if it hurts when he does that."

I heard some murmured voices and, after a few seconds, Gabe came back on. "Yeah, that hurts."

"I think it's appendicitis. Listen, Gabe, I'm going to call for an ambulance to come to the house. You'll have to let them in. Ask them if you can go with him to the hospital. I don't want you to be home alone."

"Aunt Kate," Gabe's voice was shaky. "I don't want to go in an ambulance."

"It'll be okay," I tried to reassure him. "They'll know what to do and you'll be fine until I get there. I'll go straight to the hospital."

I rang off and called the emergency number. The dispatcher assured me an ambulance was on its way. Leaning forward, I asked the taxi driver to go as fast as he could. The car surged forward. On the front dash, an assortment of figures with nodding heads snapped into frenzied motion. Most of them were dogs and cats, but an Albert Einstein, a Buddha, and a Christ nestled among them, nodding wildly as the car sped along the fast lane of the M40. I wondered what to make of the driver's bobbing head collection. Was he a scientifically-inclined agnostic who was hedging his bets with a choice of religions?

I welcomed the brief distraction from my concerns for Aidan. It was likely that I was overreacting. I briefly envisioned the conversation I'd have with Leo later. It wasn't a pretty image, but better to face that than take any risks. I wondered if I would have sent for an ambulance if it weren't for the aura. I decided probably not. In fact, I wouldn't have texted the boys at all had it not been for my constant anxiety about a threat to Aidan.

It was twenty minutes before Gabe called back. My taxi had already left the motorway and was weaving in and out of evening traffic on the Oxford ring road.

The ambulance man wants to talk to you," Gabe said. The paramedic's tone, when he came on the line, was calm and unhurried. He explained that they suspected acute appendicitis and were taking Aidan to the John Radcliffe hospital.

"Is he going to be okay?" I asked.

"The emergency room doctors will be able to give you a better answer on that," he replied. "I need permission to take the young man's brother to the hospital. Are you the mother?"

"No, I'm their aunt. Please take Gabe with you. He can't be home alone. Their father is at a function and I can't reach him. I'll be at the hospital in ten minutes, maybe less."

"Give me a minute," he said, and I leaned forward to tell the driver to go to the ER. Apparently enjoying the drama, he put his foot down even further. The cab fishtailed on the wet road and I grabbed at the armrest, gripping it like a lifebuoy while the car slid sideways into the slow lane. Several horns blared, drowning out the euro-pop music on the radio. By some miracle, we didn't hit anyone, but my relief was short-lived. There was a massive jolt, and the taxi surged forward, hit from the behind. My seat belt tightened across my chest. All I could hear was the driver's voice. "Shit, shit, shit."

He jumped out of the car and hurried towards the driver of the car that had slammed into us.

Realizing I'd let go of the phone, I undid the seat belt so I could feel around under the seat in front of me. When I'd found it, I looked out through the rear window to see the taxi driver arguing with the driver of the Renault that had hit us. Behind them, a line of cars had come to a halt, their headlights blazing in the darkness.

The Renault driver loomed over the little taxi driver, swinging his heavily-muscled arms around. I was relieved to hear a police siren rising and falling as it came closer. Blue lights whirling, a

Range Rover pulled up behind the disabled vehicles.

A glance at my watch showed that it had been nearly ten minutes since I talked to Gabe. Damn. I opened the back door, and squeezed out in the narrow space between the car and a guardrail on the side of the road. A policeman was talking to the taxi driver and the owner of the Renault, while traffic eased past in the fast lane.

"I'm sorry, but I have an emergency," I said to the police officer. "I need to get to the ER."

The policeman glanced up at me. "Are you injured, ma'am?"

"No, no. It's not for me. My nephew's been taken to the ER. I need to get there immediately."

"Just a few minutes, and we'll be done here," he replied. "But it may take a while for the tow truck to get here."

"Tow truck?"

"Can't drive the taxi. Both rear lights are smashed."

"Will you take me?" I said to the Renault driver. "It's an emergency."

"What do you think I am? A bloody taxi driver? No freakin' way, I'm already late for my date."

"The tow truck will take you," said the policeman, with a glance of disapproval at the Renault driver. "I'm sure it won't be long before it gets here."

In my previous life, I'd had little to no contact with policemen. Now, in the last few weeks, I'd spent time in a police station, had coffee with a detective, had my fingerprints taken. Any awe and veneration I'd had for the uniform was quickly dissipating.

"You're not listening," I said. "I have to get to the ER. Right now."

The policeman's head shot up from the ticket he was writing. His eyes locked with mine, but I didn't flinch. Finally, he nodded. "I'll take you there myself. Two minutes."

I told the taxi driver I'd talk with his boss to make sure he got paid and, feeling a little sorry about leaving him to deal with the crazed Renault driver and the tow truck, I got in the back seat of the police Range Rover.

"ER at Radcliffe?" the policeman verified.

When I nodded, he turned on his lights and siren and pulled out into traffic. I tried calling Leo again but got no answer. Aidan's phone also clicked to voicemail. I hoped the two boys were safely at the hospital by now. My heart raced.

It was only a few minutes before we were at the hospital entrance. "Hope things go okay, miss," the officer said.

Thanking him for the lift, I hurried inside, blinking in the dazzlingly bright lights. The ER waiting room was busy. People waited on plastic chairs, some of them watching a flat panel television hung on the wall, others dozing or looking at their mobile phones. A baby screamed. I tried Leo's number again while joining the back of a line at the registration desk.

"Come on Leo. Check your phone," I said, realizing I was talking out loud. After five minutes, I'd had enough of waiting, and walked up to the desk, to the muttered annoyance of the people standing in line.

"I need to find my nephews. One was brought in with appendicitis. Aidan Benedict. And his little brother is here somewhere."

"Please wait your turn, ma'am," the receptionist replied, raising her bulbous yellow-brown eyes to stare at me. Her sallow skin was very wrinkled, folding its way down her face to a pendulous dewlap. She reminded me of an iguana.

I leaned forward over the counter, eighteen inches of formica that separated those who waited from those who controlled how long they would wait.

"I want to know where my nephews are. Please check your computer and tell me. Now."

The lizard woman harrumphed, but pecked at the keyboard with long green-painted nails.

"What was the name again?"

I told her and she peered at the screen. "Benedict. Yes, he's been admitted and is on his way to surgery."

"Where?"

"You can't go down there," she began and then rolled her reptilian eyes, as if to acknowledge that I would extract the information from her one way or another. "One floor down, Suite B, but they won't let you in. There's a waiting room where ..."

I hurried towards the elevator, punching the call button impatiently. When it finally arrived, I had to wait for two nurses to push out a gurney, its occupant as pale as death and perforated with tubes. An aura floated above the man's head, and I turned away, unable to give him a second thought. I was too focused on Aidan.

The elevator moved slowly down one floor, hissed to a halt, and the doors opened slowly on to a long, brightly lit corridor. A sign in front of me indicated Suite B was to the left. My boots squeaked on the linoleum floor as I hurried past closed doors, finally reaching a room marked with a B.

The door was shut and I stopped dead in front of it. Aidan was on the other side, on the operating table. I wished I could send him a message, letting him know I was there. Now I'd arrived, I didn't know what to do. I leaned against the wall, suddenly aware that my shoulder hurt where the seatbelt had tightened over it. Going back upstairs was pointless; I had to find Gabe. The thought of the little boy being alone somewhere in this vast hospital made me feel sick.

A nurse in greens scrubs strode towards me, a few dark hairs bristling out from a white surgical cap. Her furrowed brow reminded me of my high school principal on a bad day.

"Can I help you?" the nurse asked.

"I'm looking for my nephews," I said, standing up straight. "Aidan Benedict, and his brother Gabe."

"You're the aunt," she said. She was wearing a nametag with 'Cindy' printed on it. "Come with me."

She led the way further down the corridor to another door, which she pushed open, standing back to let me go in first.

"Aunt Kate!" Gabe jumped out of a chair and threw himself at me. His little body was trembling.

The nurse smiled, some of her scariness melting away. "This is Maude, one of our volunteers," she said, introducing me to a kind-looking woman in her sixties. "She's been keeping Gabe company."

"Thank you," I said. "Do you know how Aidan is doing?"

"He's just gone into surgery." Cindy said. "It could be some time before we know anything; I'll come back as soon as I have any information."

Maude quietly withdrew, leaving Gabe and me alone in the small room. There were four or five chairs upholstered in brown fabric, along with a table that held a pile of dog-eared magazines and a tub of plastic toys.

"Are you okay?" I asked him. He nodded, but it was an uncertain gesture. Taking my hand, he pulled me over to a chair, and then sat in the one next to me, leaning into me over the wooden armrest.

"How was Aidan doing when they took him into surgery?"

"Not too good. He was really white and he wouldn't talk to me. Just sort of groaning a lot. At least he stopped being sick before the ambulance men came." Gabe shivered. I tightened my arm around his shoulder.

"He'll be okay, I promise. We need to find your Dad somehow. Did he tell you where the dinner was being held?"

Gabe scrunched up his face in thought. "Well, he took his fancy gown and cap with him, which usually means it's at one of the colleges. He said he would keep his phone on and we could text him but he never answered. I called twice and texted a lot."

"OK, I'll try calling the Porter at his college to see if he can give us any help."

Damn, I should have thought of that earlier. I made some calls, finally reaching a master who said he knew where Leo was. Unaware of the urgency, he started to tell me that the dinner was being held in honor of some visiting mathematician from Sweden, but I cut him off.

"Please find Leo. It's very urgent. Ask him to call his sister." I gave him the number. Gabe looked as though he was going to cry.

"Your Dad will be here soon, don't worry. Do you want to look at a comic? They seem to have a few."

"Uh huh." He nestled closer against me. I had to shift him slightly to get to my phone when it rang.

"What's the problem, Kate?" Leo's voice was low. I heard voices and the clinking of plates and glasses in the background. There was no mistaking the ill-concealed irritation in his voice.

"It's Aidan," I said. "He's okay, but he's in surgery. Appendicitis. Can you come? I'm at the hospital with Gabe."

"Oh my God," said Leo. There was a long pause. "My phone battery died. I didn't realize until the Porter came to tell me to call you. I'm using a colleague's phone. I'm really sorry. Is Aidan okay?"

"We don't know anything yet. Just come as fast as you can."

"I'm on my way."

"Your Dad's coming," I said to Gabe. "He won't be long now."

He leaned his head on my shoulder and I stroked his hair. "Will Aidan be all right?" he asked after a while. "I'm scared."

"He'll be fine. The doctors know what they're doing and they perform these operations all the time."

"He'll have a scar, won't he? I bet it'll be bigger than the one on my elbow. Do you want to see it?"

I laughed. I'd seen it before; it was the result of a fall from a bike when he was little. "Yes, show me," I said, happy to keep him occupied and his thoughts off Aidan.

I heard the squeak of shoes on the lino floor in the hallway and stood up, expecting Leo. It was Cindy, her expression serious.

"What is it?" I asked.

"Aidan's appendix had ruptured, so there is some infection. The doctors are working on it."

"Oh my God. Is it serious?"

"Peritonitis is always serious, but he's in good hands. The best, really. Doctor Patel has handled many, many of these cases."

The doctor's experience was no consolation. My stomach clenched as though a wire had tightened around it.

"There's a cafeteria on the third floor and a vending machine on the second," she said, with a glance at Gabe. "Perhaps a drink or a snack would help to pass the time?"

Before I could explain that we were waiting for Aidan's father, Leo arrived in a rush, out of breath and red in the cheeks. He held out his arms to Gabe, who ran into them, tears streaming down his cheeks. The two of them hugged for a minute, then Leo pushed him gently back so he could talk to the nurse.

"Do we know anything about Aidan?"

Cindy told him everything. When she mentioned the peritonitis, Leo's face blanched. He sat down with his head in his hands. After a minute, he looked up.

"Can I see the doctor?"

"Not yet. These surgeries can take a while. Please be patient," she said.

"That's funny," said Gabe. "Aidan is the patient, but we have to be patient."

It was the first time he'd smiled since I'd arrived. I thought of explaining the origin of the word to him, but it seemed like too many words for my tired brain to string together.

Ruffling Gabe's hair, Leo turned to me. "How did you end up here?"

I gave him a succinct version of how I'd talked to Gabe, called for an ambulance, and got a taxi up from London.

"I'm so sorry." Leo paced the room. "I should have noticed that Aidan was sick before I left. I should have checked my phone during the evening. I can't believe I let my phone run out of power and didn't even know. Stupid of me."

I tried to reassure him. "It's not your fault, Leo. Aidan would be in surgery even if your phone had been working."

"He wouldn't be if it weren't for you, Kate. You were the one that checked in and got him to the hospital. If you hadn't done that, God knows what would have happened to him. Thank you."

I felt the coldness in my veins melt away with Leo's words. All the conflict of the past weeks was gone. In spite of my fear for Aidan, I felt a little better, happy that Leo and I were not fighting any more.

Time passed very slowly. Gabe sat on the brown carpet, pushing legos around with no real interest. Leo paced, sat for a while, and paced some more. I stared at a magazine, but didn't read a single word. The door opened. A nurse in green scrubs poked her head around it. "Dr. Benedict? Your son is out of surgery. You will be able to see him in a few minutes. The doctor would like a word with you first."

Leo squeezed my hand before hurrying after Cindy, leaving Gabe and me alone again. It was past midnight. Gabe should have been in bed.

When Leo returned a few minutes later, he looked pale and drawn.

"How is he?" I asked. "You should sit down. You look a bit wobbly."

"He's okay. Recovery will be slow because of the damage done by the ruptured appendix, which released a lot of bacteria. They have him hooked up to IVs for fluids and antibiotics and are moving him to a room now." Leo rubbed his eyes with his fist. "It was hard... he looked so fragile."

"I need to see him," I said.

"You need to get home to bed. You can see him in the morning."

"No." When I shook my head, I felt as though a wave of water had sloshed from one ear to the other. I flicked a glance at Gabe, who was clutching a handful of lego bricks and looking at us both intently.

"I really need to see him now." I had to see if the aura had disappeared, but didn't want to say anything in front of Gabe. I saw understanding dawning on Leo's face.

"Okay. Just for a minute," he said.

The trek to Aidan's room took forever, along corridors, in elevators, and through more corridors that were lined with doors open to darkened rooms where patients slept.

Aidan's room was still lit and partitioned into two by a curtain. Low voices murmured on the other side. He was asleep, propped up, his face as white as the pillows. Several IV tubes ran into his arm. Gabe reached for my hand and squeezed it. "He looks really sick," he said in a whisper.

I leaned over and stroked the hair back from Aidan's forehead. His skin was cold and dry. I gazed at him, at the area around his head. The air was as still and motionless as he was, not a tremble or flicker of the aura remaining. I gave Leo a big smile. He expelled a huge breath and smiled back. He had never wanted to believe in the aura, but he obviously had, whether consciously or not. We would need to talk about it, but not yet. Not until Aidan was well.

Leo drove Gabe and me back home. I'd said I'd stay for a day or two, so that Leo could sit with Aidan at the hospital. When we got to the house, I carried Gabe from the car. He was worn out, but he woke up enough to ask me to sleep in his room, so I straightened the duvet on Aidan's bed and crawled in. It was soothing to sleep under the glow in the dark stars on the ceiling.

When I woke up, the curtains were dappled with daylight, but I snuggled deeper under the duvet and closed my eyes, dozing until Gabe crept into the room with a mug of tea for me.

I was sore from the fender bender, but felt my shoulder loosening up under a hot shower. I went downstairs to help Gabe, who was making bacon sandwiches for breakfast. We passed the day on the sofa, watching cartoons and drinking hot chocolate. Leo came by in the evening with takeout Indian and updates on Aidan, who was still sleeping a lot, knocked out by the morphine.

On Sunday afternoon, Leo made arrangements for his girlfriend to look after Gabe, and I headed back to London on the train. I was anxious to see Josh. I wished we hadn't fought over the glass panels; not, I reflected, that they were really the cause of the problem. The aura was the issue. I didn't blame Josh for needing some time to come to terms with it, but I missed him. I missed the way he looked at me when he thought I wasn't watching, the way his dark brown hair curled against the back of his neck. I missed him and I needed him, in a way that I'd never let myself need anyone before. But I had an uneasy feeling that he was slipping away from me. The aura visions were making me behave differently. I didn't like this new me. How could I expect Josh to?

And there was Nick. I'd texted him a couple of times and he'd responded, so I knew he was alive. But for how much longer? I needed to see him, to assess the aura to see if it was any stronger. I couldn't let him die.

CHAPTER THIRTY-ONE

I texted Josh when I got off the train at Paddington Station, but he didn't answer. Disappointed, I stopped at a convenience store on the corner of my street, where I bought a microwaveable lasagna. It didn't look very appetizing, but I needed to eat something. I had no energy to cook. I was about to turn the microwave on when the phone rang. When I heard Josh's voice, I felt a thrill of relief.

"I'll bring food and we can have dinner together?" he offered.

Happy, I threw the lasagna in the bin and ran around, tidying up.

The sound of the doorbell was jarring in the silence of the apartment. I glanced at the clock. It was only six, even though the rain-soaked darkness made it seem much later. When I opened the front door, Josh wrapped his arms around me. I leaned into him, feeling the dampness of his coat through my thin silk shirt.

"I've been really worried about you," he said, taking off his coat, which was dripping water that pooled into dark spots on the beige carpet. With the image of the bloodstains on Rebecca's carpet flashing in front of my eyes, I took a step back.

"Are you okay?" Josh asked.

"Not really. A lot has happened."

"Why don't you sit while I heat up this food and make us some drinks."

We moved to the kitchen, Josh pulling out a counter stool for me to sit on before turning his attention to a bottle of white wine. He handed me a glass.

"I'm sorry about your nephew. How's he doing?"

I'd told Josh some of the story by text. Now I filled in the details of Aidan's appendicitis and surgery. "He's going to be fine, but it was frightening for a while."

I left Aidan's aura out of the story. There was no need to bring it up and risk spoiling the newfound harmony between us.

"Any updates on Rebecca?" Josh asked. "I thought the funeral would have been sooner."

"It was delayed because of the autopsy. The police think it was murder."

A look of shock crossed Josh's face. "Murder? But who and how? I thought it was an accident?"

I told him about my own suspicions, the autopsy findings, and my meeting with Clarke. Josh put his hand over mine and held it there while I talked. I didn't say anything about Clarke's concerns for my safety.

When I finished, we sat in silence for a while. I heard the clock ticking in the living room and the muted sound of traffic from the street below. "Kate, I need to apologize to you," Josh said. "I got mad about the glass panels, which was really stupid of me. I know you weren't going around me to Alan." He sighed. "It's no excuse, but I've been running on fumes for more than a month now. Alan's working me really hard. Not just me, but Laura and Jim too. I get the feeling there's something going on that we don't know about."

"Something wrong at the top, do you think?"

"I'm not sure. I'll tell you if I learn anything."

He paused, took a sip of wine. "How's Nick doing?"

"I don't know. I make excuses to check in on him by sending him messages. So far, so good, but I haven't seen him for a week. I need to do that soon to check if the aura is any stronger. That reminds me. I saw Gary a few days ago."

I told Josh about Gary's hostility and his apparent jealousy of Nick's friendship with Rebecca.

"Do you think he could have killed Rebecca?" Josh asked.

"I don't know. I can't imagine anyone killing her, Gary or anyone else. Who could do that?"

I stifled a yawn. It wasn't late, but I was exhausted. Josh began to clean up, rinsing plates and wiping down the counter. Then he put the kettle on.

"Chamomile tea?"

Reminded of Sister Chiara, I thought I should tell him about my meeting with her, but it seemed like more words than my brain could handle. I said yes to the tea. I'd tell him about the nun another time.

"How about I sleep on the sofa tonight?" he asked.

He held up his hand when I opened my mouth to object. "I won't be in your way. I just want to be sure you're all right. This isn't a good time for you to be alone. I'll let myself out in the morning."

I had to admit to myself that I wanted the company. At the same time, I was nervous, not ready to jump into bed with Josh, and I wasn't sure if that's what he'd really meant.

As if divining my thoughts, he put down the teapot and came to take my hands in his. "Genuine offer. No strings attached," he said. "I'm used to sleeping on sofas, and I'll sleep better knowing that you're close by. Okay?"

I nodded, emotion clogging my throat. Clinging to him, I felt the smoothness of his shirt against my cheek. Then we were kissing, tentatively at first, but with increasing urgency. Pleasure collided with anxiety. I wasn't ready for this yet. I needed to keep my mind clear to solve the aura dilemma, to work out how to look after Nick. Still, I loved the feeling of Josh's mouth on mine, the firmness of his body against my fingers. Abandoning my normal circumspection, I took his hand and led him to the bedroom. The aura hallucinations made me feel vulnerable and out of control. So what? That didn't mean I had to put my entire life on hold.

I woke up a few times during the night to assure myself that Josh was still there. He was, his body curled around mine. In the soft glow from a streetlight, his hair looked black against the white pillow. He slept peacefully. I wondered if he was dreaming.

He must have got up while I slept because I woke to a gentle shake and a cup of tea on the bedside table. It was still dark, but it was that grey thin darkness that heralds the arrival of the day.

"I have to run home for a clean shirt," he said. "I didn't want to leave without saying anything. I'll see you at the office."

When I heard the front door close, I grabbed the pillow Josh had slept on, holding it against my chest while I thought about what had happened. Deciding that I felt ridiculously happy, I got up, took a shower and dressed, getting ready in record time. I wanted to be early to work.

On my desk I found a note telling me to go see Alan as soon as I arrived. Dread knotted my stomach. I knew my repeated absences had infuriated him; this final one had probably pushed him over the edge. So I dawdled, walking slowly along the corridors, hoping to see Josh, to perhaps enlist his support. There was no sign of him.

Alan kept the meeting brief, expressed his frustration and anger in colorful terms and recommended I take a month's unpaid leave to get myself sorted out.

"I'd be justified in terminating you," he said. "But I'm holding out hope that you can clean up your act and come back as a productive member of the team. Do a handover with Laura, who will be taking over your part of the project. Then get out of here before I change my mind and fire you."

I left, having not uttered a single word. Even though I'd expected it, I was stunned. I bolted back to my office, avoiding any contact with other employees. After texting Josh to let him know and asking him to come over straight after work, I packed a few things in my briefcase. When I walked out the front door, I felt unhooked, like a boat come adrift from its dock.

I crossed the road to avoid a construction site, where men in orange vests wielded jackhammers. Barricades protected deep holes in the ground and the smell of old asphalt and gas made my nostrils burn. It seemed that London was in a constant state of repair, hardly surprising, given how long it had been standing. With nothing better to do for the day, I decided to walk home, detouring here and there to pass some of the City's ancient buildings and monuments to remind myself of why I'd wanted to become an architect. I paused outside St. Bartholomews, the oldest church in the City. Built in the twelfth century, it had survived centuries of natural and human interventions, with some parts obliterated, and other features, like the Tudor gatehouse, added hundreds of years later. Admiring the Romanesque flint and stone walls, I thought of how resilient the old building was. It made me feel better. I could endure this temporary hiatus in my career. Lengthening my stride, I continued my journey through the narrow roads and alleyways of the old city, which gradually gave way to twentieth-century rows of shops and flats.

Back at my apartment, I cleaned the kitchen to the sound of the morning news on the television. The day stretched out in front of me like an interminable desert landscape. Josh was at work, Leo was teaching, Inspector Clarke was investigating. Even my retired father was probably busy writing his book. Paolo was treating patients, and I supposed that Sister Chiara was praying or gardening.

When my cell phone rang, I grabbed it, hoping it would be Alan to tell me he'd changed his mind. It was Inspector Clarke. He told me, with ill-concealed irritation, that the computer technician who worked on facial composite images was back at work. He had booked a time with Nick to create a sketch of the man thought to be Rebecca's boyfriend.

"Can you come in to take a look at it tomorrow morning?" Clarke asked. "I'm sorry to ask. I know you'll have to get to work. You can come early. Would eight be all right?"

I said yes, not wanting to tell him about my enforced medical leave. When he rang off, I sat, absorbing the silence. Being unemployed, even temporarily, felt awful. I answered on the first ring when my phone trilled again.

"Kate, it's Jack. A little bird told me that you're not at work today. What's the problem?"

"Alan put me on leave for a month."

"That seems harsh," Jack said. The line wasn't very clear. His voice faded in and out. "I'm on the train back from Edinburgh," he said. "Sorry about the signal. Listen, come into the office tomorrow. I can smooth things over with Alan. He often jumps before he looks, you know. We need all hands on deck right now. Lots going on."

"It's my own fault," I felt compelled to confess. "I've been out of the office a lot. It's hard to blame Alan for being upset with me."

"Are you ill? What's the problem with all the time off?"

I contemplated telling Jack about the aura sightings. I trusted him. Ever since I joined the company, he'd been very good to me. He deserved to know the reasons why I'd been out so much.

"I'm not ill, but I have been having some issues," I began. "Hallucinations, I suppose you could call them. That, and all the time, of course, around the investigation into Rebecca's death. I've spent a lot of time with the police."

"Rebecca Williams?" he asked, sounding as though he was in a tunnel. "Why are you involved in the investigation?"

"We were friends. I've been able to help the police with some details, and…"

The line went dead. Thirty seconds later, the phone rang.

"I'll probably lose you again," Jack said. "Will you come into the office in the morning? We can chat then. I'll square it with Alan for you to come back to work. I'll be in at eight thirty. Let's talk then."

"All right, as long as you're sure Alan won't try to throw me out. He wasn't very happy today. Oh, and there is one thing. I need to go to the police station at eight tomorrow, just to look at a sketch. I'll come straight to the office afterwards, but it may be a little later than eight thirty. I promised Inspector Clarke I'd go in."

The train must be fording a river, judging by the gurgling and whooshing noises on the line. I heard a muffled 'okay' before the call died. I felt better for having talked with Jack. I knew he could persuade Alan to let me come back. Alan could be aggressive and strident, but Jack seemed to get what he wanted most of the time.

My feelings of rejection alleviated by Jack's call, I embarked on a thorough clean out of my closet and the kitchen cupboards. When everything was shipshape and orderly, I decided to go shopping for a special dinner for Josh. Checking my watch, I realized I could beat the commute rush if I left at once. A high quality supermarket was just a couple of Tube stops away; I always enjoyed exploring the aisles of organic food and fresh produce there.

An hour later, with two full bags in hand, I headed home. It was on the escalator going back up to street level that I began to feel uneasy. Without the usual crush of commuters, the Tube station was so quiet that I could hear the rhythmic pulse of the machinery that moved the escalators. Perhaps it was the calm that heightened my other senses; the faint prickle on the back of my neck as though someone had stroked a finger across my skin. Turning quickly, I saw a young couple a few steps below me, entwined and oblivious to all but each other. Behind them, a man in a dark wool coat rested his fingers lightly on the moving handrail and appeared to be reading the advertisements on the walls. His studied absorption in the posters seemed artificial but, although I watched him for a while, he didn't turn his head to look at me. I must be imagining things.

I passed through the turnstiles in the windswept entry hall and took the exit on to the high street, pulling my scarf tighter around my neck against the sudden blast of cold. There were plenty of pedestrians about, and the shops were busy. I stopped to look in the window of a shoe store, eyeing a pair of brown leather boots I'd been thinking of buying. In the glass, I saw the man from the escalator walk past me. I turned my head to watch him. He was quite tall, broad-shouldered, with sandy hair. He was moving slowly. Now I was sure he was following me. I reached for my cell phone, dialed Inspector Clarke's number, and heard a recorded voice, telling me to leave a message.

In the time it took me to listen to it, my heart rate had slowed and my breathing had returned to normal. The man in the overcoat had disappeared into the crowds, so I left a short message for Inspector Clarke, asking him to call me back when he had time.

Walking home, I decided I was overreacting. Still, when I reached my building, I stopped and looked around before opening the front door, then slipped inside and pushed the door closed behind me. With no sounds to reassure me that anyone else was home in the downstairs apartment, my heart thudded against my ribs as I climbed the stairs. The dark shadows at the end of the hallways were suddenly full of imaginary assailants. I almost ran up the last flight of stairs, grocery bags in one hand, keys at the ready. Once I was in my apartment, I did a quick tour of the rooms, even swishing the shower curtain back in the bathroom. I'd always had a vague fear of what might lurk in a curtained-off bath, probably from watching *Psycho* so many times.

Certain that I was alone and that no one had followed me, I chided myself for being a coward. I was still trying to decide whether I was making too much of the man in the black coat when my phone rang. "Aunt Kate? It's Aidan."

"Aidan, sweetheart, it's so good to hear your voice. How are you feeling?"

"Hungry. I'm still on IV fluids and ice chips, but tomorrow they're going to let me have some real food. And they might let me go home by Friday, which would be brilliant because I want to watch the Chelsea match on television. It's really boring here."

I leaned against the kitchen counter listening to Aidan recount his memories of coming out of surgery, the details of the hospital routine, and the loud snoring noises emanating from the other patient in his room. He said his school friends had made a huge card for him and sent it with a bunch of balloons.

"And Dad keeps coming in and staring at me like he's never seen me before. Can you tell him to stop doing that? It's creepy."

I laughed. "No, I don't think I can. You had us all very scared there for a while, kiddo. Your dad's just happy that you're alive and well."

"Dad said things could have been pretty bad if it wasn't for you, Aunt Kate. That you were the one that got the ambulance to come. So thanks for doing that. Lucky you got me this cell phone, huh?"

"Yes, that was lucky."

"OK, I have to go. The nurse is here to change my IV. Will you come and visit soon? Maybe this weekend?"

"Of course. I can't wait to see you. Maybe we can watch the soccer together. Love you."

"Yeah, bye."

I stared at the blank screen on my phone for a full minute after Aidan hung up, reliving the terror I'd felt when I saw the aura, the panicked trip to the emergency room, and the overwhelming relief when Aidan came out of surgery and the aura was gone.

After unpacking the groceries, which kept me occupied for all of two minutes, I set about preparing dinner. The cell phone rang again; this time it was Inspector Clarke.

"Kate. Are you all right?" There was a sharp edge of urgency in his voice. I felt guilty about alarming him.

"Yes, I'm fine. I thought I was being followed, but now I'm not so sure."

Clarke made me describe the man and said he'd look into it.

"For now, keep your door locked."

"Of course. Is there anything new?" I asked. "Any leads on who Rebecca's boyfriend might be?"

"Nothing concrete. We found wire transfers into Rebecca's bank account at the beginning of each year for sums that would cover six months' rent. So that explains how the boyfriend was paying for the apartment. But the remitting bank is based in Switzerland and we don't have a name for the account holder. I'm working on it but it could take days-- if not weeks. It's well nigh impossible to deal with the Swiss when it comes to disclosing information on bank accounts."

"Do you think he's deliberately obscuring the trail of money?" I asked. "To hide something?" This was a lot more elaborate than I'd imagined.

"Possibly. It could be some rich guy who's paying for the rent out of untaxed money. My people are working on it." He paused. "You're sure you're okay? You sounded a little rattled when you left that voicemail."

"I'm fine. I panicked. Maybe I'll see you in the morning when I come in to look at the identikit picture."

"Maybe. It depends on how much murder and mayhem the night brings. If I don't see you, be sure to call me. I'm hoping you will recognize the man in the sketch."

I promised I'd call.

Thinking about Rebecca and the boyfriend, I went to find the drawing of Rebecca's room that I had kept and stored in a drawer in the kitchen, I stared at it for ten minutes while I made and drank some tea. Nothing new jumped out at me. I just kept running through the same scenario in my head. Rebecca and her boyfriend had argued, he'd held her by the wrists, trying to reason with her, and then, angry, had pushed her away. She'd fallen on to the glass table, and lay bleeding on the shards of glass. Then what? With frightening lack of compassion, the boyfriend had waited for her to die, ignoring her effort to pull herself up, not helping her, not calling for an ambulance. And then he'd added the props of the wineglass and wine bottle in an attempt to provide a reason for her fall.

He must have known that the police could check for alcohol in Rebecca's system, so the window dressing was just that, a red herring. But why? To give him time to run away? To leave the country? Was that what had happened? I pondered the enigma of Edward, who traveled frequently and didn't seem to exist except in a few mentions of his name. No photos, little evidence of his presence in the apartment. I wished I'd been more pushy, got more details from Rebecca.

I thought back to my conversation with the Williamses. There was something nagging at me, little tugs at the edges of my brain, trying to attract my attention. But I couldn't pin it down.

Thoughts of Rebecca and the boyfriend dissolved when the doorbell rang. It was Josh. "Can I come up? It's tipping down out here."

I buzzed him in and heard him bounding up the stairs. He was earlier than I expected, but that was fine with me. "I heard about Alan putting you on leave," he said before he'd taken his coat off. "Everyone wants you to come back. We're missing you."

"Even Ben?" I asked with a smile.

"Okay, everyone except Ben. He's so insecure that nothing would make him happier than being the last one left on the payroll. Then he could be confident he's the best."

"Yeah," I agreed. "Poor Ben."

I told him about the call from Jack while we made dinner together and drank some wine. I lit some candles and set them on the kitchen island. We'd just sat down when the doorbell rang.

"Now what?" I said, not moving to answer it.

Josh looked at me inquiringly. "Shall I get it?"

I shook my head. "Sorry, I'll do it." I didn't tell him that my first thought had been that it was the sandy-haired man in the black wool coat. In fact, it was Inspector Clarke.

"I just wanted to check on you," he said, when I opened the door. "I didn't want you to think I was dismissing your concerns about being followed."

"Thank you. I'm fine, though." There was an awkward silence and then I stepped aside to let him in. I saw him take in the scene: Josh, the bottle of wine, the candles. His shoulders stiffened and I could feel a coolness fill the air between us.

"I didn't realize I was interrupting your dinner," he said, taking a step back towards the door. "I'll see you at the police station tomorrow."

"Would you like to stay for a glass of wine?"

His mouth twitched as though he were trying to force a smile and failing. "No, that's very kind, but I'll be going."

I closed the door and leaned against it, feeling guilty for no reason I could explain, as though I'd been caught cheating.

"Who was that?" asked Josh.

"Inspector Clarke. He's investigating Rebecca's death." I sat down and took another bite of food.

"I didn't know detectives made house calls," Josh said drily.

"He's just doing his job," I said. I put my hand on his arm. "I didn't tell you before, but he's worried that Rebecca's boyfriend might come after me. So he was just checking up on me to make sure I'm all right."

His look of concern touched my heart. "Are you in danger?"

"I don't know. I don't think so, but Clarke is being cautious. Because Rebecca was so secretive about who she was seeing, the police haven't been able to track him down yet. The Inspector is worried that if the boyfriend thinks I know who he is, he'll consider me a threat. I know, it all sounds a bit melodramatic."

"Maybe, but if there's any risk at all, you have to take it seriously."

"Perhaps that's what the threat to Nick is as well?"

"What?"

"If the boyfriend thinks you might expose who he is, then it's possible he thinks Nick might know enough to identify him as well."

"But why Nick and not Gary? Gary doesn't have an aura."

"You said that Nick claims to have seen the boyfriend on the stairs a few times? Maybe Gary wasn't there, and didn't ever see him. So he's not a threat."

I put my fork down. "Josh, if that's the case, and Nick's aura means he's in danger from this man, then maybe I was right about being followed. Perhaps I have an aura too?"

Sliding down from the counter stool, I hurried to the bathroom and stared into the mirror, turning my head slowly trying to catch a glimpse of moving air. I'd checked before, of course, but this time I did it with intent. Josh came in and stood behind me. "Can you see anything?"

"No, but that might not mean it's not there."

Turning around, I leaned into Josh. I felt better for having his arms around me. "What did you mean about being followed?" he asked.

I told him about seeing the sandy-haired man at the Tube station.

"I'm going to keep an eye on you until the police work out who this boyfriend is," he said. He hesitated. "If that's okay with you, of course? I came prepared this time and brought a toothbrush. And a clean shirt."

That made me laugh. It felt good to be happy. Memories of the man in the black coat evaporated. We picked a movie, sat together on the couch, Josh's arms around me. Watching it, I was able to forget, for a couple of hours, about the aura, even about Rebecca. We brushed our teeth in the bathroom together while Josh related snippets of the day's activity at the office. Later, in bed, he turned off the lamp. Within minutes, I was asleep.

I woke to see the clock's red numbers showing that it was three in the morning. I'd been dreaming of Rebecca again, and Toby, and Sophie, weird dreams where they were all together. My heart pounded; the adrenalin had thoroughly wakened me. I lay on my back, listening to Josh's soft breathing, thankful he was there. I slid closer to nestle up against him. He smelled good, like fresh air in the mountains on a clear spring morning. A thought traversed my brain; something to do with scent. I couldn't quite grasp it. Then I remembered. It was the scent of aftershave. The smell of Amouage, the aftershave I'd seen in Rebecca's bathroom cabinet.

CHAPTER THIRTY-TWO

The person who'd been wearing the aftershave was Peter Montgomery. I gently turned back the bed covers and padded across the carpeted floor to find my purse. I hadn't cleaned it out for days, so I was sure Montgomery's business card was still in there somewhere. Clutching the bag, I tiptoed along the dark hall to the living room. The moon was still blanketed by cloud, and only a faint glow from a streetlight bled into the room. Fumbling in the darkness, I pulled out the card and sniffed it. Yes, there was the faintest hint of the scent. I used my cellphone to illuminate the card, which read Peter E. Montgomery, CEO, followed by a list of qualifications that indicated a lifetime of achievement and showed no lack of ego.

I flipped the card over in my fingers several times and then looked at it again. The middle initial stopped my breath. E. Could that stand for Edward? It was possible. Montgomery was attractive, powerful, wealthy, a magnet for a young woman like Rebecca. And it would explain why she'd been so careful to keep it quiet. An affair with the CEO wouldn't be something she'd want to broadcast. Neither would he. I knew he was married. His wife appeared regularly in the society pages that reported on fundraisers and charity events.

I leaned back against the cushions and hugged my knees, still clutching the card in my hand, trying to recall anything Rebecca might have said that would point to Montgomery. Nothing came to mind. I thought yet again how incredibly discreet she had been. What had Montgomery said about Rebecca? She was a valuable asset. Could he really be dispassionate enough to say such a thing or was it just his way of covering up real grief?

But, if it were Montgomery, then I had only been imagining that the man in the black coat was following me. That thought, at least, was comforting. I felt the muscles in my neck and shoulders relax a little. I glanced at the time. I couldn't call Clarke at this time of night. I'd do it first thing in the morning. Wishing Josh was awake so I could share my discovery with him, I slipped the card back into my purse and crept back to bed. I pulled the duvet over Josh, stretched out on my side of the bed and drifted off to sleep.

A sound woke me. I bolted upright in alarm before remembering that Josh was in the apartment. It was still dark outside, and the clock showed that it was just after seven. Josh must be getting ready to leave for work, and the least I could do was make him some breakfast. I could tell him about my suspicions while I made tea. Pulling on my bathrobe, I went into the hall. The bathroom door was slightly ajar and the light was on.

The fist came out of nowhere, slamming into my abdomen and knocking me off my feet. Gasping for breath, I flailed at my attacker in the semi-darkness, swinging my arms, trying to land a blow, then grabbed at a sleeve, feeling the rough wool cloth. It was him, the man from the Underground, I was sure of it. The fist came at me again and I rolled to my side, pulling my knees up to my chest, swallowing against the nausea rising in my throat. Seeing the flash of a blade, I rolled away from it. He lifted the knife again.

I heard a shout, saw Josh coming up behind the attacker, who swung around, knife in hand and lunged at him. I screamed, clawing my way towards the living room on my hands and knees. I needed to get to my cellphone to call the police, but the effort was just too much. I felt warm, sticky blood leaking from my head, dripping into my eyes and down my cheek.

Josh was on the floor, trying to get up. The attacker stood over him. I watched in horror as he raised the blade, watched the sharp point sink into Josh's leg.

Shouts clamored from the landing. I wanted to yell back but couldn't find the energy. I twisted my head around to see Josh leaning up against the hall wall, grasping his leg, and the attacker coming towards me again. The shouting got louder, the attacker aimed a kick at my head, and everything went dark.

When I came round, I was lying in a hospital bed in a curtained cubicle. I touched my temple, feeling the dressing that covered my stitches. I was aware of white curtains and beige tile floor, the smell of disinfectant, and quiet murmurs from the other cubicles. I thought I remembered Aidan in the hospital, a meeting at work, my evening with Josh. Had it all been a dream? It felt real and yet, at the same time, vague and chimerical. I struggled to sit up, aware of an IV in my arm dragging against my skin. Colored lights danced in front of my eyes, like the illuminations at a fun-fair, bright and whirling. I felt sick and clasped my stomach, trying not to throw up.

"Nurse!" I called. "Is anyone there?"

A nurse in blue scrubs pushed through the curtain. "You're awake. That's good. You need to lie down, please." She gently pushed me back down.

"I feel fine," I protested. It was almost true; the nausea was subsiding.

"That's because you're on pain meds. Believe me, you need them. You have severe bruising, a couple of cracked ribs, and a wound to your head. Fortunately, no serious damage to the organs. So please lie back. The doctor will be in to see you later. Oh, and there's a detective here who wants to talk to you about the assault. I'll send him in."

The assault. Now I remembered the man inside my apartment, punching and kicking me, trying to stab me. I felt a sudden rush of fear for Josh.

"Where's Josh?" I asked.

"The young man who came in at the same time as you?"

"Yes, can I speak to him?"

The nurse frowned. "Not yet, dear. He's in surgery."

"What?" I sat up again. "Is he badly hurt?"

"Stab wounds, I believe, but I don't have the details. Now please lie down. You've been through a traumatic attack and your body needs to rest. I'll be back very soon."

I took a couple of deep breaths, trying to calm my pounding heart. Last night there had been no aura around Josh. That meant he wouldn't die. But he was hurt, and it was my fault. Tears welled in my eyes. I looked for a box of tissues but couldn't see one. I wiped them away with my fist, my bathrobe was folded neatly on a chair, and there was no sign of my purse or shoes. I realized I was dressed only in a hospital gown, but I didn't remember arriving at the hospital. I didn't remember anything after that last brutal kick. I dabbed at my nose and face with a corner of the bed sheet, waiting for Inspector Clarke to arrive.

It was hard to swallow my disappointment when my visitor came in. Not Inspector Clarke, but someone called Hopkins from the local police station. He looked around, and moved my clothes to the bottom of the bed so he could drag the chair over closer to me. He was stick thin, with sparse hair combed to one side and a voice that sounded as though he was speaking through a mouthful of sand.

"When the police responded to an emergency call, we found a young man bleeding and you unconscious in the hallway of your flat. The door was open. Yet there was no sign of forced entry or of a robbery. Do you remember what happened?"

"Only that I was attacked by someone in my apartment. He kicked me and stabbed Josh in the leg. Can you find Inspector Clarke at Scotland Yard? This is to do with a case he's investigating, I'm sure of it."

Hopkins, not replying, wrote something down in a notebook.

"Please listen to what I'm saying," I said. "I need to talk with Inspector Clarke. The man who attacked me had been following me earlier in the day."

"Local jurisdiction," was all he said, still scribbling with his wretched scratchy pencil. "What else do you remember?"

I wanted to tear the notebook from his hands, shred it, and break his pencil into tiny pieces. He looked up with an eyebrow raised, waiting for an answer.

"Can I borrow your phone? I really need to call Inspector Clarke," I begged.

"When I've finished asking questions, I will try to contact him for you. So, tell me about this man that you say was following you. What did he look like?"

I described him. "I think it was the man who attacked me because I saw he was wearing a wool coat. I felt it just before I passed out."

"Half the men in London are wearing wool coats. It is winter. Although strictly speaking, it's autumn, but you know what I mean." Hopkins scribbled again. "And what do you think this has to do with the other case you mentioned?"

"It's complicated. If I could just talk to Inspector Clarke, that would be easier. I have something really important to tell him."

Hopkins sighed. "Do you have his number?"

"No, I don't have my phone with me."

Hopkins stuck his pencil in his pocket and pushed himself to his feet. For such a thin man, he made the action look like hard work, as though he were moving a heavy weight.

"Give me a few minutes."

He pushed his way through the curtain, which caught on his shoulder and trailed after him until he moved out of reach. It fell silently back into place. Alone again, I lay back on the pillows and tried to convince myself that Josh would be all right. It seemed to take a long time before Hopkins returned, cell phone pressed to his ear.

"Right," he said. "I see. Yes, sir. I will." He gave the phone to me. "The Inspector wants to talk to you."

"Kate, I'm so sorry." Clarke's voice faded in and out on a weak signal. "I'm going to come to the hospital as soon as I can. Do you know how long they plan on keeping you in?"

"No. I'll ask the nurse when she comes back. How long will you be? Can you get here soon? I have something I must tell you. It's important."

There was a short silence, as though Clarke were deciding whether to change his plans.

"Something has come up that may be relevant to Rebecca's case. I need to deal with it, and then I'll come."

He sounded distracted, and very serious.

"I want to speak to Hopkins again. Can you pass me over?"

From Hopkins' side of the conversation, I gathered that he wasn't happy. His face flushed red, he answered in monosyllables. Finally he snapped the phone shut.

"I have to stay with you until DI Clarke gets here," he said. "For your own protection, in case your alleged attacker comes looking for you."

I hadn't thought about the possibility of the man trying again. The thought churned my stomach. "What about Josh? Will he be safe?" I asked.

"I imagine so, in a surgery room with half a dozen doctors," Hopkins replied. I caught the sarcastic tone in his voice and glared at him.

"I'm tired. I'm going to try to sleep." I closed my eyes. In fact, I was wide awake and jittery. I wondered if the pain meds had that effect. But pretending to sleep was better than talking to Hopkins.

***

When I opened my eyes again, I had no idea how much time had passed. In the windowless cubicle, the light was the same, but my IV bag was nearly empty so I guessed I must have dozed for a while. Hopkins glanced up from his newspaper when I stirred.

"You're awake," he said, stating the obvious as though declaring the discovery of gravity. He looked at his watch. "It's been two hours. Inspector Clarke should be here soon."

He nodded towards a tray of food on the table next to the bed. "They brought that in a few minutes ago. If you don't eat it, I will. I'm starving."

"Help yourself," I said, nauseated by the thought of food. Just as Hopkins took his first bite of something white and glutinous from the plate, Inspector Clarke came in through the curtains. He gave Hopkins a dismissive look before moving to my bedside. "You okay?"

I nodded. "Just some bruising and a couple of broken ribs, they say. But Josh was stabbed. Have you heard anything about him?"

Clarke's face was impassive. "Yes, I checked. He's out of surgery. Fortunately no major arteries damaged and he will mend quickly." He paused. "Lucky for you he stayed the night, from what I heard. He probably saved your life."

I nodded.

"Your neighbors heard a lot of noise so they called emergency services. The suspect ran past them on the stairs and was gone well before the ambulance arrived."

"Oh my God." I felt the tears coming again. Clarke handed me a clean white handkerchief. He must have a huge supply of them somewhere.

"You said that something else had come up?" I asked, trying to focus on something other than an image of Josh lying hurt and bleeding. "Something to do with the case?"

Clarke perched on the edge of the bed. "Yes, but it's not important right now. All that matters is that you're safe."

"I'd rather you tell me. Is it Nick?"

He stood up and hands behind his back, stared at the monitor that beeped away in the corner of the cubicle. He turned back to look at me.

"I'm afraid so. He was killed last night. He fell under a train at the Oxford Street Tube station."

CHAPTER THIRTY-THREE

I sat upright and stared at Clarke. "Oh, my God," I said.

He patted my hand soothingly.

"I'm sorry. I know it's a shock. His partner Gary identified him this morning."

A shadow passed over his face and I thought again of how hard his job was. He must have dealt with so many grieving relatives. Thinking about Nick, and the aura over him. I groaned. Clarke's brooding expression changed to one of concern.

"Are you okay?"

I would never be okay for as long as I could see the damned auras with no way of saving the people that had them. I knew one thing for sure, though.

"It wasn't an accident," I said.

"We don't know that yet. We're still sifting through witness statements to see if he jumped, fell, or was pushed. Gary insists that Nick wouldn't commit suicide, says he was happy, a little shaken up by finding Rebecca like that, but not depressed. Still, I've seen enough suicides to know that it's often impossible for family members to see it coming. Someone's happy as a lark in the morning, and dead at nightfall."

"Not Nick," I said. "Remember how worried he was about Caspian? He insisted on taking the cat home with him. I don't see that as the action of someone about to kill himself. Did he leave a note?"

"Not that we know of."

"And how many people accidentally fall onto the lines in a Tube station?"

"Not many," he agreed. "Hardly any. But it can happen, especially if the platform is very crowded, as it was at Oxford Street yesterday evening."

"Too coincidental," I said. "I don't believe it."

Clarke nodded his head in agreement. "I am going to assume foul play until we learn otherwise," he said. Standing up, he paced around the enclosed space.

"Where was Gary when it happened?" I asked.

"At a cocktail party. Lots of alibis. Let's go back to what happened to you. Can you provide a detailed description of the attacker?"

"Definitely," I said. "I saw him during the day before he got into the apartment."

Clarke stopped pacing and stared at me. "The man who you said was following you? Dammit. I should have got on to that more quickly. I'm sorry, Kate."

"I wasn't sure he was following me. It could have been coincidence. Now I know it wasn't, of course."

I shivered. Clarke came back to sit on the bed. "Can you go over the details? I know the time of the attack. The emergency call came in at five past seven this morning. What happened before then?"

The business card, the aftershave. Was I going to tell Clarke about my amazing deduction that the boyfriend was Peter Montgomery? In the stark light of the hospital room it seemed rather ridiculous. Plenty of men used Amouage, obviously, or there wouldn't be stacks of bottles on shelves in London's department stores. It wasn't Montgomery, but the man in the wool coat who had been Rebecca's boyfriend. I tried to remember whether there'd been any hint of aftershave on him, but couldn't remember. All I remembered was the smell of my own blood. My hand flew to my temple and I felt a bulky dressing there.

"Are you all right? Do you need a nurse?" asked Clarke.

I shook my head, and wished I hadn't; the room started to spin. When it settled again, I related the details as I remembered them from the moment I woke up, hearing the noise in the hallway. Clarke took some notes.

"The front door was jimmied open," he said. "That's how the attacker got in."

That surprised me. What kind of technology consultant knew how to break down doors?

"Do you think the man who attacked me also killed Nick?"

"It's possible. Nick died at eight pm the night before. There was plenty of time."

"So, here's the deal." Clarke looked at his watch. "A police officer will be stationed here to keep an eye on you until you're discharged. Then I'd like to get you out of London, preferably somewhere no one would be able to find you. Do you have family you can go stay with?"

"My brother. But I don't want to put him or his boys at risk. They've been through enough already. Besides, I'd rather stay in London. I can't leave the investigation and all that."

And I can't leave Josh. The words swam around in my head. It was my fault that he was injured. I had to stay close to him.

"Okay. I'll get a twenty-four hour guard organized at least for a day or two, until Josh is ready to be discharged. We have to keep you safe until we catch this guy, whoever it is."

He stretched and then pressed his hands to his back.

"Are you hurt?" I asked.

"No, just spending too much time hunched over my desk and a pile of paperwork. I could do my job so much better if I never had to fill in another form, but that's the way it is. We figure that a petty crime uses up one tree. An investigation like this one chews up a whole forest."

The curtain opened to reveal a young uniformed officer. He had short dark hair and a serious expression. He stood at attention until Clarke told him to relax.

"I'll come back in later. You'll be in good hands with PC Wyatt here."

With that, Clarke was gone. I lay back on the pillows, suddenly aware of pain in my shoulders and ribs. My head ached. A quick glance at the bag attached to the tubes running into my arm confirmed that my pain medications were running down. I didn't want to be a wimp, but I hoped the nurse intended to get them going again soon.

PC Wyatt sat, staring at the curtains as though expecting an armed killer to burst through at any second. That was his job, I knew, but it seemed a little dramatic. It was hard to believe my assailant would risk coming to such a public place. Then again, Nick had been killed in the most public of locations. I felt a lump forming in my throat. Nick had done nothing wrong and he was dead. And Josh could have died. I couldn't bear to think of him being hurt. I wanted to see him.

I lay back on the pillows but it was impossible to get comfortable. My mind was whirling. I needed to get up and move around for a minute.

"I have to use the bathroom," I said. "I suppose you'll have to come with me, at least as far as the door."

"All right," Wyatt said, shifting on his chair, looking embarrassed.

On the table next to me was a plastic bag with a pair of socks in it. I managed to open it and slid them out. They were blue, thick and fluffy, emblazoned with the hospital logo, and had silicone dots on the soles so that my feet wouldn't slip on the polished floor. I pulled them on with one hand, the other still restricted by the IV tube. Wyatt stood up to help me.

My legs felt shaky. I pushed the IV bag on its portable stand, welcoming the support it offered. We went out through the curtains, past other cubicles, into a wide, well-lit hallway. Wyatt asked the way to the bathrooms, and a harried-looking nurse directed us to the left.

"Just a few yards," she said. "Will you be all right?"

I nodded and set off in that direction. The overhead lights were bright and blinding after the dimmed illumination of my cubicle. Their reflection bounced on the glossy beige walls and made my eyes hurt; the dark floor shone like an oil slick. Wyatt and I walked slowly. We'd just reached the bathroom door when I saw my nurse bearing down on us like an approaching thunderstorm.

"Miss Benedict, what are you doing up and walking around by yourself?"

She turned an iron gaze on PC Wyatt, who straightened his shoulders and stared back.

"She's not by herself. I'm taking care of her," he said. "She needed the restroom."

"Stay right there. I'll get a wheelchair." Turning abruptly, she disappeared round a corner at the end of the hall.

Wyatt gave me a conspiratorial wink. I leaned against the wall, swaying under the bright light, feeling the slightest pull of the sticky socks on the floor, tenuous threads holding me to the ground.

At the other end of the corridor, a group of people appeared, walking slowly, and as they came closer, I saw that two male orderlies were supporting an elderly man who shuffled along in a plaid bathrobe and beige slippers. His thin white hair was only a shade lighter than his skin, which was blanched and waxy. But he was smiling and joking with the men, telling them that he used to run marathons and planned to do another one once they let him out.

I watched them go into the elevator. Their voices faded as the doors closed with a loud ping. In the ensuing silence, which felt deep and unnerving, I bent to massage a cramped calf muscle. Footsteps caught my attention, I glanced up to see a man striding along the corridor, fast and determined. Maybe a doctor in a hurry, I thought, dropping my gaze back to my leg, and giving it another rub. Then realization jolted me like an electric shock. It was the sandy-haired man from the escalator, the man who had attacked me. He stopped abruptly, obviously surprised to see me in the middle of the corridor, but kept coming, one hand going to his coat pocket.

I seized Wyatt's arm and screamed, "It's him. The man who attacked me."

Wyatt moved in front of me. "Get in there," he said, pushing the bathroom door open. Leaving Wyatt to face a man with a knife seemed cold-hearted, so I stayed at the door, shouting for help. The man with the black coat turned and ran, the policeman in pursuit. Wyatt was talking into a radio and had something in one hand that looked like a gun but I knew that wasn't possible. It must be a taser. The attacker ran through a set of double doors at the far end of the hall, leaving them swinging wildly on their hinges. I stopped yelling when Wyatt reached them. Banging through them, he disappearing from view. Silence fell like a shroud.

Seconds later, it was broken by the squeak of wheels on linoleum; the nurse came round a corner with a wheelchair. She pulled it to a stop, put the brakes on and guided me into it, tutting the whole time. Her kindly face was flushed pink, whether with exertion or dismay at the situation, it was hard to tell.

"Where is that policeman? I understood he was supposed to stay with you? What's he doing going off and leaving you standing here alone? I'll report him to his superiors."

"He chased after the man who attacked me in my apartment."

"The man was here? In the hospital? Oh my goodness."

The nurse looked up and down the corridor as if expecting him to jump out at them. "Should we call for help?"

While we waited there, uncertain what to do, the double doors swung open again. I stiffened, and the nurse put both hands firmly on the wheelchair handles. But it was Wyatt, still talking on his radio and hurrying towards us.

"He got away," he said, panting slightly. "But I've got a couple of units out looking for him."

He took his cap off, ran his hand through his hair, and put it back on. "I should have used the taser, but I never got close enough."

"You were very brave," I said. "And he had a big head start on you."

The nurse guided my foot onto the footrest. "I'm taking you to your bed. We need to get you back on your medications. Will you be coming with us, Constable?"

Wyatt nodded, following behind us. It wasn't until I was back in bed that I remembered that I still needed to go to the bathroom.

CHAPTER THIRTY-FOUR

Later that day, I sat in my wheelchair next to Josh's bed. PC Wyatt, looking uncomfortable on a plastic chair, sat facing the door. His back was straight; both feet, in their black polished shoes, rested firmly on the floor. Opposite the bed, a small television hung on the wall, running soundless BBC news commentary. A window with the blinds drawn up showed an oblong of blue sky and the tips of branches bearing decaying remnants of their once vivid foliage.

The room was gray and white: white sheets and blankets, gray walls, gray and white floor and a gray metal bed frame. The only splash of color was a potted red begonia that I had bought for Josh at the hospital gift shop, together with a brown teddy bear with a red ribbon around its neck. Probably too cute, but I'd fallen in love with the little fluffy toy and its big brown button eyes. It made Josh smile when I gave it to him. He'd propped it up on the pillow and draped an arm around it.

Josh had three stab wounds, two on his arms, which he had used to defend his body against the knife slashes, and one, more serious, in his thigh. He had lost a lot of blood, but transfused and stitched up, he was no longer in danger. His face was paler than usual, white against his dark hair, which was still tousled from a night of medication-induced sleep.

We were going over all the details, trying to fill in the gaps for each other on what had happened in the apartment the previous morning. Josh had got up early, planning to let me sleep in. When he was in the bathroom, he had heard me scream and rushed out to see a man with the knife.

"God, I feel awful about putting you in danger like that," I said. "I shouldn't have let you stay the night."

"Don't be silly. I just wish I could have stopped him from attacking you. I did my best but I never knew how much a knife cut could hurt and bleed."

"I hardly remember any of it. It's a blur from the moment he kicked me."

"Just as well the neighbors heard all the commotion and came up the stairs to investigate," Josh said. "I think he would have killed us both if he'd had more time."

He leaned back, tired from talking, looking wrung out at the memory of what had happened. I rested my head on the back of the chair, realizing I was tired too. A knock on the door brought me upright.

Wyatt jumped to his feet and relaxed when Inspector Clarke walked in. He stayed near the door.

"I hope I'm not disturbing you," he said. "They told me at the nurse's station that Kate was here."

"Come in, join the party," said Josh.

"I thought you'd like an update," said Clarke, sitting on the chair next to Josh's bed.

"Did you catch the man who attacked us?" I asked.

"No, not yet. But we will. Wyatt put in a valiant effort to apprehend him but we lost him. However, I do have some news. We have a witness who saw a man push Nick onto the rails at the Tube station. She's made a statement and given us a description. We're reasonably sure that it's the same man who attacked you, based on your preliminary description."

He paused when there was a tap at the door. An orderly poked her head in. "Tea trolley. Anyone want tea and biscuits?"

Wyatt raised his head so expectantly I had to say yes. Anyway, I needed caffeine and sugar to stay awake. The woman poured four cups of tea that looked strong enough to clean drains with. She handed them round and left a plate full of custard creams and digestive biscuits on Josh's bedside table. For a minute, an appreciative silence filled the room while everyone sipped their tea.

Less numb now than I had been the previous morning, I felt the pain of Nick's death more acutely. The man who'd come to my apartment had come with intent to kill, there was no doubt. With

Nick, he had succeeded.

"This man, who we think is Rebecca's ex-boyfriend, wanted to get rid of Nick and me because he thinks we know who he is?"

"That's the assumption, yes." Clarke said. "We'll need you and Josh to give us a detailed description of the man."

I thought back, trying to remember what the man looked like. Light blonde hair, medium height, but I hadn't really seen his face. He'd been wearing a scarf when I'd spotted him at the Tube station street. In the darkened hallway, I'd hardly seen him at all.

"Wyatt got a good look and that's going to help us," said Clarke.

"What next then?" I asked.

Clarke drained the last of his tea and put the cup down on the table. "I have to get back to the station. I'll keep you posted on the investigation. I'm going to have Wyatt stay here until you're both released. Kate, where will you go? I don't think you should be in your apartment by yourself yet, until we can get more information on our assailant."

"My brother's coming to get me later this morning." Suddenly, I remembered something. "But it's Rebecca's funeral tomorrow. I should be there."

"No way," said Clarke. "I'm sorry, but that's not a good idea, at many levels."

"Why?"

"You're hurt and can hardly stand up by yourself, for one thing. And the murderer could make an educated guess that you'd be there. It wouldn't be hard for him to have another go at you. No, I'd like you to be somewhere out of the way for a while."

"I'll go to my brother's in Oxford for a few days then. But you will stay in touch and let us know if you find the attacker, won't you?"

"Of course. I have your cell number. What about you, Josh? We can't rule out a repeat attack even on you, now that you can identify the man who did it."

"I'm going to Gloucestershire to stay with my parents until I can walk again," Josh said.

He looked at me. "This is going to make Alan very unhappy. His Montgomery project team is disintegrating."

Thinking of Alan and Montgomery reminded me of the business card and the scent of aftershave. I was sure now that I was wrong, but I might as well tell Clarke what I'd been thinking in the middle of the night.

"There was something I was going to call you about this morning," I said to him. "Last night, I realized that Peter Montgomery wears that aftershave, the one that had been in Rebecca's bathroom. I could still smell it on his business card."

Clarke looked thoughtful. "Do you have the card?"

I didn't have the card with me. It had been in my purse, which might be in my hospital room, although I couldn't recall seeing it.

"It can't be him, though, can it?" I asked. "Not if the man who attacked us is Rebecca's boyfriend?"

"I'd like to see the card," he said. "Can we go find it?"

"As long as you're happy to push my chair."

I patted Josh's hand. "I'll be back in a minute."

Clarke was silent for the trip to my room. I was quiet too, a little embarrassed about being wheeled along by him. He stood at the door while I pushed myself in and found the card in my purse.

"What do you think?" I asked, handing it to him. "Take a look at his name too. His middle initial is E, which could stand for Edward."

Clarke sniffed the card before staring at the print on it. "I think this is a good lead, Kate. Come on, I'll take you back to Josh's room. You can tell me what else you know about Montgomery."

I described Montgomery's company, and the contract for the new building. "He's too slick for my taste," I concluded. "But I could see him being Rebecca's boyfriend. He's good-looking. I suppose some would think him charismatic. And he has loads of money, which might explain the luxury apartment."

We reached Josh's room, where Clarke positioned my chair next to the bed. Josh pushed himself up on his pillows. "Well?"

"I'm going back to my office to follow up on this," said Clarke. "I know it sounds obvious, but let me know if either of you hear anything from Montgomery." He walked to the door. "I'll be in touch."

Josh lay back, with a grimace of pain.

"I should leave you to rest," I said, stroking his arm.

"No, please stay," he said. "I'd like you to stay, and so would Marmaduke."

I raised an eyebrow. "Marmaduke?"

Josh picked up the brown bear, rested it against his chest and closed his eyes. It was only a couple of minutes before he was asleep, the stuffed toy rising and falling to the rhythm of his breathing.

I wheeled my chair over to the window and looked out. The sky was crystalline, a vitreous blue so delicate it looked as though it could shatter at any moment. The sun shone small and pale as though unsure it was ready to come out of hiding, and a thin layer of frost coated the walkways. A clear wintry day was a welcome respite from the interminable weeks of rain.

On the other side of the road was an office block of steel and smoked glass, with miles of conduit snaking up and down the exterior. It looked as though the building had been turned inside out. The odd architectural design made me think of Bradley Cohen; I wondered what was happening there. Josh was right that the Montgomery project was losing its team, but I was sure Alan would pull in Laura and Jim.

A noise at the door disturbed my thoughts and woke Josh. Wyatt snapped to full alert but stood aside when he saw the couple in the doorway; a petite brunette dressed in tailored pants and a loose floral blouse, carrying a basket of fruit and a couple of magazines, and a man who could only be Josh's father. He had the same lean build, long legs, and light eyes.

"How's my boy today?" he asked, striding across the room to pat Josh gently on the shoulder.

"Don't touch his arm," exclaimed the woman, depositing the gifts on the bedside table. "It must hurt. Does it hurt, sweetheart?"

"Mum!" Josh succumbed to the kisses she planted on his forehead.

"Hi, Dad," he grinned. "This is Kate."

I wheeled my chair back towards the bed, and Josh's mother leaned over to give me a hug.

"You poor girl." Tears welled in her eyes. "Josh told us some of what happened when we came in last night, but not everything. He was still coming round from the anesthetic. Are you all right, my dear? It must have been terrifying for you. Just look at the bruises on your face."

"Mum, not too many questions. Kate's still tired. I can tell you more..."

He was interrupted by the arrival of another woman, carrying a box of chocolates and a helium balloon that said Get Well Soon.

"Aunt Tilda. What a surprise." Josh threw a quick look at me and pulled a face.

"Sorry, I wasn't expecting the whole tribe," he whispered.

"I should go actually," I said. "I need to get showered and dressed before Leo comes."

"Please don't leave because of us," said Josh's mother. "I'm sure Josh would rather have you here than us anyway."

"Mum, really..." Josh started.

"Truly, I don't want to keep my brother waiting. It was lovely to meet you all." I leaned over to squeeze Josh's hand. "I'll talk to you soon. Take care of yourself."

Wyatt took the handles of the wheelchair. "I'll take you back to your room," he said.

I turned to wave goodbye to Josh but he was hidden by the figures of his parents and his aunt. I wondered how long it would be before I saw him again.

An hour later, I sat in the lobby of the hospital, waiting for Leo. In the shower, I'd been able to examine the bruises on my legs and torso, explosions of color against my pale skin. The hot water had woken me up, but hadn't dissolved the hazy, disconnected feeling I'd had since the attack. I looked at the people around me. Two of them had auras. I felt sad for them.

I was already missing Josh. Tears pushed at my eyes. I tried talking to Wyatt to distract myself but he answered in polite monosyllables. I wondered if he was impatient to get back to his real job, which probably didn't involve babysitting weepy women. Then I saw Leo coming towards me across the lobby. Happy to see him, I smiled and waved.

He bent to kiss me on the cheek.

"We have to stop meeting in hospitals," he said. "It's becoming a bad habit."

CHAPTER THIRTY-FIVE

The next day, I slept in late, watching television with Aidan, who was still off school recuperating. My pain had quickly diminished to a pervasive stiffness and soreness. I took a nap in the middle of the afternoon, missing a call from Inspector Clarke. When I called him back an hour later, I only reached his voicemail.

That evening, Leo arrived home a little earlier than usual, loaded with bags of groceries. "Olivia's coming for dinner."

"So I'm the third wheel on a date? I'd be happy to take my dinner upstairs and stay out of the way."

"Rubbish. I want your opinion. See if you like her. Oh, and she's interested in talking with you about your experience with the aura."

"You told her about it?" I was astonished. "And she still wants to meet me? Your crazy sister?"

"It might be helpful," he said. "She'll understand it better than I can. We'll let the boys eat and watch television in Aidan's room."

I thought about changing for dinner but the effort seemed too much. Instead, I kept on my grey sweatpants and black cardigan and pulled my hair up into a ponytail.

I regretted not trying a little harder when Leo's guest arrived. Olivia wore an ivory silk dress and leather flats. Her glossy black hair was cut in a sleek shoulder-length bob with heavy bangs that grazed perfectly arched eyebrows and kohl-lined eyes. Gold bangles encircled her arm. She certainly didn't look like a psychology professor, not my vision of one at least.

As we sat in the living room, I sipped my wine and looked at

Olivia over the rim of my glass.

"I'm happy to meet you, Kate." Her voice was soft and velvety. "I'm very sorry about the assault. That must have been a ghastly experience."

"Thanks," I said, shifting in my chair. I didn't do well with overt sympathy. It made me feel as though I was fake, unworthy of the attention.

"From what Leo has told me, you've had a rough few weeks. I hope you don't mind that he told me about the aura." She leaned forward. "It's fascinating."

Gabe poked his head round the door. "Can I get something to eat? I'm starving."

He slipped through the living room and into the kitchen, where I heard the fridge open and close, followed by the clink of plates. I hoped he hadn't heard Olivia's comment about the aura. I waited until he walked back with a plate piled high with cheese, ham and a packet of chips. Leo didn't comment on the quantity of food. I realized he was looking at Olivia. He had a wistful expression on his face, which meant I should be nice to her. I didn't want to mess up any chance he had of being with a partner again. Even one that seemed to be channeling her inner Cleopatra.

When Gabe's footsteps on the stairs faded and Aidan's bedroom door slammed shut, I told Olivia about the aura sightings. Before I knew it, I was pouring out the whole story of Rebecca, her murder, and the attack in my apartment. Olivia appeared to be listening intently, sipping her wine from time to time.

"And this all started after you saw your mother in Tuscany?"

"Yes, I have to believe that there's a connection, but I don't understand it," I said.

"I think it's something to do with Toby," said Leo suddenly. He'd been uncharacteristically quiet.

"What about Toby?" asked Olivia.

"Kate, you told me that Mum mentioned Toby when you, er, talked with her?" he said, looking with embarrassment at Olivia. "This is all beyond the scope of comprehension for my fact-based mind."

Leaning forward, Olivia looked at me questioningly. "Did she?"

I nodded. "She said she was with Toby now and happy. Something like that."

"Leo told me what happened to Toby." Olivia paused, leaned

back in her armchair, and crossed one slim leg across the other. "He also said that you apparently shouldered the burden of guilt for his death. Did you? Do you feel that it was your fault that he died?"

"Yes," I said. The word came out far louder than I'd intended.

Leo put his glass down on the coffee table. "But it wasn't, Katie," he said quietly. "You said often that it was your fault, even to the point of making Mum and Dad angry with you for keeping on about it. You must remember? At the funeral, you told the vicar that you'd killed Toby. Caused quite a stir, I have to say."

"I was supposed to be watching him. It was my fault he drowned." I picked at a loose thread on my cardigan and watched the wool unravel, leaving a small hole in the black fabric. My skin showed through, white as ice.

"You were only ten years old!" Leo exclaimed. "And don't you think Mum and Dad felt they were the ones at fault? For leaving Toby with Mrs. Parry, for not being there when it happened? They tore apart every decision, every action, and they lived with "what if?" every day after that one. Kate, they took complete responsibility for what happened. And so did Mrs. Parry. She suffered from depression for years, you know."

I tried to speak but my throat had closed up. Leo patted me on the knee.

"I'm sorry, sweetheart. I don't want to upset you, but it's important for you to know that Mum and Dad never blamed you, ever. I know they never talked about it all very much and maybe in that they were at fault, but I know how much it upset them to remember. We all fell into the habit of silence."

He glanced at his watch, and stood up. "I'm going to finish getting dinner ready."

When he'd left the room, Olivia seemed happy to sit quietly sipping her wine. After a while, she put the glass down. "Kate, from what I understand from Leo, you blame yourself for your mother's death too."

I didn't want to talk about it. It was all too raw and painful to even think about.

"I'm sorry Olivia, but I can't discuss that."

Olivia shrugged, a slight upward movement of one silk-clad shoulder. "That's okay. I'm sorry if I'm interfering. I'll go and help Leo get dinner ready."

She stood up, smoothing imaginary creases from her dress with the palms of her hands. I watched her. So graceful, self-confident, just the kind of woman Leo deserved.

"I appreciate your trying to help," I said. "Perhaps some other time when I'm feeling a bit more stable."

"Of course. I can understand how difficult it must be for you. I hope you can at least feel some comfort in the fact that you saved Aidan?"

I looked up at her. "I suppose so."

"That's good."

She turned towards the kitchen.

"Olivia," I called her back. "Why do you think I can see these auras? What have they got to do with Toby and my mother?"

Olivia adjusted one of her bracelets, turning it around her wrist. "My opinion is that your mother's death triggered a revival of guilt about Toby. Add to that your conviction that you were to blame for the car accident that killed your mother, and you were buried under an avalanche of remorse. Think of the way your mother appeared to you, in a car that caused you injuries. That was no coincidence. It's almost as though you wanted to be the one that had been killed by the car, not your mother."

My skin chilled, and my heart fluttered as though in despair.

"You don't believe I saw her up there?"

"Oh yes, I'm sure you did. Encounters with loved ones who have passed on are not as unusual as you'd think. But I believe you conflated the run-in with the car and the encounter with your mother in your mind."

The room was quiet apart from the clink of dishes in the kitchen.

"The auras?" I asked. "What about them?"

"Not everything can be explained in the context of what we think of as the real world," she said. "There are mysteries we can't explain with science, although we have a pretty good stab at them. There's a scientific basis for energy fields around us, for example. Some people can see them, the vast majority can't."

"Will I always be able to see auras? Will they go away?"

A frown passed over her face. "I don't know. I should go help Leo with the cooking,"

Leaning back in my armchair, I thought about what she'd said. From the kitchen came the clatter of crockery and a low murmur of voices. When my cell phone buzzed, I noticed it was a London number. It was probably Inspector Clarke.

"Hello?" I answered.

"Kate, how are you?"

It took a minute to place the voice. It was Peter Montgomery.

"Fine," I said, my automatic reply to the question, a typically British response. I'd once had a friend from Russia who took the question literally and would launch into a detailed description of her health and mental status in response. But a monosyllabic answer seemed appropriate under the circumstances.

"Can you give me a couple of minutes? I have some questions," he said.

"Questions about what?" I couldn't imagine any reason why he would want to talk to me. "If it's about the project, I don't know anything. I haven't been at work for a week."

"Why not?"

"It's complicated."

I stood up and stretched my legs, which were cramped from sitting down.

"I want to talk about Rebecca," he said. There was something in the way he said her name that made me know indisputably that he had been her lover.

"You were the last one to see her," he continued.

I paused, my skin prickling. I could be talking with a murderer. I probably shouldn't be talking with him at all, but I was curious. "I wasn't the last one to see her," I said. "As far as I can tell, you were. You must have been there when she died."

There was a pause so long that I thought we'd been cut off.

"I wasn't there," he said finally. "Why would you think I was?"

I hesitated. I shouldn't say anything to tip him off.

"Listen, never mind," I said. "I really can't help you because I don't know anything. I should go."

"No, please. Give me a minute. I need to know what happened to her."

"Ask the police. I'm sure they'll be glad to talk to you about it."

"The police? Why are they involved? It was an accident, from what I heard, wasn't it?"

Damn. I really shouldn't have said anything. "I don't know. I should go."

"Wait. There's something else. It's important. I need to know if she made up her own mind to break things off, or if you had anything to do with it. Did you encourage her to leave me?"

"Of course not. I didn't even know who you were. She told me her boyfriend's name was Edward."

I thought I heard a sigh. "Just something we came up with to keep everything under the radar. It's my middle name. She couldn't go around telling anyone she was dating someone called Peter. They would have guessed it was me. That doesn't matter now. I can't believe she left me. It was on the Saturday morning before... before she died. She told me she was embarrassed that she was living off my money, tired of not being able to tell anyone about us. She told me she needed time to think things through, that she could see our relationship was going nowhere and it was time for her to start living her own life. And that she was going to Italy with you."

"I didn't tell her to do anything," I said. "I'm hanging up now." I ended the call, sank down on a chair, catching my breath. My heart pounded. I needed to call Clarke right away to let him know that Peter Montgomery had been Rebecca's boyfriend. It seemed incredible. Irrationally, while I dialed Clarke's number, I thought of how upset Alan would be when he found out his most important client was a killer.

CHAPTER THIRTY-SIX

The following morning, I sat in a meeting room in the Oxford police headquarters. Inspector Clarke was on his way from London, apparently; he wanted to hear first hand about my phone call with Montgomery even though I'd made a statement to a WPC the evening before. Through the glass walls of the room, I watched a group of about ten men and women writing up reports, peering at computer screens, or standing around drinking coffee. It was like watching television with the sound off.

I stifled a yawn and took a gulp of the coffee from a thick china cup bearing the logo of Oxford's Division Two football team. An almost imperceptible tremor ran through the larger room; eyes lifted towards the door, then shifted back to computer screens. Clarke had arrived. I watched him shake hands with a detective wearing a crumpled blue suit before crossing the area to the meeting room. He looked tired, with dark circles under his eyes and a five o'clock shadow even though it was before noon.

He slid his arms from his raincoat as he pushed the door open and came in, carrying cold air with him.

"How are you, Kate? I'm surprised to see you up and about so soon. You have some coffee? Good."

He took the chair on the opposite side of the table, put his briefcase on one corner and settled back into his seat.

"Did you arrest Montgomery?" I asked.

"No. He's out of the country. In Switzerland, in fact."

"Did he run away?" I was shocked.

Clarke smiled. "Not exactly. His secretary said this was a

planned business trip. He must have called you from Zurich. I have your statement here. Can you take a look?"

He handed it to me. I scanned the text, thinking it was strange to see my own words in print like that, right down to the 'er's and 'um's that I didn't realize I used so much. I nodded. "That's what he said, yes. But, I'm confused. If Montgomery was Rebecca's lover, then who is the man who attacked me?"

Clarke steepled his fingers under his chin and looked at me. "That's the big question and the main reason I'm here. Did Montgomery say anything at all that would hint at an accomplice?"

"He didn't, but it's possible that he would have someone do his dirty work for him, isn't it? He has plenty of money."

"Maybe."

"But I don't think this man, whoever he is, was the one who killed Rebecca," I said. I'd wrestled with this all night, lying on the sofa bed in Leo's study, unable to sleep.

Clarke raised his eyebrows. "Why not?"

"Why would Rebecca let a stranger into her apartment? There was no sign of forced entry or of a struggle, no damage except to the coffee table. Whereas, in my flat, the man left plenty of evidence of a fight. I'm sure Montgomery killed her himself, but he hired the other man to go after me and Nick."

"The problem with that theory is that Montgomery was at a wedding in Hastings with his wife and kids from Saturday evening until late Sunday. Then he drove straight to Heathrow for the flight to Zurich."

"He was there for the whole time? He could have slipped out to see Rebecca. It's only an hour and a half from Hastings to London."

Clarke shook his head. "Even with priority security and boarding, he'd have had to be at the airport at about the time that Rebecca was killed."

In the long silence that fell between us, I was aware of a low buzzing noise from the fluorescent light fixture overhead, and the gentle hum of traffic on the road below. If not the man in the black coat or Montgomery, then who?

"Gary?" I asked.

Clarke shook his head. "Rebecca died some time between five and seven on that Sunday evening, maybe eight at the latest. Gary showed me validated tickets proving he and Nick were on the fast train from Brussels that got into St. Pancras at 8.25pm. No way Gary could have done it."

I propped my chin in my hands, elbows on the table, fighting the urge to sleep. I wanted Montgomery to be guilty. I despised him for having an affair with Rebecca. I'd thought a lot about what he'd said about Rebecca changing since she met me. I remembered when she'd make a joke about loving money and had then fallen silent as though wondering if money was really enough. Was she really planning to change her lifestyle and leave Montgomery? I wished she'd had a chance to do that. I wished she'd told me what she was planning.

A young man in a leather jacket knocked on the glass door and poked his head in.

"Sorry to interrupt, Matthew, but we just got the message about that ID you've been waiting for."

He came in to hand a slip of paper to Clarke, closed the door quietly behind him, leaving the two of us in a soft shell of silence. Clarke read the message. "Good, good," he murmured.

"Something to do with the case?"

"Yes, Gary, Nick's partner, told me that he saw a man going up to Rebecca's apartment about a month ago. An older man, not the boyfriend. He's still very cut up about Nick, of course, and it's taken him a few days to come forward with this. But, as there appears to be a link between Rebecca's death and Nick's, he said he'll do whatever he can to help. He's coming into the London station tomorrow to work on the composite facial image."

"Do you trust Gary?" I asked. "Doesn't it seem convenient that he's coming up with this picture now?"

"He's motivated to find Nick's killer," Clarke said. "It makes sense to me. More often than not, witnesses don't come forward unless they have a personal interest in a case. There's an understandable reluctance to get involved. Some are nervous around police officers, others worry about how much time it might take. But when the victim is a family member, a lover or a good friend, then people open up. They want to talk about the person they knew, to make sure the police understand why it's important to find the killer."

Standing up, Clarke stared out of the window. I thought about Peter Montgomery and Rebecca. According to Montgomery, she'd broken things off between them on Saturday morning, yet I'd seen on her Sunday and she hadn't said a word about it. In fact, she'd told me she was seeing her boyfriend on Sunday evening. That was why she'd canceled our movie outing. Why would she lie?

Strictly speaking, I thought, she hadn't told me she was seeing Edward on Sunday. I'd assumed that she was, and she hadn't denied it. Which meant one of two things. One was that she'd decided she didn't want to go to a movie with me. I dismissed that idea. All she had to do was say she didn't want to go. The other was that she was seeing someone else that evening, someone she couldn't tell me about. A new boyfriend? It was possible. Perhaps she'd found someone else; that was her motivation for dumping Montgomery. But then why wouldn't she tell me about him? For some reason, she had kept the identity of her Sunday evening visitor a secret.

"Nice view," Clarke said turning round and leaning on the windowsill. "But I never liked Oxford."

"Why not?"

"I don't know, it's very clubby. Exclusive, as in excluding anyone who isn't part of the university system."

"That's funny. I'm not sure my brother would agree with you."

His cheeks flushed red with embarrassment. "Sorry, I forgot he's a professor here. Well, if he's like you, I'm sure he's a good guy."

It was my turn to blush, and I bent my head over an imaginary speck of dust on my jeans.

Clarke pushed himself away from the windowsill and came back to his seat.

"Montgomery will be back in London in two days. I'll bring him in for questioning then, but I don't think he's our killer."

"We'll see," I said. "So many secrets." I was still thinking of the ambiguity about Rebecca's Sunday evening commitment.

"Everyone has secrets," he replied. "In my line of work, you come to think of it as normal."

"Not everyone."

"I think you do," he said. I felt warmth flood my cheeks.

"I don't believe that you killed Rebecca or Nick, but I am certain that you're hiding something. If it's something that could help the case, I'd appreciate your honesty."

"It's not. There's nothing."

"Okay. Will you come into the station tomorrow afternoon to look at Gary's sketch?"

"Of course. How's he doing? Gary?"

"Not so well. I can only imagine his pain," said Clarke. "To find someone to love and to imagine spending your life with him, only to lose him like that. It's devastating."

My heart vibrated with the emotion in his voice. And I knew what his secret was.

"Does everyone know?" I asked. "About you?"

A momentary look of surprise crossed his face. And then he laughed. "Not everyone. Just those that need to know. My boss, my assistant, a few others. And now you."

"Why do you need to keep it a secret?"

"I don't," he said. "But I don't feel the need to go round informing everyone either." He checked his watch. "I have to get back to London. Take it easy. And let me know if you think of anything at all that might help. I'll be in touch, of course."

I watched while he stood up and put his coat on, noted the way he did up the buttons, and pulled the collar up. Every movement was precise and efficient. I supposed that made him a good detective, organized, calm. He moved around from behind the desk, briefcase in hand, and paused to look at me for a second.

"Be careful. I'll see you soon." He smiled, but I couldn't reciprocate. And then he was gone and I was alone in the glass-walled room.

I pulled on my coat and scarf and made my way through the busy police station to the front entrance. Under heavy, piercing rain, I strode quickly to the bus stop. I could have called Leo or Olivia to come to fetch me, but I was content to be out and about and by myself for a while. As I passed a fish and chip shop, the enticing smell of frying oil and vinegar made me realize I was hungry.

The warm, steamy interior was a welcome respite from the biting cold. An Indian woman, wearing a green and yellow sari underneath a blue anorak, waited for her order. She was listening to an iPod, the telltale white cables dangling from her ears. She smiled, but it wasn't clear if the smile was meant for me or was in response to something she was listening to.

While I waited for a small order of chips, the door opened with the jangle of a bell, and a blast of cold air. A middle-aged man went straight to the counter, almost pushing me aside. He was talking to himself and banging his leg with a rolled-up umbrella. His jeans and lumberjack jacket were worn and dirty. He also had an aura. When he saw me staring at him, he bared his teeth at me. I envisaged him dying in an alley somewhere, hungry and freezing in the middle of the night.

I handed the shopkeeper some money. "Can you give him a double order of whatever he'd like, and a carton of milk?" I asked him.

"Whatever you say, miss."

The man took the food and headed for the door. He turned his head very slightly and growled "thanks" before exiting and slamming the door behind him.

CHAPTER THIRTY-SEVEN

"You need to call Josh," Olivia said over breakfast the next day. "He'll want to know about your call with Montgomery." She'd been staying at Leo's, driving him to work in the morning, while I made breakfast for the boys and took them to school. For a few days, the routine had been surprisingly pleasurable, but I was beginning to feel the need to get back to London. I missed Josh, I missed my job. I wanted to resume some sort of normal life.

My cellphone rang while I was putting my plate in the sink. I thought it might be Jack. He'd tried to reach me a couple of times, but I'd missed his calls. To my surprise, it was Alan.

"Kate. When are you coming back to work?"

"You want me back?"

"Want isn't exactly the word I'd use. But I need you. We still have work to do. I can't do it all myself."

"Okay," I said. I was ready. I assumed that Jack was the cause of Alan's change of heart. I was grateful; I'd take Jack out for lunch as soon as he was available. "But I may need time off occasionally to deal with some things related to the murder inquiry, and other issues. If you can handle that, I can start again tomorrow."

"Hold my feet to the fire, why don't you? You'll be asking for a raise next."

"Well, actually..."

"Just come on back and get some work done. Then we can talk."

"I'll see you in the morning."

I was up to my elbows in dishwater when the phone rang again, dancing around on the countertop. I leaned over to see who was calling. It was Josh. I rushed to pick up the phone and it slipped out of my soapy hands, slid along the counter and balanced precariously for a second before tipping over the edge. I caught it with my foot, breaking its fall before it hit the tile floor. Wiping my hands on my jeans, I picked it up. It was still intact and working.

"Everything all right?" asked Josh. "It sounded as though you were playing football with the phone."

"Well, I dropped you but then I caught you," I said. "The phone, that is."

"I was thinking of coming to Oxford to see you, if you're up to it?"

"Of course. But are you? Your injuries were far worse than mine."

He told me the doctor had signed him off the day before, said it was okay for him to walk, but not too much.

"I love my parents," he said. "But I need to get out for a while. I'm missing you. And there's something I want to talk to you about."

We agreed that I'd meet him at the station at three that afternoon.

I spent the rest of the day cleaning and shopping, and prepared dinner for the family. It was the least I could do to thank Leo and Olivia for looking after me. I washed my favorite jeans and shirt, polished my boots, and blow-dried my hair. Stepping outside, I took a deep breath. The weather had changed in the past few days, the rain and mist giving way to clear skies. It was very cold, but I preferred that to the rain.

When Josh came through the ticket barrier, my heart fluttered. I felt warm from head to toe. We hugged, our heavy wool coats getting in the way.

"Do you want to go for a coffee to warm up?" he asked.

The cafe was crowded, the tables piled with open laptops and steaming mugs; a faint aroma of unwashed clothes mingled with the smell of coffee. A group of students in one corner appeared to have set up an informal debate club, arguing loudly about climate change and population growth. At a table nearby, a professorial-looking type talked earnestly with three young women who jotted words in spiral-bound notebooks.

Josh bought us both coffees and scones while I found a table for two next to the window. For a few minutes, we talked about Josh's doctor visits and how he was feeling. He looked good. The pallor was gone. He seemed to be walking well, apart from a slight limp.

"What did you want to talk to me about?" I asked.

He reached over to take my hand in his. "I missed you so much. It's time to get back to London so we can spend some time together."

I smiled. That's how I felt too.

"But you did say there was something you wanted to talk about?" I reminded him.

He glanced around, as though checking that no one was listening.

"Remember your last full day at work, when I was stuck in Alan's office for hours?"

"Hmm. I think so. What was going on?"

"Alan and Jack told me that there was some financial risk to continuing with the Montgomery project. They didn't elaborate, but I've had plenty of time to do a bit of research. And I talked with my Dad. He used to be a corporate attorney, so he knows about this stuff."

"Okay," I said slowly.

"Montgomery Group is probably the tenth largest real estate developer in London right now. Maybe a little higher in the rankings if you take into account their foreign investments. Five years ago, they weren't even in the top twenty. They've been gobbling up real estate in the city and elsewhere in Britain, taking over foreclosed buildings, investing in new ones, and improving some of their older properties."

"That sounds expensive," I said.

Josh nodded. "Very. A lot of those projects were financed with five- to seven-year financing deals, and many are coming up to be refinanced right now. But there's no money available. The banks have had their fingers burned and they're not ladling out money the way they used to."

"Which means Montgomery will default on some of their loans?" I asked.

"Exactly. Some very big loans. It's not just Montgomery, of course. A bunch of other developers are in the same boat. There's roughly two hundred and eighty billion pounds' worth of real estate debt due to mature in the next year to eighteen months and some of the analysts believe that about a third of that could become delinquent. There are a lot of fortunes about to be lost."

I sipped my coffee, which tasted burned. "So what does that have to do with Bradley Cohen exactly?"

Josh ran his finger around the rim of his cup, glanced around the cafe and leaned in towards me. "Montgomery represents nearly fifty percent of Bradley Cohen's revenues for this year."

"That's crazy, Josh. Alan always said that we'd never be dependent on one or two clients, that we'd always have a mixed portfolio that would protect us from risk if any single company failed to pay us."

"I know. That's what I thought too. But wait until you hear this. It was Rebecca who told them-- Alan and Jack-- about the state of Montgomery's finances. She told them completely off the record that the budget Peter Montgomery had given us for the development on the Islington building was outside the range of acceptable risk."

"Huh? What does the range of acceptable risk mean?"

"Well, any property developer has to analyze the total return for each asset. How much rent they can charge, for example, and what it costs to run the asset, with property taxes, utilities, security, whatever. And they try to project the value of the final disposition to make sure that it is a sound investment."

"Explain 'final disposition'?"

"The ultimate sale of the property. So they calculate how long they should hang on to it and what it will be worth if and when they sell."

"Was that part of Rebecca's job? I knew she was responsible for budgets but didn't realize there was so much more to it."

"I'm sure she worked closely with other managers in the company, but she certainly understood the risk of continuing with the project, both for Montgomery and for Bradley Cohen," Josh continued. "She was sure they would run out of money before the building could be leased and start to generate revenues. And if Montgomery ran out of money, then we wouldn't get paid."

"So what happened when she told us her concerns? We didn't pull out of the project?"

"Apparently not. Did Rebecca say anything to you about any of this?"

"No, nothing. I would have told you if she had."

I thought back. She and I hadn't talked about work much at all. I'd told her a little about what I did, but she'd never really described her job. She said she liked it, that she enjoyed the challenge. But that was all.

"And the vast majority choose to ignore scientific fact," shouted one of the students, slamming his fist on his table, pulling me back to the present.

"So should we be worried?" I asked Josh. "Are our jobs at risk? Alan called me this morning, asking me to come back. He said there's loads of work to do. Of course, we do have other clients apart from Montgomery, so maybe he meant that I'd be working on some of those."

"He told me the same thing," Josh said. "For now, at least, I think the company is safe and solvent. But losing the Montgomery project would take a serious toll."

"Talking of Montgomery," I said. "He called me." I told him what he'd said. When I'd finished, Josh looked stunned. "So he was Rebecca's boyfriend. Did he kill her?"

"Inspector Clarke thinks not. He has an alibi for the time that Rebecca died."

I sipped my coffee. "I wanted him to be the killer. I really dislike him."

"I suppose being an awful human being doesn't make you a criminal."

We sat quietly for a minute.

"Er, how's the aura thing going?" he asked after a while. "Any more sightings?"

"Yep. Still there, not that it's doing me any good."

"You saved Aidan," he said. "That has to count for something."

"But not Rebecca and not Nick."

"No."

I invited Josh to come to Leo's for dinner, but he said his mum would kill him if he didn't get back home soon. Finishing our coffee, we linked arms for the walk back to the station. Now he'd been out for a while, his limp seemed more pronounced and he looked tired.

"When will I see you again?" I asked.

"Soon. I told Alan I'd come back to work in about a week."

The train was at the platform when we reached the station and I was irrationally annoyed. Trains ran late all the time. Why not today, to give me a few more minutes with Josh? I knew he needed to go home, but I was reluctant to let him leave. He made me feel safe, dispelled my doubts, and made me believe that one day I would be able to forget the trauma of Rebecca's death and the attack at my apartment. But there the train was, with a conductor walking along the platform, slamming the doors closed. Josh got into the nearest carriage and turned back to wave goodbye. I watched until the train disappeared around a bend in the tracks.

CHAPTER THIRTY-EIGHT

The following morning, after an early start, I got to the office just before nine. Annie waved at me from the reception desk, looking pleased to see me. I'd chat with her later. For now, I wanted to get to my desk quickly, to demonstrate my good intentions to Alan.

He'd left a sticky note on my computer screen telling me to go see him as soon as I arrived. With some trepidation, I walked to his office.

"Come in," he said. "Bloody mess this has been, losing you and Josh at the same time."

"I'm doing much better, thank you," I said, smiling sweetly.

He flushed. "Well, I'm sorry about that attack in your apartment, and not just because it's fouling up our projects. You look okay. How's Josh?"

"Good. He's looking forward to being back next week. So, what do you want me to work on?" I hesitated. "Is the Montgomery project still going ahead?"

"Of course it is," he said. "Montgomery might be a jerk, but we can lower our standards to work with him."

"What makes you so sure he's a jerk?"

Alan raised his hands. "Gossip. Rumor. Apparently, he was having an affair with that young woman who was his Financial Director."

"News does get around quickly," I said. "I only found out about that a few days ago."

"Yeah, well, the police have been crawling around here, asking everyone questions, wasting time. Bloody inconvenient."

"They do have a murderer to catch," I said.

Alan muttered something under his breath.

"I'm glad the project is still on," I said. "Although Josh mentioned a problem with Montgomery's finances."

I braced myself for Alan to rage about confidentiality of information or something. Instead, I saw him looking over my shoulder. I turned to see Jack in the doorway. Elegant as ever in his bow tie and expensive suit, he took a seat next to me.

"Kate, my dear, how are you doing? I'm so sorry about the attack in your apartment. Dreadful. I hope you're recovering? Have they identified the man who did it?"

"No. But they're confident they'll find him. The sooner the better. He's a lunatic. He killed Rebecca and Nick, and hurt Josh. I'd like to snap the cuffs on him myself."

Jack patted the back of my hand. "Very understandable. But let the police do their job. We don't want you to put yourself in more danger. Are you sure you should be here? Don't you need more time to recuperate?"

"Oh, I'm doing so much better. I'm looking forward to working again. Thank you both for letting me come back."

"Well, if you're sure," Jack said. "You shouldn't overdo things."

"Kate's young and she can handle it," interrupted Alan. "Speaking of which, we have lots to do and no time to sit around here talking. Here you are, Kate."

He handed me a piece of paper. "Those are the project codes. Check the status report for each one, create an action list and prioritize. You know what to do."

I stood up, excited to be back, thrilled to be needed. And I was relieved to hear that Alan wasn't concerned about Bradley Cohen's finances. Perhaps everyone had initially overreacted, or maybe Josh had misconstrued what Alan had told him.

When I got to the door, I remembered something. "Alan, I promised Inspector Clarke that I'd go into the station some time today. It shouldn't take long."

Alan frowned. "Really? What now?"

"He wants me to look at a sketch of a man seen visiting Rebecca. A neighbor saw him on the stairs apparently. It will only take a few minutes. I'll take a short lunch break and be right back."

"OK. I hope this investigation winds up soon. It's taking up far too much of your time."

The morning passed in a blur of activity. Seeing that we'd fallen behind on several of our client projects, I created worksheets listing what needed to be done. Just before lunch, I was able to give Alan an updated project status and had started some catch-up work on a new shopping complex east of the City. As soon as that was done, I took a cab to the police station. Clarke wasn't there, but a constable showed me the sketch that Gary had worked on. It was a good likeness of someone, I was sure, but not of anyone I recognized. Although I thought he resembled someone I knew or had seen somewhere, I couldn't work out who it was. Rather irritated by the time I'd wasted, I hurried back, detouring to Alan's office, where he and Jack were poring over blueprints spread out on the desk.

"Just wanted to let you know I'm back," I said. "It only took thirty minutes. I'll stay a bit later this evening."

"Did you finger the bastard?" Alan asked.

I shrugged. "No, he looked familiar, but I didn't recognize him. Maybe it will come to me later."

The afternoon passed quickly. Alan called me at six to tell me he was on his way to a dinner meeting and would see me in the morning. I thought I heard him mumble 'thank you for your help today' but that seemed so unlikely that I decided I was imagining it.

The overhead lights flickered as darkness gathered at the windows. A few team members dropped by to say goodnight.

"Good to have you back," said Laura. "You want to go out for a drink?"

"Tomorrow," I said. "I'm going to get a little more done here."

I listened to their voices fading as they walked away towards the elevators. There was something eerie about the empty office building. I'd worked late nights and weekends a few times before, but usually preferred to take my work home with me. I was glad to hear the sudden roar of a vacuum cleaner further up the hallway. At least the janitors were around. I decided to leave when they did.

"Kate."

I jumped, feeling a jolt of adrenaline coursing through my chest and stomach.

"God, Jack, you scared me."

He was standing in the doorway of my office, leaning against the doorjamb.

"I'm sorry," he said. "Why are you working so late? You should be resting, you know."

"I'm feeling good, really. And there's so much to catch up on." I glanced at the time. "But you're right, I should go home. I'm starving."

"Good, I'll walk down with you. You need to be taking more care of yourself after all you've been through."

I gathered up my papers and stuffed them into my briefcase.

"Stairs?" he asked.

"Elevator," I replied. "I'm tired and this case is heavy."

We walked to the end of the darkened hallway and waited for the elevator to arrive. I could still hear the vacuum cleaner, but no one was in sight. Jack was unusually quiet, so I tried to draw him out on the subject of an upcoming marathon. Questions about running usually elicited an enthusiastic response.

Once we were in the elevator, Jack leaned against the back wall and I looked at him curiously, wondering what was wrong with him. The lights recessed in the ceiling above him flattened the angularity of his cheekbones, casting a rubescent glow on his skin and hair.

I felt as though someone had punched me in the stomach. A short gasp escaped me and I tried to conceal it by coughing loudly. In this light, his resemblance to the man in Gary's sketch was obvious.

"Sorry," I said. "I hope I'm not getting sick."

He straightened up, giving me a quizzical look. "What's wrong?"

"Jack, I don't know how to tell you this, but you have an aura. You're going to die."

It wasn't true. There was no aura, but I wanted to distract Jack, find an excuse to use my phone.

"What?"

I felt in my pocket for my phone. "I'm calling for an ambulance."

"I don't know what the hell you're doing, Kate, but I don't need an ambulance."

Fumbling with my phone, I hit the speed dial for Clarke's number and got his voicemail.

"Emergency services?" I said. "I need help urgently at Bradley Cohen, in the lobby."

Jack was suddenly right next to me, yanking the phone from my hand. It tumbled to the floor. He stepped on it with the heel of his black, polished shoe.

"What are you playing at?" he said.

"You look terrible, Jack. I can see auras that predict death. Rebecca had one, and so did Nick. And you know they both died. You will too."

The elevator stopped in the lobby. This was my chance. I had to make a run for it. But when the doors opened, my exit was blocked by the man in the black wool coat.

"Get in, Ernie," Jack said, pressing the button for the garage in the basement.

The two men talked during the short ride down, but I couldn't hear the words for the roaring of the blood in my temples. My heart was trying to break out of my ribcage. When the elevator stopped, I inched towards the door. Making a run for it seemed like the only option. I swung my briefcase at Ernie's knees. Barely flinching, he slammed a gloved hand against my mouth.

"You're a hard person to kill, Kate," Jack said. "But I think this time we'll succeed. Put her in the car, Ernie."

Ernie dragged me out of the elevator. The garage smelled of oil and fuel, and was lit with orange lights that cast a creepy glow across the expanse of empty concrete. There were only three vehicles left, two Mercedes parked next to each other, and a van I thought must belong to the janitors. One of the Mercedes' was Jack's and the other was Alan's. Alan hated public transport, but sometimes used taxis to get to restaurants in town when he was meeting clients. Maybe that's what he'd done this evening.

Jack seemed to be consciously detaching himself from the scene, keeping a distance between himself and Ernie, refusing to look at me. So Ernie would do the dirty work while Jack kept his hands clean? That was what had happened before, I could see it all now. But why? Why would Jack need to kill Rebecca? And me.

I realized my thoughts were rambling. I needed to concentrate, to work out how to get out of this mess. Ernie, knife in hand, grabbed my arm, dragging me towards Jack's car.

"This won't work," I said to him quietly. "Jack will get away with everything and you'll be the one who gets arrested."

"Shut your mouth." He aimed a punch at the side of my head.

I staggered back against the car nearest to me. The alarm went off, strident and terrifying in the low-ceilinged space.

"Turn that off," Ernie yelled at Jack.

"I can't. It's Alan's car."

"Fuck," said Ernie, and pushed me towards the other Mercedes.

Jack clicked it open. Ernie threw me into the back seat. Something had to happen, I thought. Alan would come back. Someone would hear the alarm and come to investigate. Clarke would get my message in time.

But right now, it appeared that no miraculous rescue was coming my way. Pulling some handcuffs from a pocket, Ernie tried to clamp them on to my wrists, but I slid across the seat to the far side.

"Forget it," Jack said. "The alarm's going to attract attention. Let's get out of here."

Ernie slammed the door closed and got into the driver's seat. Jack sat on the passenger side. I tried to open the back door, but it was locked. I kicked the seat in front of me in frustration.

Ernie reversed out of the space and accelerated towards the exit. I slid over to the seat behind him, leaned forward, grabbed hold of his short dirty-blonde hair and yanked his head back against the headrest.

Jack reached over to slap my hands away, but I hung on, moved my fingers down to Ernie's neck, and squeezed the soft flesh. Ernie lifted his hands off the steering wheel, tried to peel my fingers off one by one. He used his knees to steer, but the car was weaving, coming dangerously close to the painted concrete pillars that supported the garage ceiling. Jack grabbed the steering wheel, but that only seemed to make things worse. Ernie eased up on the accelerator.

Jack undid his seat belt, turned around and clawed at me. "Jesus, Ernie, you should have tied her up."

I pressed hard on Ernie's windpipe. He gagged and coughed. Whether deliberately or accidentally, he suddenly accelerated. The car shot across the garage at an angle, clipped the side of a pillar, spun around and slid head-on into the pillar again. The impact threw me back in my seat and knocked the breath out of me. Ernie's head, freed of my grip, struck the window; blood flowed down the glass. Ernie slumped forward over the steering wheel. Jack threw his door open and jumped out. He ran across the garage towards the staircase that led back up to the lobby.

I was having trouble breathing and my neck hurt, but I scrambled between the seats and out through the passenger door. Ernie might be unconscious, but I didn't want to spend another second in the car with him.

I stumbled out of the car, heading for the exit. I needed to find a phone, call emergency services.

"Kate!"

I turned to see Jack sitting on the stairs that led to the lobby. One arm hung limply at his side.

"Kate. I need a doctor."

"You destroyed my phone, remember?"

Wary, I took a few steps towards him. He had a cut on his brow that dripped blood on to his starched white shirt. His blue bow tie was undone, a strip of crushed silk hanging around his neck. Wincing, he moved his good hand, found his cell phone in a pocket. He held it out towards me. "Please, call for an ambulance."

I stood still, ten yards away from him, leg muscles twitching, ready to run. He put the phone on the ground and kicked it towards me. "For Christ's sake, Kate. I could die here. I think I'm having a heart attack."

His face was ashen, starkly white against the red of the blood on his forehead. He didn't have an aura, but I didn't want to risk it. Whatever he'd done, he had been my friend. The phone was just out of reach. I dashed forward, retrieved it, backed up. After I'd made the call, I put the phone in my pocket.

He patted the step next to him. "Come and sit. I can't hurt you."

After hesitating for a few seconds, I accepted his invitation. My legs were wobbly, my knees felt like jelly. Sitting down seemed like a good idea. The coldness of the concrete seeped through my wool pants.

"Why, Jack? Why did you kill Rebecca?"

He shook his head. I couldn't tell if it was meant to be a denial or a sign that he was too beaten up and ill to talk. He clutched at his chest.

"I feel like I have a goddamn elephant sitting on me."

Taking off my jacket, I rolled it up and put it behind him. "Lean back," I advised. "The ambulance will be here soon."

He did as I suggested, and closed his eyes. After listening to his erratic breathing for a minute, I jumped to my feet, and pulled the phone from my pocket, trying to decide who else to call. The ambulance should have come by now. Just then, I heard a siren, distant at first and suddenly deafening as an ambulance appeared at the top of the ramp, washing the garage with blue and red light. With a squeal of tires, the vehicle pulled up behind me, disgorging two paramedics in yellow vests. One ran to the crashed car, the other towards Jack. Feeling sick, almost faint, I sat on the concrete floor, resting my head on my knees.

A hand on my shoulder made me jump. I looked up to see Alan staring down at me, with a look of utter confusion on his face. "What the hell is going on?"

He helped me to my feet just as two police cars screamed down the parking ramp, pulling to a halt feet away from where we stood. Inspector Clarke jumped out of one, while uniformed police officers surrounded the crashed car. Ernie was on a stretcher. A medic was giving Jack oxygen.

"Are you all right, Kate?" Clarke asked. "What happened here?"

"Jack and the man in the black coat tried to kidnap me. They forced me into that car." I pointed to the mangled Mercedes. "They were going to kill me."

Clarke's lips were set in a thin line as he turned towards Jack. Alan looked stunned. "What's going on? Why the fuck would Jack want to kill you?"

"It's a long story. I don't really know all of it yet."

We watched in silence while Jack was put on a gurney and rolled to the ambulance where Ernie already lay unconscious. A medic slammed the doors shut; the siren wailed as the vehicle sped away towards the exit with one of the police cars following closely behind.

Clarke came back to us. "I hope Jack makes it. He looked as though he was having a coronary."

"He'd better make it," said Alan. "I have a few questions to ask him."

"I do too," said Clarke. He looked at me. "You should probably go to the hospital to get checked out."

"Oh no. I've spent more than enough time in hospitals recently, thank you. I'll be okay."

"Good, then I'd like to hear what happened here."

"So would I," said Alan. "We can sit in my office. I need a drink."

The three of us took the elevator up to the second floor, where the vacuum cleaner was still going. The janitor waved to us over the din. I sank into the comfort of the luxurious leather visitor's chair in Alan's office, while he poured himself a whisky from a decanter on the credenza behind his desk. He waved the decanter in our direction, but the detective and I declined.

"Tell us what happened," instructed Clarke.

"Jack killed Rebecca," I started, stopping when he held his hand up.

"Whoa, wait right there. Did he tell you he did?"

"No, but… I'll start at the beginning, then you'll understand why I'm sure he did it."

Clarke nodded. Alan knocked back his glass of whisky and refilled it.

"I was working late," I began. "Jack came by my office. We chatted for a minute, he walked me to the elevator and we rode down to the lobby together. That's when I realized it was him. Because of the sketch that Gary provided of the man he'd seen on the stairway in Rebecca's building."

"But you'd seen the sketch before," said Clarke. "You saw it yesterday. You didn't recognize him then?"

I shook my head. "It was to do with the lighting. Rebecca's building is a very high-end house divided into three luxury apartments. The lighting in the hallways and stairwells comes from sconces on the walls. No cheap fluorescents or anything like that. You remember?"

Seeing his expression of confusion, I hurried on. "The sconces have dark red shades. The sketch showed that the man's hair had a reddish tint. And the lighting softened the contours of the face, smoothing out the age lines. Gary hadn't seen this man outside or under a different light, so he just described him as he saw him in that particular environment."

I paused, searching Clarke's face for any sign of understanding, but he sat still, sphinx-like.

"Gary said the man he saw was of medium height," I continued. "But Gary is what, six foot three or four? Most people look short to him. Even someone who is actually quite tall."

"Six feet," said Alan. "Jack's an inch taller than I am."

"Why would Jack be visiting Miss Williams' apartment?" asked Clarke. "Were they having an affair?"

I shook my head. "I can't imagine it was that. I tried asking Jack, but he wasn't in any condition to answer questions."

"So you recognized him as being the man in Gary's sketch. Then what happened?"

I told them about the man in the black coat getting into the elevator. "Jack called him Ernie," I said. "He's a brute. He manhandled me into the car."

The memory of it made my heart thump around in my chest. I recounted how I'd attacked Ernie and caused the car to crash into the pillar.

"Bloody hell." Alan had turned pale. "This is Jack, my partner, we're talking about. It doesn't seem possible."

"And you, Mr. Bradley, have no idea what might have happened between him and Miss Williams?" Clarke asked.

"I most certainly do not. And if he dies before he can tell us what was going on, I'm going to kill him myself."

Alan stood up to pour himself another whisky. He didn't drink it, just swirled it around in the glass, gazing at the amber liquid as though it might hold the answer to the mystery.

I didn't want Jack to die of a heart attack. More than anything I wanted him to explain everything, and I wanted him to be punished for killing Rebecca. Deep down, too, I still cared about him, whatever he'd done.

Clarke looked at his watch. "I should get back. I've got paperwork to fill out. I'd appreciate it if you could both accompany me to the station so that we can take statements."

"I don't have time..." Alan began. I shot him a warning glance. It was time for him to start taking this seriously.

He nodded. "All right."

CHAPTER THIRTY-NINE

Alan drove me back home after we'd been interviewed by a couple of police officers at the station. Wishing Josh were with me, I paced around the empty flat, my head buzzing with questions until I was exhausted. Finally, I found some ibuprofen, took two with a glass of wine, and went to bed. I didn't wake up until my cellphone rang at seven the next morning. It was Alan.

"Jack's fine," he said. "He had a panic attack. Combined with the injury to his head and his arm, he's feeling crappy, but he's going to be okay. They're keeping him in for another twenty-four hours for observation. He was moved from Accident and Emergency to the men's cardiac ward last night."

"How come you know all that? I thought they only talked to next of kin or something?"

"Jack and I signed consent forms when we formed the partnership." Alan's voice was raspy. If I didn't know better, I'd have thought he'd been crying. "Besides, he doesn't have any kin to speak of, apart from an estranged brother. I'm probably his closest friend."

That made me sad. I pushed the duvet back, pulled my knees up to my chest.

"I want to see him," I said. "I have to find out what happened."

"Take a ticket. Clarke's on his way in there now, apparently. That's what the nurse on duty told me. I asked when I could visit and she said late morning, maybe."

"Okay, I'll come into work soon. I'll go see him later."

"Don't be daft. Stay home. Rest. Work can wait."

I never thought I'd hear those words from Alan. I decided he must be in shock. When he rang off, I lay back on the pillows, trying to order my thoughts.

Three hours later, I stood at the door of Jack's room at St. Thomas's Hospital. He was sitting up in his bed, with a thick bandage around his head, and his arm in a sling. He managed a weak smile when he saw me. "Come in."

I pulled a plastic chair to the side of the bed. "Did you talk to Inspector Clarke this morning?"

"No, I pretended to be asleep. He'll be back soon enough, I'm sure." He fiddled with a loose thread on the sling. "I'm sorry, Kate. For everything."

"I don't understand any of it," I said. "Why did you kill Rebecca?"

"I didn't kill her. Not exactly. I don't really want to talk about it."

"You're going to have to talk at some point, Jack. The police will be back. And I think you owe me. The least you can do is explain."

He nodded, grimacing in pain.

"It was all about money," he said after a long pause. "As is the case with most of the world's ills. Montgomery is having financial problems. Rebecca Williams was the one who told me about it. She said she had a plan that would make sure we got paid for the work we'd been doing on the new Montgomery construction project. But she wasn't doing it out of the goodness of her heart."

I leaned forward to listen. His voice was quiet, not much above a whisper.

"She was expecting a kickback. She'd get us to the top of the list to be paid each month for the duration of the contract, and we'd pay a little extra on the side, directly to her. Five percent. She told me some cockamamy story about how she planned to split up with her boyfriend and needed another source of income to maintain the lifestyle to which she'd become accustomed.

"A week later, she called me. Told me to bring three thousand in cash to her flat. When I got there, she gave me a Montgomery Group check for the first payment against our contract."

"No!" I gasped. "Rebecca wouldn't do that."

Or would she? Rebecca had been willing to let Peter Montgomery pay for her luxury flat, had acquiesced to a relationship that would hurt his wife and his children. She'd lied to me, and others, about his name. Those weren't crimes, like accepting bribes, but it was an indication that she'd been willing to bend the rules to suit herself.

Jack eyed me wearily. "You're smart, but naive, Kate. Although, to an extent, you're right. A couple of weeks later, I went to see her again, with more cash in return for another check, or so I thought. When I got to her apartment, she said she was having second thoughts about taking the money and that she couldn't guarantee that we'd get paid another penny."

"So you killed her because she changed her mind?"

"No. She insisted that she couldn't go through with it, that she was sorry she'd ever mentioned it. She said she was planning to change jobs and move out of that apartment, and that she didn't care about the money any more.

"We argued. I said I'd go to Peter Montgomery and tell him everything. I wanted her to stay in her job long enough to get some payments made to us, but she was so stubborn."

"Jesus, Jack. What were you thinking?"

He pressed his fingers to his brow.

"Do you want me to get a nurse?" I asked.

"I'm fine. Let me finish. I want you to know I didn't mean to kill her. I was upset, desperate really, and I grabbed her wrists to make her listen to me while I described what the impact would be on my company if we didn't get the money. She took a step back. The table was right behind her and she fell on to it. It shattered and…"

Tears welled in his eyes. "It was just bad luck. A piece of glass must have cut a major artery. I've never seen so much blood. I should have called for an ambulance, but I was in shock. I just stood there. She moaned and tried to lift herself up from the floor, tried to grab the sofa cushion, but she had no strength left to do it. I watched her die. It was terrible. I knew that if I called for help, I'd be accused of killing her, and the whole sordid story of debt and bribes would come out. I couldn't risk that. So I did what I could to make it look like an accident, planted the wineglass and bottle, and went through the living room, the kitchen, the hall, the front door, wiping every surface so my fingerprints wouldn't show up."

"And Ernie?" I prompted.

"He's my nephew. Yes," he said, seeing the look on my face. "My brother didn't do as well for himself as I did, and makes his living as a fence for stolen goods. He thinks I don't know, but I do of course. Mostly, I keep my distance from him, but I knew Ernie could do what I needed."

"Why did you kill Nick? And why did you try to kill me?"

"Nick?"

"Rebecca's neighbor. He lives – lived – in the apartment downstairs from her."

Jack waved his good hand as though pushing something to the side.

"That was an error on Ernie's part. I knew that one of the neighbors had seen me on the stairs a couple of times. After the... accidental death, I was worried he might describe me to the police so I sent Ernie after him. I just told him to get rid of the man from downstairs. But he got the wrong one. How was I supposed to know that there were two men living in that apartment? Ernie's not so bright.

"As for you, Kate, I hadn't realized that you were friends with Rebecca until Alan mentioned it. I realized you could be a threat, that maybe Rebecca had told you about the arrangement and the bribes. Then, when you talked about looking at the ID sketch, I thought it was likely that you'd recognize me. I didn't want to hurt you, but the risk was too great."

"So you sent Ernie after me."

Jack closed his eyes. Already pale, his cheeks blanched a shade lighter. He looked like a cadaver. The thought of death made me shiver. I could be dead now, if things had gone Jack's way. Briefly, I wondered how Ernie was doing. I decided I really didn't care.

"Ah, you're awake, Mr. Cohen. May we come in?" Clarke stood at the door, with another man at his shoulder. I stood up, feeling my legs shake underneath me. Clarke would undoubtedly hear everything I'd just heard. Jack would go to prison.

CHAPTER FORTY

A week later, I sat on a bench in Hyde Park not far from Clarke's office. I hadn't seen Clarke since the day he arrested Jack, but he called me occasionally with updates, and I'd spent some time at the police station going over my statement. Funny how a place I'd never previously visited or even thought about was starting to feel like home.

I wrapped my hands around my styrofoam cup of coffee, trying to get warm. The sleet that had been falling on London for the past few days had stopped, but there was no doubt that winter had arrived. Autumn had fled, chased away by ice and frost, and even an unseasonably early snowfall. For an hour or two, the city had glistened under a coat of sparkling whiteness, but it wasn't long before the pristine snow had turned to grey slush that clogged the gutters and dripped from rooftops.

I looked up to see Clarke striding towards me. He was wearing a dark blue coat and a green scarf that matched his eyes. He sat on the bench next to me.

"Thanks for meeting me," he said. "Are you feeling okay?"

When I nodded, he said, "I wanted to thank you in person for your quick thinking. We've filed charges against Jack and Ernie."

"Jack seemed happy enough to confess everything," I said, thinking back to the evening in the garage. It felt surreal now, but it had really happened. Yellow Do Not Cross tape was tacked up across Jack's office door. The police had taken away several files of paperwork and cancelled checks. Apart from that, though, life at the office had fallen back into its usual routine. We had dumped the Montgomery project and were suing Peter Montgomery for payment of the debt he owed the company. Alan was working hard to juggle expenses and bring in new projects. A few days earlier, Josh and I had celebrated Josh's major promotion. Alan made it clear that Josh was being groomed to become a partner in the firm.

The last time I'd chatted with Inspector Clarke, he had told me that everyone has secrets, but I knew that Josh didn't. There was nothing counterfeit about him. Unburdened by artifice, he told the truth, acted without deceit, and was honest with his emotions. And, strangely, Alan too was an open book, for all his bluster and arrogance. He said what he thought, however brutal, and cared deeply about his company. With Alan and Josh at the helm, it would be in good hands.

"I have a question," Clarke said.

I tensed, knowing what was coming.

"Jack said you told him he had an aura and was going to die, that evening in the elevator," he said. "Where did that all come from? What's an aura?"

I'd thought about this for days. Whether to tell Clarke about my ability to see auras. I'd talked to Olivia about it and her advice was to come clean.

"It will explain some things to him," she'd said. "He'll realize how wrong he was to treat you as a suspect. Besides, you'll probably never see him again, so no harm can come of it."

I found it depressing to think I wouldn't see him again; I hoped we could be friends. So, despite my reservations, I did my best to explain, and told him about Francesca, little Sophie and my nephew.

"I wanted to protect Rebecca," I finished. "But I failed. Same with Nick."

He leaned back on the bench with an expression of utter confusion on his face, and I knew I shouldn't have said anything.

"Kate, I don't pretend to understand. Auras that predict death?"

He sounded like Leo, but Leo had come to accept the reality of the auras, even though he didn't understand them. I sensed, though, that Clarke never would. There was already a distance between us, an intergalactic space that couldn't be crossed.

"It's okay," I said. "I know it's hard to believe. I just wanted you to know."

He nodded. "I'm glad you told me. It explains my gut feeling that you were hiding something; it made no sense that you were involved. I knew that, but I couldn't put my finger on what it was that felt off."

"I'm glad to have enlightened you."

He acknowledged the sarcasm with a quick grin, but then looked serious again.

"One thing I have to ask," he said. "Your statements are factual, aren't they? I mean based on what really happened?"

"Yes. Absolutely. Everything in the statements is true."

"And you won't mention these auras in your testimony as a witness on the stand."

It was an instruction more than a question.

"No, I won't." I knew that would be enough to get the cases thrown out. "I'm not stupid. I want to see those men punished."

He smiled and, to my surprise, leaned forward and took my hand in his for a moment. "Thank you."

Letting go of my hand, he leaned back, legs stretched out in front of him. He had an uncanny ability to look comfortable wherever he was, however unlikely the setting.

"I'm very sorry about Rebecca," he said at last. "I mean, all that stuff about her taking bribes. It must have been hard to find out about that."

I nodded. "It was. Looking back on it, so much of what she told me was a lie, or a pretense at least. I think that secrets had become the norm for her. Montgomery's wife couldn't find out about them and no one at work could know. The apartment that she couldn't afford, the promotions she got that were probably unmerited. She probably couldn't distinguish between truth and lies, appearances and reality any more. She thought that money would save her, offer her a different life from the one her parents lead.

"But you know what saves me from despairing for her is that she was trying to make a change. She'd told Montgomery that it was over between them. She was going to look for a new job. I truly believe that she was trying to put her life back in order."

"I agree, and I think you should take some credit for that."

"But I'd only been seeing her for a few weeks, not enough time to make a difference."

"True, but if she'd already had some doubts about what she was doing, perhaps her renewed friendship with you was just enough to light the torch paper. She saw that you had a good job without sleeping with the CEO, if you'll excuse my crassness, that you had the respect of your colleagues, and enjoyed a high degree of independence. You became a sort of role model for her."

"It was all too late," I said. "She never had a chance to see what life might have brought her. It's very sad."

We were quiet for a couple of minutes. Traffic on the roads beyond the park provided a muted backdrop to the frantic honking of a flock of geese that rose from the lake in front of us. The surface of the water, momentarily agitated by the departure of the geese, quickly settled, flat and dark under the pewter sky.

"How are you doing?" I asked Clarke.

He looked surprised. "Me? I'm good. Not many people ask me that."

"It must be tough. Dealing with all that death and violence, grief and anger. Doesn't it depress you?"

"I don't let it," he said. "If I did, I couldn't do my job. My work means more to me than anything. I love it." He smiled. "I meet interesting people, like you."

I smiled back. Perhaps he would forgive me for my strange aura-sighting ability and we could be friends after all.

He looked at his watch. "I should go. I'm meeting Gary for lunch, to go over his statements and prepare him for Jack's trial."

Raising an eyebrow, I nudged him in the arm. "Really? As a key witness, I've never warranted a whole lunch, just a couple of coffees in dingy cafes and a freezing cold park bench. What does Gary have that I don't, I wonder?"

I turned to look at him. The flush in his cheeks and the brightness of his deep green eyes left no doubt as to his feelings.

"Good," I said. "Give Gary my regards."

He stood up and re-knotted his scarf.

"You take care of yourself, Kate. I'll be in touch again soon."

CHAPTER FORTY-ONE

Alan gave us time off for Christmas and New Year, so I asked Josh if he would come to Italy with me. Leo and Olivia were planning to join us there with Aidan and Gabe. When Josh said yes, I felt like a bird let out of a cage, nervous about what the future held for me, yet excited and happy.

Nonetheless, my mind kept wandering into unwanted places. The horror of Rebecca's death was still vivid, memories of her bloodied body still weaving through my dreams, disrupting my sleep. I had an image, like a photo in my head, of the moment when the train had hit Nick at the Tube station. My distress over little Sophie's death was still raw. Still, I was determined to enjoy the holiday with Josh and my family. I ran down the steps from the plane to the tarmac, eager to see Dad again, excited to introduce him to Josh.

Once we were in the car, weaving through traffic, Dad spoke. "They found the car that hit you on the hill that day."

I turned in my seat, saw his face in profile, eyes on the road. He was getting older, I thought sadly. But his grey hair was still thick and he wore it as he always had, a little too long so that it curled against his neck at the back.

"It belonged to a young man from Florence, apparently. He was hiding stolen goods in the old farmhouse."

I glanced back at Josh to see if he'd heard, but he was gazing out of the window, taking in his first views of Tuscany.

"How did they find the car?"

"A villager reported a car driving fast on that road. Almost hit her, apparently. So the police took a look, found the stuff in the farmhouse, and waited for him to come back, which he did. Same car, silver, tinted windows. The one you tried to grab hold of, that day."

"I tried to grab hold of it?"

He glanced over at me, a look of surprise on his face. "You must remember? That car came speeding over the top of the hill. You yelled at the driver to slow down. When he didn't, you caught hold of the back door handle and tried to open the door. The police said you were very brave, trying to apprehend him like that, but, honestly, Katie, it was very frightening. You could have been killed if you'd fallen under the car."

We drove in silence for a few miles until Josh asked questions about the landmarks we were passing. I was happy to switch into tour guide mode. It saved me from thinking about what Dad had said.

***

The next day was the winter solstice, the shortest day of the year. The pale sun hung low in the sky, timid and ready to scurry back into hiding. The light was metallic and brittle, and thick frost formed a veneer of white over the trees and paths. I stamped my feet a few times, trying to move the blood through them.

For the third time my father asked, "Are you sure you don't want one of us to come with you?

"No, thanks. I'll be fine and I have my whistle." I held up the silver object to reassure him.

Josh blew on his hands to warm them. "Don't take too long. Your Dad and I will be waiting for you in the cafe in the village."

A few days earlier, I'd had the idea of walking the maze again. I didn't know what I thought it would achieve but, once rooted, the idea had grown. As soon as we'd reached Dad's house, I had called Professore Bertagli to ask permission to visit.

The maze made me think back to the day I had met Sister Chiara up on the hill. It was she who had taken me to the overlook and shown me the labyrinth below. Over the past weeks, I had left several messages at the convent, but whoever answered the phone always told me Sister Chiara wasn't seeing visitors, that she hadn't left the convent for over a month.

I walked to the entrance, turning to wave to Josh and my father before going into the maze, where thick cypress hedges leaned ominously over the narrow path. A few steps brought me to the first turn, and I was suddenly alone, out of view and, it seemed, out of touch with the world outside.

The anemic sun threw gauzy shadows across the pathways and the grass underfoot was crisp with frost. There was no birdsong, no breeze. The intense silence was unnerving. I walked as fast as I could while still keeping track of my right and left turns. I was cold, and my toes were numb. I wondered if this was a pointless exercise. What could I learn from being alone in here? I could be drinking coffee and eating pastries with Josh and Dad in a nice cozy cafe.

Surprisingly, I didn't bump into any dead ends and kept making progress towards the center. Eventually, I noticed a brightening in the air ahead of me; fewer hedges throwing shadows must mean I was close to the heart of the maze. Encouraged, I walked on, rounded a corner and emerged into a small grassy clearing. In the middle was a stone bench with lions' paw feet.

Sister Chiara sat on one end of the bench, her black robe in stark contrast to the milky white stone. Her eyes were closed, face turned up towards the pallid sun. I stopped, astonished at seeing the nun there. Professore Bertagli had said nothing about anyone else coming today.

As if sensing my presence, Sister Chiara opened her eyes and looked at me. She patted the bench beside her and I went to sit down. The stone surface was icy cold.

"I've been trying to reach you," I said. "I wanted to see you."

"Yes, I know. I'm sorry, but I've been rather preoccupied," said the nun. "I'm glad to see you, my dear. So much has happened to you since we last met."

I looked at her in surprise. "To me? How do you know? Did you talk to my Dad? Or Paolo?"

Sister Chiara smiled and shook her head. "And you still have that aura. I was hoping to see that gone by now."

I jumped as though I'd touched a live electric cable. "Aura? I have an aura? What does it look like?"

"Don't be alarmed. It is not the aura you are seeing that signifies death. But it saddens me that it is still there."

"Please tell me what it looks like. I can't see it. What color is it?"

"It's dark grey, heavy around your head and shoulders and chest.

It's weighing on your head and your heart."

"But what does it mean?"

"It's guilt, my dear." She held her hand up when I began to speak. "Not guilt for anything you have done, but guilt for what you think you have done. It's always been that. First there was your little brother. What was his name? Toby. You carried the burden of his death on your young shoulders for so many years. And now, there are others who are dead and you think you could have saved them. Why don't you tell me about them? We have plenty of time."

I related the events of the past few months, from my first meeting with Rebecca to the arrests of Montgomery and Jack Cohen. I stumbled over my words when I came to describing Rebecca's death, and Nick's. My voice shook when I talked about the attack in my apartment and Josh being injured.

The whole time Sister Chiara watched me intently, nodding occasionally to show that she was listening. When I had finished, she leaned back and folded her hands in her lap. "While you were talking, your aura vibrated and turned darker, but it was not your fault that those people died. Do you believe that?"

I thought about it. "I'm not sure. I felt I could have done more to protect Rebecca. And Nick."

"That's not the way I see it, Kate. And I don't think anyone else would, either." She paused, and smoothed out the folds in her black robe. "You saved an elderly man in the fish and chip shop, do you remember him? He would have died that night but for you. And there's Aidan, of course. In saving your nephew, you also saved Leo, who would otherwise have plunged into unassailable grief and depression. And his relationship with his lovely fiancée Olivia would have come to an end."

"Oh, they're not engaged," I said. How could Chiara know about Aidan, or Olivia, or the homeless man? What was she doing here at the center of the maze, as if waiting for me to arrive?

"So you have achieved a great deal of good, Kate, but what you are doing now is focusing on the negative. You have so many wonderful attributes and you care deeply about people, but you can't let that empathy cross the line into responsibility for others. I'd like you to promise me that you will start to take care of yourself, to do what is right for you. Be a little selfish for a change. When you do that, everything will fall into place. And your mother will be freed from worrying about you. She wants you to be happy and then she can be happy too. She deserves that, don't you think?"

"Yes, she does."

Sister Chiara sat, with concern in her eyes, while I tried to regain my composure. I watched the sun, like a mountaineer attempting to summit, grappling towards its apex. I felt a hint of warmth on my face, as the deep silence was broken by a drip of melting ice. The clear notes of a skylark rang through the clearing and roused me from my reverie. I glanced at my watch. It was almost noon.

"I should go. My father and my boyfriend are waiting for me. Will you come with me? We could have lunch."

"That is kind of you, but no thank you, Kate. You go ahead. I'd like to stay here for a little longer and enjoy the sunshine."

I stood but didn't move away. "I'd like to see you again soon. It's Christmas in a few days. Perhaps you could come for dinner?"

"Perhaps, my dear, perhaps. Now you go and join the others. We don't want them to be worrying about you."

Still I hesitated. I didn't want to leave Sister Chiara alone.

"Goodbye, Kate. Remember what I said."

The nun's words seemed like a dismissal, so I nodded and turned away reluctantly to find my way back to the exit.

When I emerged into the garden, blinking in the brightness after the shadows of the towering hedges, I looked around for Professore Bertagli. There was no sign of him. I'd wanted to ask him if he knew that Sister Chiara was in the maze. I was still astonished that she had been there on the very day I went back.

I walked out along the long driveway into the village. On each side of the unpaved road, green hills topped with cypress trees rolled into the distance, punctuated here and there with ploughed fields awaiting the spring planting. The rich earth was dark, the color of espresso.

My conversation with Sister Chiara ran like a recording in my head. I needed some time to think about it all; there was so much I didn't understand. When I reached the cafe, Josh stood up to give me a hug.

"Did it go okay?"

"Yes," I said. "Let me warm up a bit. I'll tell you all about it."

Dad had already ordered me a cappuccino and a slice of panettone. I devoured them as though I'd just returned from an expedition in the wilderness. I felt the warmth of the little cafe percolating into my bones, smelled the fragrances of coffee and baking, and listened to the soft hiss of the milk steamer and the music of the conversations around us. Aware that both Dad and Josh were looking at me expectantly, I pushed my plate away.

"I saw Sister Chiara in the maze," I said.

"Funny that she would be there the same day as you," said Josh, waving at the waiter to bring more coffee. "Did you talk to her?"

"Yes, it was strange. I asked her to come home for lunch, but she seemed to be enjoying the sunshine, so I invited her to visit sometime over Christmas. That's okay, isn't it, Dad? If she comes?"

"Of course. Ah, here's Paolo." Dad stood up to grab another chair from the empty table beside us. Paolo came in, taking off his coat and unwinding a green paisley scarf from around his neck. Without being asked, the waiter brought a macchiato and set it down in front of him.

He took a sip. "Sorry I'm late. I was over at the convent. Sad thing, one of the sisters passed away a few hours ago. I had to sign the death certificate."

I had a knot in my stomach. "Who was it?" I asked.

"You met her, I seem to recall. Nice lady. Sister Chiara. She'd been having heart problems for a couple of months, which led to a fatal myocardial infarction. One of the sisters found her in her room after she didn't make an appearance for noon prayers."

CHAPTER FORTY-TWO

Two days later, Josh and I stood together at the back of the small chapel. It was packed with mourners. The sheep-wool smell of damp clothes was interlaced with the stronger fragrance of incense and the odor of lilies. Lamps suspended from the vaulted ceiling, formed pools of greenish light on the travertine floor, while a bank of votives flickered at the entry to the side chapel. The dark walnut wood coffin gleamed in the glow of the altar candles. Vases of pink and white flowers sat on the altar top.

Italian funerals were typically somber affairs that took a long time. After a few minutes, my attention wandered to a pretty fresco on the wall of the apse behind the altar. Finally, when a rustling and shifting signaled the end of the service, everyone stood to follow the coffin to its resting place in the cemetery.

Memorial plaques were stacked three high in the walls, each bearing a photo of the deceased, and a small votive that was lit day and night. The congregated mourners were silent while the coffin was pushed carefully into the long, narrow niche in the wall. Two nuns placed vases of flowers on the sill; later, when we'd left, the opening would be sealed closed and a marble plaque fixed into place.

I had struggled to make sense of it all for three days now and was no closer to understanding. But it didn't matter. I had to accept the fact that I had sat on the bench in the maze and talked with Sister Chiara several hours after she had died.

The priest turned away, his work done, and a nun knelt briefly for one last prayer. Tears trickled down my cheeks, warm on my cold skin. Josh reached out to brush them away. He gave me an encouraging smile. He'd smiled a lot since we arrived in Tuscany, although he was suitably solemn for the funeral.

The convent bells began, ringing out over the valley, startling a murder of crows that flew up in a noisy panic from the old oak tree in the center of the convent grounds. I linked my arm through Josh's for the short walk back to my father's house.

***

That night, Leo and Olivia arrived with the boys and the house was full of voices and laughter, warm with crackling log fires, festive with Christmas lights. Presents were piled up under the tree that Josh and Dad had cut and trimmed.

I could tell that Dad liked Josh. Only Josh was allowed into his study to look at the draft of the Book, as we called it, the gardening book he'd been working on. Huddled over drafts and layouts, they closed the door after me when I took in cups of tea or glasses of wine.

I spent most of my time in the kitchen. Paolo had volunteered to be my assistant; we baked, rolled out pasta sheets, and cooked multi-course feasts, while Olivia sat at the kitchen table, drinking tea and flipping through recipe books for new culinary challenges to give us. Leo and the boys kicked a ball around on the frosted lawn, or played video games with the volume turned as high as it would go.

On Christmas Day, flutes of prosecco in hand, Leo and Olivia announced their engagement. Olivia said they planned a quiet wedding ceremony in the early spring and were hoping to get away for a week to somewhere exotic like the Seychelles or the Maldives. Sister Chiara had been right when she referred to Olivia as Leo's fiancée.

After dinner that evening, while Leo, Josh and the boys played Gabe's new video game, I sat with Olivia to tell her about my visit to the maze and my unearthly meeting with Sister Chiara.

When I'd finished, she nodded, as though agreeing with something I'd said.

"It makes sense. You had to puzzle your way through the maze to get to the revelation at the center."

"I spoke to a dead nun, Olivia."

"I don't think you did, actually. You received her message, of that there's no doubt."

"You mean she wasn't there? I imagined sitting on that bench with her and talking?"

"Perhaps. But that doesn't mean that what she told you isn't real. That's what you have to focus on. It's what Leo's been telling you too, if you think about it, that you have to let all that guilt go. Get on with your life. Put it all behind you. It doesn't mean you have to forget those you've lost, just that you have to accept they've gone and that it wasn't your fault."

She gave me a mischievous grin. "Josh is lovely. Be happy, enjoy being with him. Don't let him slip away."

"And the auras? What do I do about those?"

She leaned over and took my hands in hers. "You're going to be all right, Kate, I'm sure of it. One day these auras will make sense to you. Meanwhile, I have a plan. I'm going to keep you totally engrossed in wedding planning. I have a zillion ideas, but I need your organizational skills to execute them. We'll have fun, don't you think?"

She stood up, went to the dining table, and came back with a white three-ring binder and a bottle of wine.

"Let's get started."